WITHDRAWN

ALSO BY MARGO CANDELA

More Than This

good-bye
to all that

Margo Candela

A Touchstone Book
Published by Simon & Schuster
New York   London   Toronto   Sydney

Touchstone
A Division of Simon & Schuster, Inc.
1230 Avenue of the Americas
New York, NY 10020

First Touchstone trade paperback edition July 2010

TOUCHSTONE and colophon are registered trademarks of Simon & Schuster, Inc.

For information about special discounts for bulk purchases, please contact Simon & Schuster Special Sales at 1-866-506-1949 or business@simonandschuster.com.

The Simon & Schuster Speakers Bureau can bring authors to your live event. For more information or to book an event contact the Simon & Schuster Speakers Bureau at 1-866-248-3049 or visit our website at www.simonspeakers.com.

Designed by Akasha Archer

Manufactured in the United States of America

10 9 8 7 6 5 4 3 2 1

Library of Congress Cataloging-in-Publication Data
Candela, Margo.
  Good-bye to all that / by Margo Candela.
      p.   cm.
  1. Women in the professions—Fiction. 2. Man-woman relationships—Fiction. 3. Corporate culture—Fiction. 4. Los Angeles (Calif.)—Fiction. 5. Chick lit. I. Title. II. Title: Goodbye to all that.
  PS3603.A5357G66 2010
  813'.6—dc22   2010013368

ISBN 978-1-4165-7135-3
ISBN 978-1-4165-7215-2 (ebook)

For Monica

one | TRUE LIES

Forces of Nature . . .

It's true Los Angeles doesn't have real weather. It's usually sunny, mild, and picture-postcard perfect the closer you get to the beach, where the air quality is better and the real estate more expensive. It can get a tad chilly in the winter and occasionally it even rains in the spring, but you can get away without ever having to buy a winter coat much less rain boots. Warm coats and rubber boots are more for the sake of fashion than for the sake of necessity. But generally, outside of a Hollywood soundstage, you won't find rainstorms, lightning, and especially snow.

Well into my teens I assumed trees only changed color and lost their leaves in movies, seasonal TV specials, and in the promotional calendars the local auto body shop sent every third week of December. In L.A. palm trees are always tall, skinny, and green and only sway with any sort of drama when Santa Ana winds decide to blow in.

My defining experience with real weather occurred during a weekend trip to Tempe, Arizona. I was in the tenth grade and attending a cheerleading competition. The twelve of us and our coach arrived a day early, checked into a local motel, and spent most of the night cowering in bathtubs as a lightning storm raged outside. What I saw, between running from room to room, was awesome. The storm was a true force of nature—unpredictable, dangerous, and beautiful. I was as scared witless as the rest of my teammates, yet drawn to the windows at the same time.

I get the same sort of thrill standing off to the side of the paparazzi pen as they strain against the metal barriers that separate them from their willing prey. Bursts of light from their cameras illuminate the curvy, but still very thin, blonde as she takes her first tentative steps onto the red carpet. It's almost as if they can smell it—fresh meat. Nicolette Meyers is the perfect blonde, hazel-eyed, twenty-three-year-old girl next door who happens to have a pair of tastefully done C cups.

Nicolette has a minor but crucial part in the movie that's premiering tonight, *Risk Management III*. She delivers a poolside drink to Redford Henson, megastar of *Risk Management I* and *II*. About twenty-two minutes into the movie she appears and in her bikini top is the pinkie-size supertechno doohickey Redford needs to carry the plot into the second act. When Redford plucks the device from in between her cleavage, her top comes off and Nicolette then joins the chosen few as a Boob Girl. It's nothing more than a gratuitous skin shot, but it's become a hallmark of the *Risk Management* franchise.

As Nicolette reaches her mark, a piece of duct tape centered on the carpet so cameras will catch the movie poster in the background, she shrugs off her trench coat. The paparazzi roar to life, and all it takes is a little thigh and shoulder. If I could bottle up their barely contained intensity, it could run my air conditioner for an entire weekend.

"What's her name?" one of them yells. "Is she a Boob Girl?"

"Nicolette Meyers! M-E-Y-E-R-S," I yell back when I notice the Belmore Corporation public relations bunny is too busy fawning over some B-list movie actor to do her job. "It's Nicolette Meyers!"

"Nicolette! Nicolette!" the paparazzi yell, as if they have her name on a loop. "Nicolette! Nicolette!"

That they had no idea who she was until a few seconds before is no matter. Nicolette's name is going to be on everyone's lips and her boobs on everyone's mind tomorrow morning. But she's going to have to do more than pose demurely in her borrowed designer frock. The paparazzi won't turn away from a budding starlet, but they're not going waste time giving her posing lessons either.

I edge myself toward the metal barrier that separates the mere humans from the stars and other very important people who know they're somebodies even if your average *Us Weekly* reader doesn't. This group includes my boss, Bert Floss, who has just stepped out of his limo and onto the carpet with his new trophy wife on his arm.

Bert is the vice president of Marketing for the Belmore Corporation, the company behind *Risk Management*. Of anyone here, he'll be the one to notice Nicolette isn't causing the splash the marketing report assured him she would. And it's my job, as his trustworthy, hardworking, and indispensable assistant who wants to be promoted out of her current job to junior exec, to make sure the marketing research is proven right. After all, I'm the one who wrote the memo that said Nicolette Meyers would be a big deal.

I push forward, shoving bodies out of my way, not bothering to apologize to the guy I just rammed my elbow into. The paparazzi are used to it—they have the manners of a pack of hyenas. But they have their uses, and I've been to enough premieres to know how to give them what they want so that Belmore can get what it wants.

I fumble underneath my jacket to pull out my employee ID and all-access event pass. I'm wearing both around my neck on a lanyard, but I'd tucked them away, hoping to go incognito. My task is to catalog reactions to every aspect of the night's event. From the color of the red carpet to the popularity of the mini–truffle burger that will be served at the after party. Once I get enough information, I'll write up a memo and have it on Bert's desk well before he shows up for work at 8:30 tomorrow morning.

"I need to get through." I wave my credentials at the security guard. I'm not anything near short, standing five eight in flats and five ten in my usual two-inch heels, but this guy towers a good foot over the top of my head.

"No one gets on the carpet that doesn't pull up in a limo," the security guard says over the noise of the crowd.

He's not even close to being impressed by a no-name starlet who's crashing and burning a few feet away from us. He's especially not impressed by some equally no-name twenty-five-year-old in a rumpled corporate lady suit. My go-to little black dress is in the trunk of my car with the rest of the stuff I meant to drop off at the dry cleaner's days ago. That I didn't get the chance to slip into it is no great loss. There's really nothing sexy about a three-quarter-length-sleeve dress with a slight cowl neck. Really, I could wear it to the Vatican for tea with the Pope and still be kosher. It's the kind of dress that gets the job done without getting in the way of me doing my job.

I've learned to downplay my looks, which got me on the homecoming court in high school and referred to as pretty often enough so I feel fairly confident that I am. I have a heart-shaped face with good cheekbones, big brown eyes under strong brows, and shiny brown hair, but now I control how I look instead of letting my looks control how other people see me.

For a long time, most of my life really, I'd been happy to be a pretty face in a sea of the same, confident that my looks would get me somewhere in life until I realized that would be somewhere I didn't want to go. A pretty face with no motivation equals a restaurant hostess and not much else in this town.

My goal in getting dressed every morning is to find a balance that will allow me to succeed at Belmore and not have to wear thick-framed glasses and go without Frizz-Ease to prove I have working gray matter in my head. But seeing myself through the security guard's eyes, I know I've stopped swimming in a sea of pretty and settled firmly in the land of frumpy. In the scheme of things, it's a sacrifice that's worth it if it gets me where I want to go.

The last thing I want is someone thinking I'm too attractive to be good at my job. I dress unobtrusively with simple hair and makeup to match because I want to be taken seriously. I don't want to stay Bert's assistant forever, and I can't let something as distracting as cleavage get in the way of my career advancement. Once I make it into my own office, I'll upgrade from my staid suits and two-inch nun pumps to something with a bit more personality. I might even show some collarbone again.

Case in point, Nicolette Meyers's looks (and boobs) have gotten her where she is, but she's going to need my brain (and chutzpah) to get her any attention.

"Please! I'm on the list. Please check it," I beg the security guard. "I'm supposed to escort her inside the theater."

I look toward Nicolette, who can sense by the diminishing pops of light that she's losing the interest of the paparazzi. The wattage on her smile dims with each millisecond that her picture isn't taken. A handler, her agent, manager, or even an overinvested parent would tell her to do something, anything—even something cheesy, like blowing a kiss—to keep the paparazzi snapping.

I'm able to see my stressed-out face in the security guard's sunglasses. He's wearing them because they're a movie tie-in. Ray-Ban has issued a specially designed pair called, fittingly enough, the Redford. While Redford Henson doesn't wear this particular design in the movie, he's been sporting a pair for the last few weeks. They're completely sold out, and Ray-Ban is rushing to get another shipment to stores. The sunglasses were my idea, something I mentioned to Bert after visiting the *Risk Management III* set last year. Redford was wearing sunglasses to hide his bloodshot eyes—he was going through a nasty divorce and custody battle at the time—but what I saw was a marketing opportunity. Bert took the credit for my idea, which I presented to him in a memo, but it still earns me points in my promotion account. An account I want to settle in the very near future.

The security guard compares the photo on my Belmore Corp. ID to the face on my, well, face. Satisfied I'm not pretending to be Raquel Azorian because that's who in fact I am, he then scans my all-access pass with the electronic reader attached to his belt. The light flashes green, proving it's legit. He then checks the master list, which is printed on, of all things, old-fashioned paper. This list has all the names of who is and who is not allowed past the metal barriers. Mine isn't on it.

As this is happening, I'm forced to wait. The worst thing I could do is throw attitude his way. He can keep me here all night if he wants to. He has this power because his orders are to keep anyone off the carpet who doesn't belong there.

"Is this chick going to do something besides stand there?" a raspy-voiced paparazzo asks.

"Where are the Ward twins?" another yells, lowering his camera. "Move it, honey. Get outta the way!"

Nicolette has sense enough not to relinquish the prime spot of real estate even though she's being motioned to move along. She's had her moment in the false sun of media celebrity, and now it's time for someone more important to take a turn.

"Don't move," I scream. My voice cracks with anxiety, but she hears me. Nicolette scans the crowd. A picture-perfect smile is still on her face, but desperation is creeping into her mostly vacant eyes. She knows she's drowning but is trying to look good while it happens. Bless her. "Stay right there!"

Finally the security guard motions for another to help him move the metal gate. My feet in their sensible pumps go from standing on anonymous concrete to sinking into plush red carpet. Ignoring everyone and everything, I sidle up to Nicolette and hiss in her ear. "Turn around, stick your ass out, and look over your shoulder. Now."

She does it, and the paparazzi go nuts. I step back, melting into the crowd again so I can enjoy the storm from a safe distance.

Nuts, Bolts, and One Shiny Cog . . .

Less than eight hours later I'm sitting in the marketing department conference room on the seventeenth floor of the Frank Gehry–designed Belmore Corporation Tower. I spend more time here than I do in my apartment, located just a few miles away. In fact, I still have boxes of clothes sitting in my living room that I've given up on ever opening two years after moving in. I've been meaning to call Out of the Closet and have them picked up, but it's one of the many things not related to my job that I haven't gotten around to taking care of. I'm not entirely sure what's in there, but I hope my forsaken clothes might be of some use to someone who doesn't mind secondhand Gap jeans and never worn Belmore promotional T-shirts.

"This could be a major cock-up, ladies and gents." Bert Floss says this with a proper amount of gravitas, which comes with the thirty years of marketing experience under his strained leather belt.

"A major cock-up," he repeats with an especially hard *k* on the *cock*. "The shitstorm is coming, folks, and my umbrella is only big enough for me."

That's a new one, I think as I jot it down. I have a notebook where I keep a running list of Bert's business-related aphorisms. Very few things Bert says can be embroidered on pillows, but he rarely fails to amuse and educate at the same time.

"Can anyone see what I'm seeing?" Bert asks, more for his own benefit than for that of anyone else. He doesn't expect anyone to answer his question, but he does expect a solution.

Bert uses his ever-present laser pointer to direct attention away from BlackBerrys in laps to the PowerPoint slide on the screen behind him. On it is the image from the DVD cover sleeve for the season three compilation of the *Twin Tales* television series.

Stars Cat and Cara Ward, Belmore cash cows, look a tad on the bovine side. Their side ponytails, cropped jeans, and white T-shirts under denim vests only serve to accentuate the baby fat that pads their middles and fills out their cheeks. The photo was taken when the girls had a brief awkward period that shortened season three from the usual twenty-four episodes to twenty. By the time season four started taping, they'd morphed into the lithe, hollow-cheeked fashionistas we've all convinced ourselves they've always been. But right in front of our noses is the very obvious proof that they look chubby, and the Ward twins cannot be chubby.

To come out and say that the twins look fat is not only

wrong but monumentally stupid. Even Bert is smart enough to keeping from calling the elephant in the room an elephant. Anything he says will get back to the twins. And even though Bert is the vice president of marketing and sits three chairs away from the president of Belmore, Cat and Cara are Hollywood royalty. While he wouldn't lose his head, he wouldn't be sitting at the head table of any corporate function for a very long time. It's scary to think two nineteen-year-old high school dropouts have that kind of power, but they do. In this town, celebrity outranks just about everything except bigger celebrity.

"Tell me I'm not the only one who sees what the issue is here," Bert prods. It's a rhetorical question only a fool would answer, and that fool's name is Cris Fuller.

"With all due respect, I don't think there's an issue," he says.

Fuller is the senior exec in charge of marketing the *Twin Tales* DVDs, and he's number two in the department. He clears his throat and waits for Bert to acknowledge what he's said. But Bert ignores him until Fuller raises his hand and follows proper protocol.

"Fuller," he barks, giving him permission to speak.

"Mr. Floss. As I said, I don't—"

"Fuller"—Bert cuts him off without looking at him—"you're in charge of this fuckup, so anything you say should bring us closer to rectifying this mess. Speak, Fuller. What solution do you have to offer us?"

For a moment naked emotion—hate and contempt mixed in with a dash of fear—plays out on Fuller's pinched face. Botox keeps his brow from furrowing, and his tanned face absorbs the light, but it's there before it disappears just as quickly. As much as Cris Fuller despises Bert, he knows who the boss is.

"The cover image can be Photoshopped," he says through his capped and gritted teeth. "I've gone ahead and had a preliminary mock-up done for you to look at."

Fuller hands me a folder, which I hand to Bert. Inside is the tweaked image that takes the twins from chubby and normal to acceptable Hollywood standards for puberty. They're still in their Wal-Mart shopper–friendly outfits, but they look at least ten pounds thinner and a little taller, too. It's Fuller's solution, but he had nothing to do with solving the problem.

This morning, desperate to make polite chitchat when we'd ended up riding the same elevator, I mentioned how refreshing it was to see that the Ward twins had at one time looked like relatable, average human beings.

"What exactly do you mean by that?" Cris Fuller always assumes everyone is out to screw him, because screwing people over is second nature to him.

"You know," I said, regretting every word I'd uttered starting with "good morning," "they look like regular twelve-year-olds."

"Not acceptable. It won't fly." When Fuller is upset, his color rises. My little remark caused him to go two shades of red.

"I can call in a favor, Mr. Fuller," I said quickly, hoping to stave off a freak-out. "There's someone I know in Art, and they work fast."

"Fine. Do it. Get it done." He didn't have to add that I was not to tell anyone.

I'd given Fuller the retouched image right before the meeting, having sprinted up the six floors from Art to make it in time. My good deed would be neither appreciated nor acknowledged by Fuller, but now he owes me. This alone was worth more than a thousand empty thank-yous.

Bert flips open the folder, glances at the image, scribbles his name on the proof, hands it back to me to hand back to Fuller. It's the Belmore chain of command in action. Even though Cris Fuller makes four times the amount I see on my paycheck every two weeks, he still has to go through me to get to Bert.

Fuller makes to rise from his seat.

"And the audio commentary?" Bert's not through with eviscerating his wannabe successor.

There is no audio commentary because the Ward twins have grown into statuesque, platinum-haired business moguls who want to pretend they've never been the painfully normal, pudgy preteens of season three. As far as they're concerned, season three and age twelve never happened.

"It's been pushed back due to scheduling conflicts." Fuller shifts around in his seat. His designer suit, spray tan, and Botox can't hide his discomfort at being called onto the industrial-grade carpet. "They've been out of the country and—"

"We can't put out a fucking television show compilation without audio commentary, Fuller." A bulldog in temperament and looks, Bert chews on Cris Fuller like he's a mere chicken bone, splintering him into little bits until he's nothing but gummy marrow. "Or are you planning on getting voice-over actors to do it for them?"

It's actually not a bad idea, and Fuller, if he'd been paying attention to his own job instead of politicking for Bert's, could have come up with it himself. Bert knows Fuller is chafing at being the number two in the department. This is why he's called a meeting—to remind all of us Cris is just Fuller and Bert is Mr. Floss.

"Of course not, Mr. Floss," Fuller mumbles, embarrassed at being publicly put in his place.

"What was that?" Bert snarls.

Fuller flushes again. It turns his skin a terra-cotta color, but he wisely keeps his mouth shut. No one says a word in his defense because we're too busy enjoying Bert doing a little jig all over his ass. There is nothing he can say to make Bert happy because Cris Fuller hasn't done a lick of work on the project. He left it up to the junior execs, who focused on other projects they judged to be more beneficial to their own upward trajectory at Belmore.

Cris Fuller's crash and burn is an opening for me to show I can do more than just hand folders to Bert. I'm an amateur at company politics, a blood sport at Belmore, and I might get in way over my head, but he's given me the perfect opportunity to shine. I would be a fool not to take it. The rest of the marketing department may not know it or even care, but I, too, want to step up another rung of the Belmore Corp. ladder.

I take a deep breath and raise my hand. I am calm and in control. Showing any hint of fear or doubt now would be a big mistake, bigger than drawing attention away from Cris Fuller. If I embarrass myself, I'm embarrassing my boss, and that would be unforgivable. "Mr. Floss?"

"Yeah," Bert says. It takes him a moment to register that it's me, his usually silent assistant, who's been brave (or dumb) enough to say something. "Raquel?"

He's not used to me speaking up in meetings, where my function is to be there merely for his convenience. If there's a message I have to convey, I put one finger on his forearm and then whisper it near his ear. If Bert asks me a question, I answer with what he wants to hear. I save my opinions and insights for when we're sitting in his office. He stares out the window, sips his coffee, and I, as casually as possible, tell him what's on my mind about a certain project or present him my ideas.

As Bert's longest lasting assistant, having been on the job for three years, I've learned how to finesse him without making him feel like he's being worked over. This skill is both a curse and a blessing. Bert likes me, and it's good for my boss to like me, but it also means that he wants to keep me close. Wives and girlfriends have proven unreliable, but I'm like Helen Mirren's character, Mrs. Wilson, in *Gosford Park*. Just like Mrs. Wilson, I know what Bert wants before he does, and I make sure that what he wants done happens as unobtrusively as possible. And, like the perfect 1930s English servant seeing to the comfort and needs of a manor house full of high-maintenance guests, I have no life outside the life I've made for myself inside Belmore.

By speaking up, I'm forcing Bert's hand. If he promotes me, I will move on and become another person he needs to keep an eye on. We both know it's going to happen. Otherwise why would he spend so much time teaching me everything he knows about marketing?

"I have good rapport with Cat and Cara," I say.

"You do?" I'm not sure if Bert is annoyed or amused by me asserting myself outside the confines of his office. He's definitely surprised, which I hope works in my favor.

"I do." I keep my answer simple so I don't trip myself up by relinquishing too much information.

In Hollywood who you know and who knows you is invaluable currency. I've shown my boss that I am worth more than just my assistant-level salary and that Cris Fuller has been a fool to undervalue my not so obvious worth.

The truth is the Ward twins wouldn't know me if they ran me down with their Range Rover. This doesn't matter, because I know their agent, Frappa Ivanhoe. We met a year ago, during the promotion push for *Twin Tales: Freshman Year*. To keep me from burning out from the job I'd mastered and already outgrown, Bert gave me the task of showing up at the Ward twins' shared Hollywood Hills mansion to rouse them from bed and make sure they were almost on time for interviews and photo calls. Frappa and I bonded over the long hours of standing in the background, holding out our palms to accept their chewed-up sugarless bubble gum. Much to my surprise, Frappa has become a real friend—a rare thing in the smoke-and-mirrors world of Hollywood, especially since Frappa is the one blowing the smoke and angling the mirror.

"If Mr. Fuller would like, I'd be happy to facilitate scheduling a day and time for them to come into the studio." I dip my head in his direction to signal supplication, however false it might be. "Cat and Cara are available—"

"Mr. Floss, the girls are out of town," Fuller protests. He's trying to gain the upper hand, but instead he's just proving that he's dropped the ball. "They're unreachable."

Bert cuts him off with a wave. "I don't know about you,

Fuller, but I'd like to find out how my assistant has figured out how to do your job. Go on, Raquel."

"The twins came back from Europe a week ago; they're in New York until Friday and then are checking into the Chateau Marmont because they're in a dispute with their building contractor," I say quickly. This is information Fuller could have discovered himself by reading Hollywood gossip blogs or, in my case, being good friends with their agent. "I'd be happy to work with their representation and make sure they're able to commit to studio time as soon as possible."

"Could you do that, Raquel?" Amusement at Fuller's expense is evident in Bert's voice.

"Yes." I look straight at Bert as I answer. "I can do that."

In the end, Bert's is the only opinion that matters. He is the vice president of this department, and only he can promote me to junior marketing executive. Not Cris Fuller. Right now, I'd bet a month's salary that Fuller wouldn't spit on me if I was on fire.

"Good." Bert rolls the word off his tongue like it's a piece of sticky taffy. "Make it happen, Raquel."

"Of course, Mr. Floss."

I pretend to write a note to myself so I can hide the smile that overtakes my face. Looking down also helps me avoid Cris Fuller's death stare.

Flirting with Disaster . . .

A few hours later, still glowing from my morning meeting triumph, I sit down at my desk. I have some time to myself while Bert is away at his therapy appointment. Determined to make these precious minutes as productive as possible, I study the car brochures I've accumulated over the past weeks.

I've been thinking about trading in my well cared for but tired looking Honda Civic for something befitting a (future) junior exec. I've done the math, and I can afford a car payment and not have to subsist on Top Ramen pilfered from the break room. I could do something else with the money, like up my 401(k) contribution, but a new car is something every Los Angeleno recognizes as a marker of success.

All that is left is for me to figure out what kind of car I want and, of course, for Bert to give me my promotion so I can actually afford to do more than just look.

I nibble on a strawberry Pop-Tart, sip my Diet Coke, and flip through the brochures, taking full advantage of a rare lull when I don't have to see to anyone's needs but my own. I've almost forgotten what this feels like.

"Oh, crap!" I say as I catch sight of the time. Bert will be pulling into the parking lot by now and will expect a memo regarding this morning's meeting on his desk by the time he gets here. Not wanting to waste a perfectly good Pop-Tart, I take one last savage bite just as Kyle Martin walks in.

Kyle Martin, the thirty-two-year-old Hollywood wunderkind and the new vice president of Corporate, is the anointed golden boy of Belmore. He's been with the company six weeks, having come on board after Belmore absorbed his production company and its roster of successful mass-market romantic comedies; guy-friendly, smart action flicks; and wide-range TV shows. More important, Belmore bought Kyle's heat and cachet. He's a man on the move, and it was really no surprise when Walter Belmore, owner and soul of Belmore, named him to such a power position, making him the youngest vice president in Belmore history.

The only higher office Kyle can aspire to would be that of president, but Walter Belmore shows no inclination to make room for anyone at the very tippy top. Not even for Kyle, who is liked by all, even by those sworn to hate him.

Even before Kyle moved into his renovated office on the twenty-fourth floor, factions formed around and against him. Bert is firmly in the Kyle camp, even though he's told me more than once, "A guy that young and that good-looking doesn't get to where he is as fast as he has without either screwing his way there or screwing people over." I haven't bothered to put this bit of Bert wisdom into my notebook.

Judging from Kyle's self-assured saunter, none of the tension swirling around him seems to bother him.

"What's a beautiful woman like you doing hanging around in this dungeon? You should at least have a window, something nice to look at." He says this in a way that makes me think he's not talking about windows. I lost mine when Bert's new wife redid his office, but I doubt Kyle Martin would be impressed by this piece of information.

"Sorry?" My eloquence is reinforced by a piece of Pop-Tart breaking off and plopping itself onto my lap.

"That looks good, Raquel," he says, looking right at me. "Is it?"

The gossip has it that Kyle's marriage to an aspiring actress is over. His assistant, Marisa, a former model who wised up and learned the ins and outs of every Microsoft program in existence, told Jessica, assistant to the vice president of Creative, who told me that he asked for his mail to be forwarded to a sexy high-rise condo not too far from Belmore. My eyes dip to his left hand to see that the ring has indeed come off.

"Sorry?" I repeat. It's as if I've forgotten every other word in the English language except for this one.

"You are Raquel Azorian, correct?" He leans in, closer. I can feel heat radiating from under his bespoke suit. Or maybe it's just coming from me?

I nod and straighten up, determined to ignore the stain that is sure to be setting into my skirt.

Once he's gone I'll dash into the ladies' room, scrub the hell out of it, and smile stupidly at myself in the mirror because Kyle Martin has taken the time to shine his golden ray of attention on me. All the girls at Belmore, and that's what we turn into when Kyle is around, have a crush on him. Having Kyle this close makes me giddy, a feeling I thought I'd left behind once I got serious about my future at Belmore. I can't help it, though. Kyle is what my mother would consider a catch as well as a member of the small fraternity of good-looking redheaded men that includes Eric Stoltz and Ewan McGregor, both celebrity crushes of mine.

"Raquel Azorian. PowerPoint and memo mistress extraordinaire," he continues. "Bert's unacknowledged right-hand woman and Cris Fuller pisser-offer."

I say nothing. Officially my only function is to be Bert's assistant. I coordinate his appointment book, sign his holiday cards, and answer his phone. Anything else I do for him is between the two of us.

"Shopping for a car, Raquel?" Kyle asks, leaning a hip

against my desk and pinching the brochure out of my suddenly pliant hand.

"Yes." At least it wasn't another "sorry."

"Let me tell you something, Raquel. There's nothing sexier than a beautiful woman behind the wheel of a fast car." He looks at what Honda has to offer and frowns. "You don't seem like the type of woman who'd drive such a boring car."

"Maybe I am," I blurt out, finally managing a multiword reply. I clear my throat and try again. "Sometimes dependable wins over fast and fun. A woman can tell the difference between the two, and a smart one will always go for stamina over flash."

He chuckles and sifts through my pile until he gets to the VW brochure. He opens it to a picture of a cherry red convertible Beetle. Stepping behind me, he sets it on the desk, a hand on each side of me.

"Now this is the kind of car I see you zipping around town in, Raquel," he says, his minty breath close to my ear. "Breaking hearts at every intersection."

"Who says I can't do that behind the wheel of a Honda?" He's messing with me, and it sort of pisses me off in a squirming in my panties kind of way.

He leans in closer to me so our faces are only an inch apart. "I think you've broken plenty of hearts, Raquel."

Before I have a chance to answer, Bert skids to a stop just outside the door with Cris Fuller hard at his heels. His tie is askew, and his shirt has ridden up on his stomach so his undershirt is exposed. He fills the doorway, so Fuller is forced to bob his head around the available space to see what's happening.

"Kyle! Raquel? Why didn't you tell me Mr. Martin was here?" Bert is wheezing, obviously having made a dash from the elevator. Someone, most likely Fuller, alerted him that somebody important was in his office.

"I. He. We." I'm back to single-word replies.

"Raquel was just giving me an update on what's going on in the marketing department." Kyle walks over to Bert and claps him on the shoulder hard enough so Bert stumbles back into Cris Fuller. "Hey, Fuller, didn't see you lurking back there. Let's grab an empty conference room and talk about *Twin Tales*."

The three of them walk out, and I lean my elbows on my desk, my face buried in my hands. My skirt can wait. Right now I don't think I can stand up without wobbling.

"Raquel?"

"What!" My head snaps up like a firecracker has gone off under my ass.

"We'll talk horsepower another time." Kyle gives me a wink and disappears again.

I blink a few times to refocus my eyes and try to slow down my thumping heart. I tally up how many times he'd said my name—eight, no, nine, and my last name twice. He called me beautiful and paid me a professional compliment.

Kyle Martin has noticed me. *Me.* He's seen beyond my sexless A-line skirt suit, boring makeup, uninspired hairdo, and flirted with me. And I held my own. And, even better, he doesn't like Cris Fuller any more than I do.

two | ALL IN THE FAMILY

Feelings of Familiarity . . .

Instead of sleeping on my first free Saturday in months, I'm listening to my cell phone ring. Not my Belmore BlackBerry; even Bert has the decency not to call before 8:00 A.M. on a weekend. It's my other cell phone that's bleating for my attention. I want to ignore it, roll over, and go back to sleep, but I can't.

"Yeah?" I say, but it sounds more like "Yeg." I clear my throat and try again. "Yeah?"

"Raquel! I've been trying to reach you for ages." Without so much as a good morning, my sister-in-law gets right down to business. "It's like you've dropped off the face of the earth."

"Oh, hey, Cricket."

My brother, Steve, is married to a woman who willingly calls herself Cricket. *Cricket.* My sister-in-law is a former gymnast who hasn't managed to lose her penchant for coordinating Goody barrettes with whatever she happens to be wearing. Steve, usually so logical and reasonable, hadn't even hinted that he was dating anyone. Then one day he invited us all out to Señor Fish in Eagle Rock and introduced us to his already pregnant fiancée. When Cricket found out our birthdays were a few months apart, she promptly declared us spiritual sisters and insisted I be her maid of honor. (I later learned she hadn't spoken to her own sister for two years, so I felt slightly less honored to have been asked.)

"I didn't wake you, did I? I've been up for ages. I can call you back later if you're still sleeping," she says. It's perfectly obvious that the one thing I'm no longer doing is sleeping, but her manners force her to make this offer to excuse her lack of consideration. Cricket has very good manners, manners that she sometimes wields like a blunt weapon.

"What's up?" I swallow a yawn but refuse to burp up another excuse.

Something is always up with Cricket. She's a natural-born last-minute get-together organizer. I missed her last to-do—a combo Tupperware, Taser, sex toy, and book club party—but I've used up all my decent excuses. No matter what she asks, I'm going to have to say yes, please, and thank you for the sake of keeping the family peace.

Cricket has only been an Azorian for a year, and it's been a tough year for all involved. Actually, not for Cricket, who has thrived in her new role as wife and mother. She sees life as one long competition—the tougher the circumstances, the deeper she digs to triumph over them.

"I'm just calling to make sure you'll be here by three," Cricket says, her Southern-accented voice turning her order almost into an invitation. "Now, I don't need you to lift a finger, you're our guest, but I'm hoping I could trouble you for the teeny, tiniest favor?"

"Teacup Chihuahua tiny or diaphragm-size teeny?" I ask.

I amuse myself by thinking Cricket brings out the droll in me, but I know I just come off as a bitter single woman with no prospects of a man and babies in her future. Cricket is married and has been blessed with two babies, one of each, and she never lets me forget how happy she is and how sad she is for me. Cricket—all five feet, two inches of her—pities me.

"Now I'm just wondering if you can pick up some of those delicious cupcakes. I know you're supremely busy with your career and all, but I can't help thinking about them. You know the place I'm talking about?"

"Sprinkles." I supply the answer just as I've supplied the cupcakes for every little get-together Cricket has had since I've known her.

"If I wasn't so busy with the babies, I'd talk to the owner about opening up a franchise here in Pasadena," Cricket says.

In her life before Steve and the babies, Cricket was an almost Junior Olympian who taught gymnastics. Then she came out from Georgia to visit a college girlfriend, and somewhere between day trips to Rodeo Drive and Disneyland, she met my brother and got pregnant. Now Cricket says she's the CEO of her home and family. I'm not sure what this makes my brother. Maybe contract labor?

"I'll ask for the manager's card." I say this for two purposes—I want to sound encouraging, and I want to hurry the conversation to an end. "How many cupcakes should I pick up?"

"A half dozen should be more than enough," she says, pretending to give it some thought. Cricket never initiates a conversation whose outcome she hasn't already planned.

"A dozen?" I ask, even though I heard her perfectly.

"No! A *half* dozen. I'm trying to get my body back." Cricket looks the same as she did before the twins—short, with compact, piston-strong muscles. The only body that woman has is in her hair. "Bye-bye, Raquel. Try not to work so hard."

Cricket hangs up before I get a chance to offer my own "bye-bye" and piece of useless advice. As if sensing some imbalance in the familial universe, my phone rings again. This time it chimes with the special ring tone I've reserved for my mother. I call it the Darth Vader March. Whatever the proper name is, it perfectly suits dear old Mom.

"Hello, Marlene," I say.

Depending on her mood, she's either Mom or Marlene. Lately she's been Marlene. She says it makes her feel young to have her twenty-five-year-old daughter call her by her first name. And that's not the worst of it. Once the twins can talk, she's going to make them call her Glamma. And those kids will have to do it, too, if they know what's good for them.

"Don't even think of not showing up today, Raquel. If I have to go, you have to go." She's breathing heavily, and there's a low hum of vaguely familiar noise in the background.

"Are you at the gym?" I ask.

My mother doesn't exercise. She's a fan of juice fasts, fad diets, body wraps, and plain old general denial. When I go out to eat with her, which isn't often, I always order an appetizer as well as an entrée to make sure I actually get something to eat. She'll always have "just a little taste" of my food, end up eating half of everything, and then criticize me for having dessert instead of thinking about the number on the scale. Her disapproval of after-dinner sweets never stops her from digging her fork or spoon into my dessert, though.

"Why are you doing that?" I ask. Out of habit, I instantly review what I just said for potential verbal land mines I may have involuntarily planted or triggered.

"I can't afford to sit around and watch things go south." She huffs and puffs, her focus on her workout and not on the tone of incredulity in my voice. "I'm fighting every inch and pound to the death."

"Funny, because every second you spend on that machine brings you inevitably closer to it. So, really, it doesn't matter if you're sitting or jogging. Death is still going to happen."

"What? You're cutting out . . . Call me back," she says before the phone goes silent.

For a second, I debate not calling her back. I fantasize about taking a long, hot shower, then pulling on a pair of drawstring pants and an oversize Belmore T-shirt from the box in the living room I'm almost sure my bathroom scale is in. Then I'll walk down to the neighborhood café, Hello Monday, and order up a vat of coffee and a hubcap-size muffin, but I can't. All my comfy clothes have been promised to charity (and if my bathroom scale goes along with them, all the better), and my mother will have my ass if I don't call her back.

"Fuck me," I say. "Yeah, that would be nice. A nice, long, hard fuck and then some coffee. Maybe waffles made from scratch followed by a couple of hours of TV watching in the nude. I bet Kyle Martin owns a waffle iron and a bitchin' TV."

My phone jumps to life in my hand. I don't even think twice about answering it.

"I was just going to call you back." I sound guilty, as if I've been caught doing something unthinkable, like enjoying my weekend.

"I need to borrow the blouse I gave you," she says. If she's noticed I didn't instantly call her back, she's choosing to ignore it.

"I haven't had a chance to wear it yet." I eye the box the silky purple halter is packed and sealed in. Suddenly I want to shove it in my purse, fly to Vegas, and slut out for the rest of my weekend.

"Where are you going to wear it?" she scoffs.

My mother and I may not be close, but she knows me well enough. Which begs the question, Why would she buy me a blouse she knew I was never going to wear? Whatever. It's easier just to give it to her and forget about what the blouse actually says about our relationship.

"I'll bring it along with the cupcakes." I need to get off the phone with Marlene before I have a fight with my mother. "Anything else?"

"How's work?" she asks, throwing me for a loop.

"Why?" I can't help but question her motives. My mother doesn't think much of my job.

"Just wondering," she says, sounding annoyed with me. "Can't I just ask an innocent question?"

It's up to me to either give her a snippy answer and end this conversation on our usual sour note or take a chance and tell her something that actually means something to me.

"I went to the premiere of *Risk Management III* on Thursday, but I didn't get to stay for the movie or after party. I had to go back to the office and write up a memo for my boss on the status of a project. You know the Ward twins? Anyway, they have a DVD coming out and things aren't on schedule, but everything's fine now. It was a fun night."

"That doesn't sound like a fun night, Raquel, it just sounds like work." True enough, but there's really no need for her to point it out.

"You asked me about work, *Mom,* and I told you about my work."

"It's just that . . ." She trails off, waiting for me to take the bait. I don't, and after a moment she's forced to continue on without me justifying her saying what she's going to say. "Your father was a scientist at JPL, and your brother is a genius with money. I just never imagined you'd end up being some fat man's secretary. Why don't you look into becoming a stewardess?"

"Stewardesses are flight attendants, and secretaries aren't called secretaries anymore," I say. Though every so often Bert will refer to me as his secretary, and then he'll let me take an extra long lunch to make up for it. "I'm an executive assistant. Sorry if me having a real job makes it hard for you to brag to your friends about."

"I'm just trying to help, Raquel." She sighs. "If you don't want my advice, don't ask me for it."

"I don't recall asking you for advice, Mom, but thank you. I'm going to hang up now because the strange man I picked up last night has woken up with a huge hard-on and he's going to give me the business before I kick him out of my apartment."

"What? You're cutting out again," she says. "Don't be late and don't forget the blouse."

I toss the phone onto the bed and then sit up to smother it under a pillow. One of these days I'll try to have a real conversation with my mother. I'll even try to talk to Cricket without rolling my eyes. That's not going to happen today, but at least I'm willing to consider the possibility of interacting with them without getting my panties into a bunch. As far as I'm concerned, this is progress.

"Who am I kidding? Today, tomorrow, and the next time I have to see them is going to be a pain in the butt," I say as I hold a pillow over my head. "Especially in my butt, and no amount of cupcakes will make up for that."

All Together Now . . .

As I park, I'm careful not to jostle the requested box of milk chocolate cupcakes. I never bother with any other of the many flavors Sprinkles has, knowing that once I give my family options the requests will become endless.

"Don't be such a bitch, bitch," I mutter to myself. "It's not like you have to bake them yourself."

Steve and Cricket have just moved into a charming four-bedroom Craftsman in South Pasadena. It has a white picket fence, tire swing hanging from the mature magnolia tree, and is in a great school district. The house is also in a state of half-completed renovation. Along with defaulting on their mortgage, the previous owners stiffed their contractors. Right before the bank took possession, the windows were super-glued shut and a can of tuna was dumped onto the central air-conditioning unit. The soon to be exiled occupants blamed the unpaid contractors and the contractors blamed the occupants and, as these things tend to do, it went to court, but it didn't keep Steve and Cricket from buying the place. Who could possibly argue with getting a $1.5 million house for $799,529? Even I'd put up with a little glue and tuna fish sandwich smell for that kind of a bargain.

Cricket says the house will be perfect once Steve gets around to tiling the bathrooms, installing hardwood floors in the living room, and finishing up myriad other things a normal person would hire a professional to do. But Cricket is not a normal person. Cricket is a go-getting self-starter with a can-do attitude, and she's convinced herself not only that my brother is cut from the same cloth but also that he's the handy type.

"Raquel!" Cricket rushes over to me. She's wearing a crisp white apron with red piping, a puffy chef's hat, and a matching oven mitt on each hand.

We exchange kisses on each cheek with one more for luck. It's how we greet each other in my family, and Cricket wants in on all the Azorian family rituals.

"You look so sleek in black!" she exclaims over my not so special jersey dress. It's comfortable, clean and, more important, was there when I reached into my closet.

"Navy blue," I correct her. Cricket doesn't wear black because she thinks it's morbid. "But I guess it's a very dark navy blue."

"You have to take me shopping, Raquel. Ever since I became a mommy, I've been hopeless when it comes to fashion."

She lifts her apron so I can see she's wearing her usual outfit of cropped cotton candy–colored pants, an embellished

T-shirt that pulls across her muscular shoulders and, I'm sure under her chef's hat, matching Goody barrettes.

"Sure, um, we can go shopping sometime."

I'm hoping she's just trying too hard to be sisterly and isn't serious about us hitting the mall together. I'd sooner volunteer to accompany my mother on one of her take-no-prisoners marathon bargain hunts that takes her to Ross, Loehmann's, and Marshalls, capped off with a restorative jaunt around Target.

"Of course nothing that needs dry cleaning." She hooks her arm in mine, almost causing me to lose my hold on the cupcakes. "I have to be practical since I have two bundles of joy and then some to take care of."

"That is a major consideration," I say. "Dry cleaning and babies. A combination modern science and fashion never intended."

"Come see the twins. It's been ages since they've had a visit from their auntie Raquel." Cricket, her viselike grip now around my upper arm, steers me toward the portable playpen set up under a patio umbrella.

"Oh, wow, they've really grown," I lie. "I can tell the difference from the photos you e-mailed me on Wednesday."

What I can't tell is which one is Saylor (the girl) and which one is Rhys (the boy). Cricket insists on dressing them both in matching gender-neutral outfits.

"Their heads look, uh, rounder." It's a non-compliment, but I need to say something.

"Rhys's curls are coming in, and Saylor's eyes are definitely hazel. Like mine," Cricket says as she gazes down at her babies with unabashed pride. For a second I'm afraid I'll have to listen to her birthing story again. "We've all agreed on that now."

"Oh, yeah . . . Rhys has curly hair just like, uh . . ." I take hold of the tiny foot of the baby with a lone curl on the top of his head and rack my brain for some hint of family resemblance. "Rhys looks just like our uncle. You haven't met him. He lives in Minneapolis. Or at least he used to. Anyway . . . He's very handsome, just like Rhys is going to grow up to be."

"That's Saylor," Cricket snaps, scooping up her female baby. For good measure she picks up Rhys and stomps off. I'm left staring at an empty playpen and holding a single tiny shoe.

"Raquel." My mother crooks her finger at me the way she does when she wants to get a neglectful waiter's attention.

She's arranged herself on a lounge chair with a tall iced drink and a stack of magazines next to her. She obviously has no intention of getting up, and we'll have to ferry things over to her for the duration of the day.

"Nice sunglasses," I say. "Has the estate of Jackie O. finally come out with an accessory collection for Target?"

My mother peers at me over the top of them. "They're practically Chanel."

"Practically is just as good as the real thing." I bend over to kiss her, bumping into the considerable brim of her hat.

She dodges my kiss to whisper in my ear, "Cricket is a little on edge. She's a week late."

"No she isn't," I say. I have no desire to involve myself in any matters that concern Cricket, her muscular vagina, and my brother's penis. My mother, though, has other ideas. "Don't say that."

"A week. *Late*." My mother raises an eyebrow, nodding gravely. "Cricket made me promise not to breathe a word about it to anyone."

"Crap, Mom." I can't help but whine like a teenager. "Why did you have to tell me?"

"We have to help your brother before Cricket completely ruins his life." She swats me with a rolled-up magazine as if my brother's choices are somehow my fault. "You know what she told me? She said wouldn't I be so happy to have another grandbaby, and I told her that I was barely used to the idea of the ones I have now. She stopped talking to me after that."

"Marlene, please." I hold up my hands in surrender. "I just want to have some charred meat and then go home with one or two cupcakes. Is that too much to ask?"

"Raquel, your brother needs you. Try to think of someone besides yourself for once." She sniffs.

My mother is of the unwavering opinion that Steve can do no wrong, but the world is constantly doing wrong by him. He is, she insists, a fragile and special soul who would never harm a fly. This is complete bullshit. My brother has amassed a small fortune by being completely decisive and downright ruthless when it comes to money. Cricket may have fallen in love with the house, but it was Steve who went to the bank and negotiated the deal to get it at the lowest possible price.

"What is it that you would like me to do?" I ask, knowing that a relatively pleasant afternoon is now out of the question.

"You're his sister, Raquel." My mother frowns at me, disappointed I'm not going to devote myself body and soul to her crusade or at least feed the fires of the coming inquisition. "You can't let Cricket do this to him again."

"What about Steve?" I ask her. "He can control his penis. It's not like she's raping him or something. If she's pregnant, it's because Steve climbed on top. Scratch that, I think we know who's on top in this relationship. Either way, Steve knows, or should know by now, what happens when a penis and a vagina come together. It's his responsibility to cover that thing up. Not mine. Or yours."

"If you don't want to help your brother, fine, that's your choice." My mother swats me again with her *Martha Stewart Living* magazine. "Just don't complain to me when you're stuck babysitting the three of them. God forbid it's another set of twins."

"I think God has other things on his plate, Marlene, besides keeping your grandchildren to a manageable number. Where's my dad?" I ask, looking around for him.

"Your father? I haven't seen him since we got here."

My mom goes back to her magazine with a shrug and a sigh. She's pissed at him, but then again, when isn't she? If she wasn't, I'd be worried she'd had some sort of highly specific and localized stroke. Dad is happiest behind a book, in his garden, or talking about some obscure scientific study— three things my mother has absolutely zero interest in. Since he's retired from JPL, even his breathing gets on her nerves.

"Maybe he's inside rewiring lamps," I say, hoping to lighten her mood by acknowledging my father is an odd bird. "Or maybe he went for a long walk, ended up back at home, and is happily alphabetizing his drill bits."

"Shut up, Raquel. Don't be cute." My mother has no desire to be placated. She wants to pout behind her knock-off sunglasses and under her very large hat. "Go talk to your brother. Tell him he needs to convince that wife of his that now is not the time to be having—"

"Raquel!" Cricket calls over from where she's standing by

the detached garage. She must have sensed my mother is try-ing to draw me into a dark alliance. "Come see!"

"Go on," my mother says in her most put-upon voice. "Between her yelling, your father being himself, and crying babies, I'm coming down with a headache."

"I'll find you some aspirin." There's not much more I can offer her, but at least it's something.

I stumble on a patch of overwatered grass on my way to Cricket, almost falling, but keep going even though I'm annoyed with everything and just want to go home. Not one to hold a grudge when it doesn't work in her favor, Cricket thrusts one of the twins into my arms. I look down at the baby's feet and see only one shoe. It's Saylor.

"I want to show you what I gave Steve and what Steve gave me for our anniversary," she says loudly. I look around to see who she's talking to, but it's just us.

"Anniversary?" I ask, reviewing my dates. "But you guys got married in June. July? Around there, right?"

"It's our"—she lowers her voice—"first time we made love anniversary."

"Oh. Really?" What kind of woman celebrates getting laid/knocked up with a family barbecue? Maybe it's a South-ern thing?

"So much to celebrate!" Cricket chirps, her voice climb-ing three octaves.

When Cricket gets enthusiastic about something, which is often, her voice gets higher as her enthusiasm peaks. I can only imagine dogs in the neighborhood start to howl when she has an orgasm.

She hands me Rhys, and I put both babies into awkward

football holds. I haven't really spent much time with my niece and nephew, being so busy with work. Looking down at them, I realize I should make more of an effort to be a part of their life. It wouldn't kill me to offer to babysit once in a while, and I think Steve would appreciate me making an effort to be nice to Cricket.

Cricket wheels something under a flowered sheet out from the garage. I look over at Steve, who has barricaded himself behind his grill. Like Cricket, he's wearing an apron, hat, and gloves, but his are trimmed in blue. Maybe my brother is in need of rescue as my mother claims he is?

"Are you coming?" I ask my mom. She shakes her head and pulls her hat over her face. Whatever it is, she's already seen it and is not interested in seeing it again.

"Ready?" Cricket asks. I nod. With a flick of her muscled wrist, she pulls off the sheet to reveal a jacked-up bicycle. "Ta-da!"

"Oh, man," I say, staring at it. "Man, oh, man, it's a—"

"Tandem bike," Cricket says, stating the obvious.

"A tandem bike," I repeat, keeping my eyes fixed on it. If I look at anyone, I'll burst out laughing. "I don't think I've ever seen one this close up."

"We can both ride it at the same time," Cricket helpfully points out as she tugs on the thick strap of her nursing bra. Two wet spots have appeared on the front of her apron. "And we're going to get one of those kiddie trailers to hitch up to the back. That way the twins can come along, but not until they're a little older."

"How convenient." I'm wondering if this could be some kind of joke. If I was to buy a tandem bike, it would be a joke.

A very sad one, since I have no man to tandem with. "You must have saved a bundle buying one bike instead of two."

"I saw it online and knew it would be perfect for us," Cricket says, choosing to ignore my sarcasm. She reaches a hand into her shirt and shifts the weight of her breast.

"Wow," I say, unsure what kind of reaction she's looking for. I can see why Cricket would buy a tandem bike. She wants to bring herself and Steve closer together. It's the kind of painfully sweet gesture I would prefer not being privy to. No wonder my mother is keeping her distance; Cricket has outsmarted her through shopping. "It's really a unique gift."

"Just because we're an old married couple, Raquel, doesn't mean we have to stop paying attention to one another." Cricket is probably quoting word for word from *Redbook* or some other wifely magazine.

"You'll be using protection before you hop on, right?" I ask. "You know what they say—safety first in all matters dealing with the body, and especially certain body parts."

She's too busy with her leaking breasts to pay attention to me. As if on cue, Saylor and Rhys start to fuss.

"Duty calls," Cricket says, expertly taking the twins out of my arms. She deftly picks her way across the sorry looking lawn. When my mother realizes Cricket is heading her way and is about to whip out her milk-swollen breasts, she quickly raises her magazine to shield herself from the sight of Cricket nursing her grandchildren.

"I'll get you that aspirin, Mom," I say as I head back to my car. I leave my purse so I'm not tempted to get in and drive away.

Sibling Revelry . . .

I take my time looking for a bottle of aspirin I know is not in my car, but eventually I have to head back to the gathering. I sit on my mother's chaise while Cricket makes use of the other.

If dealing with my mother and Cricket on their own is taxing, dealing with the both of them at the same time is downright panic-attack inducing. They've settled into an uneasy détente, if only for each to prove she is the more magnanimous of the two. They still can't stand each other, but they can't pick each other apart, so instead they focus on my various shortcomings—actual, perceived, and projected—to distract themselves from each other.

"How's everything in Hollywood?" Cricket asks.

"Fine," I answer. People in Hollywood call Hollywood the business, but I doubt sharing this with Cricket will be of any use to either of us. "At least my little part of it is fine."

"She's married to her job," my mother comments, looking over at me as I read and send e-mails on my BlackBerry.

"Oh, don't worry, Marlene," Cricket says with false sympathy. "I was just like Raquel before I realized there's nothing more fulfilling than being a wife and a mother. It's the hardest and the most rewarding job in the world, but I don't need to tell you that, Marlene."

"Imagine the freedom she takes for granted," my mother continues, leaning toward Cricket to heighten the sense of false confidence between the two of them. "Not being stuck in the house or having to deal with the never-ending responsibilities that come with raising children and taking care of a husband. She's always going places, meeting people! Raquel is living the life we all want, so why should she tie herself down with a husband and children?"

"You're so right, Marlene. Who needs a man these days, right? I'm sure she can adopt with hardly any problems." Cricket frowns, her face awash with faux concern. "But I read China has started to tighten up regulations—no single parents over a certain age. Good thing the foster care system is overrun with kids. It would be such a good thing for Raquel to do. Give a poor, unwanted, maybe even disabled child a good home. Don't you think, Marlene?"

They both look toward me to pick a side.

"Last night I had an expired mixed berry yogurt, a corn dog, and a can of flat Diet Coke for dinner," I say, not looking up from my BlackBerry. "Then I worked until one-thirty and fell asleep in my panty hose and makeup. It's a miracle I didn't wake up with a face full of pimples and a yeast infection."

"She'll learn, Marlene." Cricket smiles.

"Hopefully it won't be too late." Mom smiles back.

"I think I'll go see if Steve needs some help with the . . . Yeah . . ." I drop my BlackBerry into my purse and then wander over to where my brother is hiding out.

I watch Steve, savoring the moment and building up his dread. He knows what's coming and tries his best to pretend he doesn't see me standing in front of him.

"What are you wearing?" I finally ask.

"An apron." He concentrates on the grill, checking the temperature and then fiddling with the grate as if his life depends on it.

"On your feet?" I say, pointing down at the brown boats that are firmly planted on the sparse lawn. "What are those *things*?"

"Crocs."

I nod thoughtfully. "And what is your wife wearing?"

"Crocs," he admits. There's no point in mounting a defense. He lost the battle the second he let his wife pick out his outfit.

"And the twins?" I gesture to where Cricket is trying to foist one of the babies on our mother along with a bottle of freshly pumped breast milk. "What are they wearing on their teeny, tiny feet?"

"What's your point, Raquel?" he snaps. For a moment, I think I see something of the old Steve flicker behind his eyes.

"I know you're still in there somewhere." I reach up and rap softly on his temple, my knuckles meeting the snug band of the chef's hat on his head. "Let's go to Vegas and gamble away the twins' college fund. I have the perfect blouse to wear in the trunk of my car. Between your brains and my cleavage, we'll clean up."

"Can you help Mom with the twins after lunch?" Steve wisely ignores my offer and counters with a request of his own.

"You mean I'll watch the twins while Mom chips off her nail polish." My mother makes sure she always has "help" when she has to babysit her grandchildren. "Where will you and the missus be?"

"We're going to take the bike out for a ride."

This is too much. My brother, always the straight man, is opening up endless avenues for ridicule. "Oh, I bet you are."

"Shut up, Raquel." Steve sounds uncharacteristically annoyed.

I pick up a long fork and give the pile of glowing charcoal briquettes a poke. "My sisterly intuition tells me something is up."

My brother has been good about not oversharing about his and Cricket's relationship. Growing up with a mother who's never encountered a drama too small to escalate or a boundary that couldn't be crossed, we learned to keep our private lives private.

"Raquel!" my dad calls out from the back porch.

My father lopes across the yard toward us. He's a tall man who's never fully embraced his height—his long limbs control him instead of the other way around. He's dressed in his usual white short-sleeved, button-up shirt, pressed khaki pants, and beat-up brown leather Top-Siders.

My mother complains that Dad dresses like an old man. He does, but that's because he is one. He was thirty-two and she barely twenty when they met and got married. My mother was in "trouble," three and a half months along with Steve, when they took a trip down to city hall. That's what they used to call getting knocked up back then, trouble. That the same thing happened to Steve and Cricket doesn't seem to matter to my mother. In her scenario, my mother was a naïve innocent who was almost in love. Cricket just wanted to hitch her wagon to my brother's bright star and is now snuffing it out with her neediness.

"Daddy! There you are. Mom has been looking all over for you," I say.

I skip over to him and make to leap into his arms like I used to when I was the appropriate age, height, and weight to do so. He opens his arms, bracing himself for impact. Instead I give him a quick hug and smooth down his hair.

"That laser comb is working, I can tell. You have at least thirty percent more hair. Wasn't that the best Christmas present ever!"

"He never uses it," my mother says.

"Give it to Steve then. He can use it." I turn to laugh at my brother, but the miserable look on his face makes me grimace instead.

"Are we on for a game of canasta later?" my father asks. Card and board games are more of my father's hobbies that Mom can't stand.

"I am," I say. "Though we'll have to stick to whatever loose change I can find in my car. I suspect Steve's embezzling my money to fund his lavish lifestyle. This is new patio furniture, right?"

"It's from Restoration Hardware!" Cricket calls out. She's changing a diaper on the chaise, much to my mother's disgust. "We're going to do the whole backyard, a flagstone patio, grass. I just jumped the gun and bought the furniture. We can't expect guests to sit on those awful plastic things."

"Dad, can you take over for a second? Don't put the steaks on yet," Steve instructs our rocket scientist father. "It's a couple of degrees off."

"Sure thing." My father takes my brother's place and leans low to get a read on the thermometer.

"Robert! You're going to singe off your eyebrows," my mother yells.

I follow Steve inside the house. We pass through the half-renovated kitchen and into the sunroom he's converted into his work space.

"Some setup you have here, Steve," I say, looking around at the mishmash of computers and portable fans to keep them cool..

It's stuffy in here. Any breeze that can come in from the backyard is blocked by that magnolia tree. It's the worst place for Steve and his beloved computers, but it's where Cricket has stuck him.

"It's just until the library is finished," he says. We both know that the library will stay a library and never become his office. Steve sits down in front of the bank of computer monitors he's set up on a U-shaped table. The usual buzz from his homemade server system is silent.

"What's up with my money? I still have some, right?" I ask. "Or has it been flushed down the world's financial toilet?"

"It doesn't take a genius to make money in a bull market, Raquel," my brother says wearily. "It's not losing that money in a bear one that proves how smart you are."

"Huh?" I say, playing dumb and not having to work very hard at it. There's a reason why my brother is in charge of my retirement fund instead of me.

"People are panicking, and when they do that, they make bad decisions," he says.

"Speaking of which . . . Is everything hunky-dory in Steve and Cricket land?" I always knew that eventually I'd have to ask how things are between them. Judging by the look on my brother's face, that time has arrived. But I need a little buffer. "And why are your computers off? Is the City of South Pasadena suffering a very specific power outage?"

"Cricket and I have agreed that weekend days are family time," Steve says. "I get more work done when everyone is asleep anyway."

"Makes sense," I pretend to agree. "After all, it's not like sleeping is going to pay for the new backyard."

"She wants us to have a nice house." Steve shrugs as if he has no say in the matter. "It's important to her."

"Is it what you want, right?" I ask. Cricket has forced Steve to grow up, but why did it have to be into someone who wears Crocs and takes family portraits where everyone wears matching outfits?

"Yes. I mean, sure . . ." Steve stares at the blank monitors longingly. "Can I talk to you about something?"

"Okay. Shoot . . ." I don't add "me," even though I want to. Something is really bothering my brother, and I'm afraid I already know what it is.

"It's just Cricket . . . She wants . . ." He pauses and tries again. "It's not that I don't . . ."

"Steve?" Cricket calls from somewhere in the kitchen. "Steve? Your mom is going to watch the twins so we can take our bike on an inaugural spin around the block. We better hurry before she changes her mind. Steve? You in your office, honey?"

"Okay, babe," Steve calls back, his voice devoid of any hint of its previous uncertainty. He stands up, ready to be the stand-up man he thinks he has to be.

"Wait." I snatch his droopy hat off. "For God's sake, promise me you'll never let anyone outside of our immediate family see you wearing this thing."

Steve gives me a kiss on the top of my head and walks briskly toward the sound of his wife's voice. Instead of following him, I peek out the window and watch my parents gather in front of Steve, Cricket, and their tandem love bike.

"Mother of Crocs," I say to myself. "My family is a mess."

three | SOUL MARKET

The Boss of Me . . .

Bert drops an approved memo onto my desk before rushing out for a meeting up on 24. I stare after him, knowing that seven floors above me he'll be spending the next hour within a few feet of Kyle Martin. And, who knows, maybe they'll come down here to talk in the privacy of Bert's office.

I reach into my purse to take a peek at my compact. I took extra time this morning getting ready, a full twenty minutes instead of ten. Besides my usual swipe of drugstore mascara and concealer, I'm wearing eyeliner, blush—Nars Orgasm—and my favorite toffee-colored lip gloss. I'll have to space out my reapplications of it since the tube is almost empty. The label is worn out, but I know it's M.A.C. Someday, when I have some time, I'll take it to the counter and hope they still carry it. Satisfied that my face still looks like I want it to, I angle the mirror so I can see the rest of my head.

Instead of gathering my hair into its usual pinned-back

twist or bun, I used my straightening and curling irons to achieve deliberately mussed waves. It seems silly now—all this effort just in case I might get to see Kyle for a few seconds as he goes about his busy day. Knowing I spent a good five minutes debating on which side to part my hair doesn't help me feel any less like a lovesick teenager. But I look nice. No, better than nice—I look good.

I've achieved a look that says, "I want to make an impression without appearing to really care what that impression is as long as you notice me, but don't get the wrong idea about why I'm here." True, I'm still dressed in my usual business lady skirt suit, but from the neck up I look as if I might have more than *The Wall Street Journal* to wake up to six mornings a week.

I'm about to allow myself the tiniest swipe of gloss when the phone on my desk rings. Instantly I shove my makeup bag into my purse and my purse into the drawer. I pick up the phone before the second ring is over.

"Thank you for calling the Belmore Corporation. Bert Floss's office. This is Raquel speaking."

How many times have I uttered this sentence over the past three years? I answer Bert's phone at least a hundred times a day. (Bert does not believe in e-mail, so anyone who wants to reach him has to call or fax.) Multiply that by number of days I've worked here and . . . well, it adds up to a lot of "Thank you for calling . . ." Still, each and every time I answer his phone, it's with the utmost professionalism. I may have outgrown my job, but I still take pride in doing it well.

"Bring up the *ECA* file and Fuller," Bert says, "to twenty-four, Big Conference Room, in ten."

"The Big Conference room in ten," I say to confirm. The Big Conference Room is reserved for press conferences, meetings Walter Belmore will be attending, and toasting successful company-related events like big opening weekends at the box office and award nominations. It's also where high-level public ass kickings take place.

We hang up at the same time, and I automatically forward my desk phone to my BlackBerry, knowing I'll be away from my desk for the next fifteen to twenty minutes. If I'm away any longer than that, I have to forward all phones to the marketing department receptionist, another temp in a long string of temps.

I unlock the door to Bert's office, using one of the three keys in existence that do so. Bert, of course, has the master key. I have a copy that he takes from me every Friday and sets on my desk on Monday but that I keep with me during the workweek. The third key is with a bonded and background-checked cleaning man whom Bert pays out of his own pocket.

I used to think Bert was just paranoid, but once I saw how much backstabbing and subterfuge goes on at Belmore, I started shredding memo drafts and password-protecting everything I saved on my desktop. Even the tiny garbage can icon on my computer is locked. Around here, people will literally dig through your trash so they can back up their trash talking about you.

Bert's office is expensively decorated but not in an obvious way. Even the Picasso and Pollack are subtle. His office is the total opposite of Bert the person, who tends to be on the loud side. It's also beyond tidy and, looking around, I can't figure out what the cleaning guy does every night between 8:30 and 9:45.

On his desk are neat stacks of files, one for each current Belmore project. Movies get red folders, TV shows blue, TV movies yellow. Books and music share the color green because they're a smaller part of the Belmore empire. No matter the color, each file contains the same things—a marketing report, a thumb drive with a PowerPoint presentation, and a memo.

For the projects Bert deems important enough to want to put his signature on, I coordinate the marketing research, which is done by junior execs, write reports based on the data, and then turn the reports into memos and PowerPoint presentations. (At Belmore, anything can be made into reality if it has the right PowerPoint presentation.) I also write memos based on marketing reports done by each of the dozen senior execs on the floor. Bert says thirty years in marketing has taught him that if it can't go into a one-page memo then it's not important.

I grab the *ECA* folder and, instead of marching directly out and locking the door behind me, I take a moment to enjoy the unusual silence and lack of sneaked cigarette smoke. Bert's office is huge, befitting a Belmore vice president, with an expansive view of Century City and the Santa Monica Mountains in the near distance. I know I can't hope for a view anywhere close to this when I get my promotion, but at least I'll be able to look out at something, even if that something is the roof of the employee parking garage.

With one last look around to make sure I haven't inadvertently left a fingerprint smudge on the glass desktop, I walk out, lock the door, and head over to Fuller's office, three doors down. His office is the second largest on 17, with a view of the office tower next door.

"Hi, Matthias, is Mr. Fuller in?" I have eight and a half minutes to get him and this file up to Corporate on 24.

"He's been in there all morning." Matthias looks over at the firmly closed door of Fuller's office. "He hasn't even come out to use the bathroom."

"That's because his office has an en suite bathroom, Matthias."

"It does?" he asks with genuine wonderment in his voice.

Matthias is, of course, an important someone's offspring. It seems fourteen years of prep school, followed by stints at Brown, NYU, and Columbia, then a couple of years wandering the globe on his parents' dime, didn't do much to prepare Matthias for the real world. Too connected for a mere internship, he's been given a real job, for which he's getting on-the-job training from me. In two weeks of following me around the marketing department, Matthias has proven himself to be as inept as a person can be without having to wear a helmet on a daily basis. But he's very good-looking—with a perfectly disheveled English schoolboy haircut and a seemingly endless wardrobe of shrunken Thom Browne suits he picked up during a stint as a New York model—and has the right last name, Pfeiffer. The Pfeiffer family owns a publishing company Belmore is looking to acquire.

Looks go a long way in Hollywood. A person can be as dumb as a rock, but if he looks good while doing it, who cares if he can't open up a spreadsheet without having to call Tech Support? I'm assuming that, despite Matthias's obvious ineptitude and lack of real-world job skills, Fuller really likes the way he looks.

"Yes, all the senior execs and veeps do," I say, admiring his peaches and cream complexion. "Why do you think you never see any of them in the bathroom?"

"That explains why Cris keeps mentioning that Bert has a steam shower big enough for two in his office," Matthias says. "I thought he was just making some sort of inside joke. Is it true? Does Bert have a steam shower?"

"It's Mr. Floss," I say. I have no idea what Bert's en suite looks like, as I stick to a well-worn path when I'm in his office. "If no one is around, we can call Bert Bert. Bert can call us by our first names, but when addressing Bert, it's Mr. Floss. Always and only Mr. Floss."

"What if I run into him at Coffee Bean or Whole Foods?" he asks. Matthias is from a socially prominent New York family and he moved out to L.A. in hopes of getting away from the rigidity of his parents' life there. The thing is, Belmore is nothing if not rigid, and he should have realized this by now. "I can't say 'Nice latte, Bert,' because that would get me fired?"

"Bert doesn't go to the supermarket or get his own coffee," I say, letting him in on another obvious truth. "Ever."

"Oh." Matthias considers this for a moment and then nods once he's processed the information. "Okay."

"So could you . . ." I gesture toward the door.

"I don't think he wants to be bothered," Matthias says. "He usually leaves the door open, but it's been closed all morning."

"He needs to be up on twenty-four in six minutes. I'm

going to need you to either call him or knock on the door, but I need you to do it now. Please, Matthias."

There is no way I can knock on Fuller's door, not with Matthias here. That would break the chain of command. I've already shown him up in a meeting today, I don't want to cross Fuller again.

"What if he yells at me?" Matthias asks, but he stands up and walks toward the door. There is a good inch and a half of bare ankle between the cuff of his trousers and his sleek leather loafers. Despite my mounting stress level, I can't help but smile. "Sometimes he yells."

"He should never yell at you, Matthias. You're much too adorable," I admit. But adorably reluctant or not, I still need him to do his job. "Just knock and say, 'Mr. Fuller, you're needed up in Corporate.' Make sure you open the door wide enough so that he sees me. He'll know what's up. Ready?"

"Okay." Matthias gives a short knock on the door, opens it, and sticks his head in. "Mr. Fuller . . . He's not in here."

"Check the bathroom!" I yelp.

"Okay." Matthias walks in, and I peer around the doorway into Fuller's office. It's overdecorated just like its missing occupant—lots of leather; dark, exotic woods; and slightly disturbing sculptural art. The bathroom door is ajar, so all it takes is a push from Matthias's finger to open it. "He's not in here either, but . . ."

"But what!" I have five minutes to get Cris Fuller's sculpted ass up seven floors or else. And I don't know what the "or else" might be because I've never, not even once, failed to come through for Bert. "But what, Matthias?"

"There's another door here . . ."

"A what?" I run in, not stopping until I bump into Matthias. "Well, slap me silly, there is another door."

Matthias steps aside and lets me do the honors. I turn the knob and see that it opens directly onto the stairwell.

"If Bert calls here looking for me, tell him I'm on my way up. Do not tell him we have no idea where Fuller is. Do not tell him about this door or that I'm about to go through it or that I've left without Fuller. Better yet, if he calls you, hang up. If Fuller shows up, you send him straight to twenty-four. Understand?"

"Okay." Matthias backs out, toward the safety of his desk. "Okay, Raquel."

I sprint up the seven flights, the *ECA* file pressed to my chest with one hand to keep my boobs from flying all over the place, my other hand holding my hair to keep it out of my face so I don't trip. I reach the twenty-fourth floor with less than a minute to go and with no hope at all of having any lip gloss left on my mouth or setting my hair to rights. If I'm lucky enough to run into Kyle Martin now, it's just my bad luck.

Attempting to catch my breath, I speed-walk toward the Big Conference Room, trying to figure out what in the hell to say to Bert. My only hope is to come up with a lie that won't be an outright falsehood and won't hint at the truth either.

As I round the corner, I skid to a stop when I come upon Bert, Kyle, and Cris Fuller standing there in the hallway shooting the breeze. Both Kyle and Cris look a little windswept and a tad on the sunburnt side. Bert just looks plain livid, but he's trying to hide it.

"There she is," Fuller says as if I'm some absentminded

novice late for morning prayers. "We were beginning to worry you got lost on your way here."

I say nothing but give him a nod and an empty half smile. Fuller can be as rude as he wants to me, but I don't have that kind of leeway. I hand Bert the file and then stand back. Whatever is going to happen has been in the works since way before I got Bert's phone call ten minutes ago.

Company Maneuvers . . .

This is a high-level meeting—senior execs and department vice presidents from Creative, Development, Publicity, Marketing, Kyle Martin, and . . . me. Instead of my being dismissed back to my desk, where I could blot the sweat from in between my breasts and under my arms, Bert has situated me in one of chairs against the wall. He wants me close, but I can't be at the table. That would throw off the seating order.

Bert is three chairs down from the head of the table where, if he were attending this meeting, Walter Belmore would sit. Since he's not here, his chair is empty. Kyle sits to the right of Mr. Belmore's empty chair, diagonally across from where I'm trying to fade into the woodwork. He is the most senior person here, and the meeting will start when he's ready.

"Raquel." Bert gestures for me to come over. I do so in a few quick steps, bending over so he can talk to me without raising his head. "When Mr. Martin is ready, start up the *ECA* presentation."

I nod, take the thumb drive from him, and make my way

to the back of the room, where there's a running laptop, to plug in the drive. I stand at the ready, waiting for a signal to double-click the PowerPoint presentation.

"All right." Kyle looks around the room, and all the murmuring stops cold. "Looks like we're good to go, Raquel."

I feel myself blush as heads swivel toward me. I'm not supposed to be here, and yet the vice president of Corporate just bothered to single me out by name. I open the file, walk over to Bert, hand him the matchbook-size remote that will allow him to control the slides, and take my seat, aware that people are watching me the whole time.

Bert clicks past a few pages, then pauses on a slide for the logo for *Extracurricular Activities,* a mindless sex farce scheduled to be Belmore's first out of the gate summer release. Bert puts the clicker down but keeps it in his hand, indicating that what's on the screen is a problem. From where I'm sitting, I watch as the back of Cris Fuller's neck turns a few shades pinker, the natural shade of his rising indignation clashing with his fake tan.

"I just want to get to the bottom of what may have happened." Bert starts by laying the potential for blame all around, just as a good vice president should. Subtly, almost imperceptibly, Cris Fuller's fellow execs shift away from him while the veeps, assured of their places on the Belmore Corp. food chain, lean forward.

"Who says there's anything wrong with the logo?" Fuller snaps. He's sitting next to Bert, as befits his number two position in Marketing, but neither of them is looking at each other.

Bert clicks to the next slide. There are two blocks of seemingly identical shades of red. All that differentiates them is the text below, which tags the right square as P199C and the left one as P200C.

"I really don't see . . . ," Fuller starts again, stubbornly emphasizing his oneness in a room full of people who have already separated him from the herd. "Really, I don't see that there is any sort of issue."

"If you would have read your own marketing report, Cris, you'd know P199C had a half point higher favorability rating than P200C with the target demographic," Bert says.

He's quoting the stat I pulled out of Fuller's report. It was the only thing I could come up with that would be of any interest to Bert. Otherwise, Fuller's report and marketing plan is spot-on. *Extracurricular Activities* is a dumb T-and-A movie full of fart and pot jokes that will either make lots of money or fade into merciful obscurity. The color of the logo is the least of its problems. This is beside the point, of course. This meeting isn't about the logo, marketing, or even the movie. Bert's pissed that Cris Fuller has played golf, gone sailing, or just plain hung out in the sun with Kyle Martin, and there is nothing he can do about it since he wasn't invited.

"If you would have read your report, you would have realized it is an issue," Bert says without hesitation as he moves in to deliver the deathblow. This might be the flimsiest of excuses to put Cris Fuller's head on the chopping block, but people have been fired for less. "As you know, the margin on this movie is knife-blade slim. Considering that you were the main proponent of this project, I would think you'd take something like this into account."

People nod, some make thoughtful faces. Now that an issue has been identified and a culprit has been named, it's safe to agree with Bert. ("A whole half a point? It's going to cost millions in domestic ticket sales!") Bert has the marketing report to back him up. Fuller has ignored said marketing report and, not only that, has overstepped his bounds by kissing up to Kyle Martin.

"What happens now, Cris?" Kyle asks, putting Fuller on the spot and leaving it up to him to reach into his designer bag of tricks and offer up something, anything.

Bert knows enough to keep his mouth shut. He's planted the seed and needs to sit back and watch while it grows and strangles Fuller.

"The art department can make the change for the DVD. The release date is far out enough for foreign distribution to make the change on the posters, too." Despite his red neck, Fuller's voice is steady. "Most of the profits were projected in overseas markets, and domestically a new trailer tested off the charts with our target demographic."

He knows what he's talking about because he knows his report, and he's smart enough to quote the part that everyone here cares about the most, the financial forecast. People now start to lean away from Bert and toward Fuller.

"If you still think we need to change the color of the logo, changes can be made, but they'll cost at least a half million. It's your call, Bert."

And it's with that single word—Bert—that the power dynamics shift away from my boss. Belmore is a very old-fashioned, some say archaic, company with many unwritten rules that govern daily interactions. Men always wear suits and keep their hair 1950s businessman tidy and tight. Women who hope to advance beyond intern or receptionist never wear slacks. Everyone above assistant is addressed as Mr. or Ms., and a junior employee, no matter how senior, never, ever, calls a veep by his or her first name.

"Sounds reasonable enough. What do you think, Bert?" Kyle asks.

He's giving Bert a chance to fall on his sword and bow out of this pissing match with some pride left. He's also called the meeting and ruled in Fuller's favor. Bert has lost and lost big. For a moment everyone holds their breath. We are witnessing the sunset of an illustrious thirty-year career.

Bert nods his head and stands up. He walks out of the room. I'm the only one who gets up to follow him.

Creative Differences . . .

I sit at my desk staring at my uneaten Pop-Tart and can of flat Diet Coke. Bert has shut himself in his office, and I know better than to ask if he wants me to have his lunch sent up from the commissary. The smell of cigarette smoke tickles my nose, and I send a spray of Febreze in the direction of his door.

News has spread of Bert's smack down, and it's as if a vacuum is hovering over this corner of the Belmore Tower as people rush to kiss the new supposed king's ring or barricade themselves in their offices to wait out the siege.

"Call in the triple S core group and send up lunch." Bert is about to go back into his office when he reaches out for the Febreze.

I wait for him to close his door, but he doesn't. He walks around the room, spraying here and there. On my computer, I bring up the list of names and extensions I need to dial. I start with the person in charge, the vice president of Creative; if he comes, everyone else will be forced to attend.

"Hello, Jessica, it's Raquel from Mr. Floss's office. Mr. Floss would like to meet with Mr. Cole in his office. I'm arranging for lunch."

"I'll check Mr. Cole's schedule." Jessica clicks off. I start counting seconds. Anything longer than twenty and it means Cole won't be coming, which means that there won't be a lunch meeting. Again. Ever. At least not for Bert at Belmore. "Raquel?"

"Yes!" I'm so stressed, I'm practically wetting myself. "Yes, Jessica? I'm here."

"Mr. Cole says he'll have a tuna on rye, an undressed side salad, and diet decaf iced green tea with candied ginger on the side. He'll be there in fifteen minutes if that works with Mr. Floss's schedule."

"That's fine. Perfectly fine. Thanks, Jessica."

"Of course . . . It's going to be okay, Raquel," Jessica adds before hanging up.

I call down to the commissary and order a sandwich platter, drinks, and bottled water along with Bert's usual chef salad and Cole's lunch. I quickly make courtesy calls to the rest of the people on my list. Some have already left their desks, and the rest say they're on their way. This is good, it gives me hope. Bert's not dead in the water, he's merely been wounded. We can recover from this. All Bert needs to do is be his usual decisive self, and he picked the right project to recover with. Triple S, as Bert calls it, is as open and shut as projects get.

Phone calls made, I knock on the doorjamb of his office. He's stopped freshening the air and is now taking in his view.

"Mr. Floss? Everyone should be here within the next few minutes. Should I bring down the screen?"

Bert nods but doesn't turn around. I click a few buttons on the console on his desk, and the screen drops from the ceiling, covering the Picasso. Bert still doesn't turn from the window, so I hold off on closing the shades. I go about arranging his office for the meeting, making sure the matching custom-made sofas are square and the armchair where Bert will be sitting is centered to the screen. I'm about to move the flower arrangement from the coffee table to make room for the food when Bert speaks.

"Raquel, move the meeting up to Creative."

I stop what I'm doing, the vase hovering an inch or two above the wood surface of the table. Under normal circumstances, say if I worked at a normal company with a normal boss and had normal ambitions in life, I would answer his request with "Are you out of your fucking mind?"

"Of course, Mr. Floss." I put down the vase, making sure it's exactly where it was before, and walk out of his office and back to my desk.

I dial Cole's extension and start talking before Jessica can say a word. "Jessica. Raquel. Mr. Floss wants to do it in your conference room. I'll reroute Catering and call—"

"Everyone's here in Mr. Cole's office. I'll let them know and will inform Catering." Jessica clicks off.

I can't take her cutting me off personally. The meeting is on her floor now, and she's the one who needs to make it happen, even if it's my boss who's called it.

Bert walks past me, shoving his beefy torso into his suit jacket while trying to keep ahold of the blue SSS folder. He pauses, one foot in the hallway, the other still in the safety of his office suite. "Are you coming or what?"

"Of course, Mr. Floss."

I follow a step or two behind and pretend not to notice as people duck into any available doorway when they see us approaching. No matter what they might have heard about what happened on 24, they still answer to Bert. As far as they're concerned, it's Dead Man Walking (with his assistant in tow) down the hall.

Bert stops in front of the bank of elevators, and it takes me a second to figure out that he's waiting for me to push the up button. I reach around him and give it a quick couple of taps. This is so unlike Bert, he's normally so self-sufficient. It's the kind of move I'd expect from Cris Fuller.

"Lunch?" he asks, naturally expecting me to understand what he means by the word.

"It's been taken care of, Mr. Floss."

He doesn't need to know how this is going to happen or who is going to take care of it. He just wants to fill the uncomfortable silence that's swallowed up his entire floor.

Mercifully, the elevator to our left pings and opens. I step to the side and let Bert get on first. Inside, I press 21 and count off the longest thirty seconds of my life. When the doors open, there's an intern waiting to escort us to the conference room. Interns always want to work Creative or one floor below, in Development, and they're willing to work for free. Since there are so many of them, most end up doing pointless tasks, but a Belmore internship looks great on a résumé.

"Mr. Floss?" Her eyes dart between us.

She's so scared of messing up that she's choking right in front of us. Her nails are bitten to the quick, and she needs a coating of ChapStick on her lips. She must be very new if she's taking her job so seriously. Bert doesn't bother to stop and acknowledge her but proceeds toward the conference room. We fall into step behind him.

"Bert!" Parker Cole, whose first name is really Marvin but who uses his wife's maiden name as his first because his name is Marvin, greets Bert outside the conference room doors.

"Parker."

They shake hands, two quick pumps and release. On cue another intern opens the doors to the conference room. Technically, Cole presides over a slightly larger department and has more cool cachet, but Bert has seniority and a closer personal relationship with Walter Belmore. Because of this, Cole is forced to ride bitch in his own conference room while Bert drives the meeting. That Cole is still toeing the hierarchical line doesn't make what he's doing any less of a kind gesture.

"We're all ready to go in here," Cole says, rocking back and forth on his heels. He can't go into his conference room until Bert does.

"Good."

Bert goes in, followed by Cole and the rest of the triple S team. I bring up the rear, just before the catering cart that's being pushed by an intern.

"So we're here to talk about *Super Suzie Sunshine*," Cole says from his spot at the head of the table. "Suzie is a tween-friendly cartoon heroine, targeted specifically at a market Belmore needs to capture to grow our animation division. We foresee marketing opportunities, from backpacks to three-D movies . . ."

Interns buzz around, distributing sandwiches and drinks. Cole's and Bert's lunches are the first to hit the table.

A PowerPoint slide comes up on the screen behind Cole. I stare at the image of the obviously excited cartoon heroine, mesmerized by her erect nipples. Despite having seen the same image too many times to count, I'm still startled by it.

"Uh . . ." An intern stands next to me. "We only have a veggie sandwich left."

"Thanks. That's fine," I say and take it. I make a mental note to send Jessica a cookie bouquet even though I know she won't eat them; she's five seven and all of 105 pounds. Cookie bouquets are an inside joke with the assistants because they're what our bosses get us on the day formerly known as Secretaries Day and now known as Cookie Bouquet Day.

"Suzie offers cartoon audiences innovative, groundbreak- ing entertainment . . ."

Despite his well-rehearsed talking points and the caliber of his PowerPoint presentation, Cole can't get around the fact that America isn't ready for this type of innovative, ground- breaking entertainment. Japan and parts of Europe would be all over Suzie and her headlights, but not Madison, Wiscon- sin. Suzie might as well have cameltoe, a tramp stamp tattoo, and a bottle of cheap gin fused to one hand while the other is flipping the bird to all that's decent, moral, and wholesome.

I know this because I've put together the marketing report and memo Bert is currently scanning. He is ignoring his salad and, from all appearances, Cole as well.

The pilot of the cartoon tested so low, Bert had me fly out

to Madison to do a second session to confirm the numbers. The numbers I ended up with were even lower than those of the first test. People were downright offended by the sight of Suzie. The smart writing, sidekicks who are likable and multicultural, and potential for product tie-ins matter for nothing when a thirty-two-year-old mother of three writes "SMUT" across her comment card.

As she's drawn, Suzie is so particular to the creative geeks who've dreamed her up, she's virtually unmarketable to their supposed target audience and, more important, to the parents who are supposed to pay for the backpacks, T-shirts, and bedsheets. Once again Creative has confused their muse with product, but we in Marketing don't have the same luxury. Marketing deals with the here, the now, and the statistically relevant. Everyone here knows *Super Suzie Sunshine* will never see the light of day, but they're still holding out hope that the memo in Bert's little blue folder will tell them what they want to hear.

Everyone follows through with the motions of the presentation, nodding at the right parts, laughing at Cole's rehearsed jokes. Bert even offers up neutral but thoughtful questions when Cole pauses for them. After these niceties, Cole and his group of fellow creatives in charge of *Super Suzie Sunshine* wait for Bert to make his pronouncement.

Bert takes his time, building up anticipation even though he already knows what it is he's going to say. It's all right there in the memo I've written for him. He clears his throat, pauses, and then speaks.

"Just because Jennifer Aniston got away with sporting a couple of headlights on *Friends* doesn't mean it won't freak out soccer moms if *Super Suzie Sunshine* runs around saving the world sporting tit erections. Sorry, guys, but you're going to have to eat this one."

I worded it a little differently, but I'm used to Bert putting his own hardened-veteran spin on my memos.

"What do we need to do to make this work, Bert?" Cole asks because he has to. Nothing goes into production without Bert's signature.

The solution to Suzie's two big problems is in the memo—she needs to go from a distracting C cup with nipples to a small A cup with no nipples. Once this is done, Bert will give his okay to retest the pilot, and then *Super Suzie Sunshine* will go into production and all those backpacks and bedsheets will be that much closer to cluttering the rooms of little girls around the country.

"Get rid of her tits," Bert says. "That's a start, Parker."

"Bert," Cole begins, but Bert cuts him off before he can try to argue that it's time for cartoon heroines to be anatomically correct.

"It's just that simple, Parker. Mothers won't let their kids watch a cartoon with a main character who has a bigger rack than they do."

Cole leans back in his seat, his pen pressed to his lips as he stares up at the image of Suzie on the screen.

"I'm sorry, Bert, but that's not going to happen," he finally says.

It takes me a moment to realize the high-pitched whine in my ear isn't an overheated hard drive or a fluorescent light going on the fritz. The noise is coming from Bert. My boss is crying.

four | WEIGHTY MATTERS

The Reckoning . . .

In between obsessively reloading Deadline Hollywood and Defamer to see if news of Bert's flame-out has leaked to the blogs, I stare at the phone, willing it to ring. I've made a deal with it—for every three times I call it, it's supposed to ring once with a real phone call.

I do, though, pick it up when I hear someone approaching. I yammer on about deadlines and deliverables, restaurant reservations and gift basket orders. Nothing more than the usual nonsense of my work-related conversations, but vague enough that it gives the appearance of being busy so whoever is walking past will think twice about interrupting me. Not that anyone is dropping by for a chat or even slowing down as they pass my door. I have what Bert has, and no one wants to catch it—career cooties.

The actual diagnosis is nervous exhaustion, but the official story is that Bert's taking a well-earned vacation. Yesterday, when Bert's current wife came to pick him up, she brought along her personal doctor. In the span of a minute, he diagnosed and drugged Bert and the three of them hurried out of the building. I'm not trying to minimize my boss's very real medical issue, but career cooties sounds a lot more jaunty and curable than nervous exhaustion. No one believes Bert is taking a vacation anyway.

Bert has the luxury of treating his nerves and cooties at home, but I have to be at my desk. I'm to go about my day and compile hourly reports on what I've accomplished, which I fax over to Bert's home office. Bert will then fax me back with additional tasks or follow-up questions on my reports. Sometimes he faxes me blank pages. I make sure to shred those right away.

My boss is now a Brother IntelliFax-4100e high-speed business-class laser fax machine.

I look down at the piece of paper in my hand. It has just two words on it—gum balls. I crumple it up and then smooth it out before I feed it into the shredder, where it joins the rest of the day's faxes.

In his office, Bert has a vintage gum ball machine. It sits next to the bookcase where he displays his myriad industry awards and commendations for all the good works he writes checks to. In case of a fire or earthquake, Bert has instructed me to save the gum ball machine, and I've never questioned his attachment to it. What I have wondered about is his issue with the actual gum balls—Bert cannot and will not tolerate blue gum balls. It's my job to fish out any and all the blue gum balls when I refill the machine. This is one of the lowly assistant tasks that Bert dignifies by being out of the office for, but today I wouldn't mind the company. Maybe I'd even ask him what he has against blue gum balls.

I've been saving this task for the end of day so I can hide in Bert's office and maybe drag it out to six o'clock. With half an hour to go, I let myself in, locking the door behind me as I've been instructed to do by an earlier fax.

I empty out what's left in the machine, tossing them into the trash bin, and then take two bowls and a large bag of assorted gum balls from the credenza. I'm about to dip into the bag when I realize I should wash my hands.

"So, Raquel," I say in a fair imitation of Bert's gruff voice, "you have two options. Let yourself out, lock the door, walk down the hall to the employee washroom, and maybe have to make awkward chitchat with the very people you've been avoiding all day, or take a look at what's behind the door three feet from you. What's it going to be?"

"Well, Bert. I'm thinking I'm going to take a chance on option two," I answer him/me.

I walk toward the closed door of Bert's en suite, the one room I've never been in, half expecting my boss to materialize to ask me what the fuck I think I'm doing. He doesn't. I open the door, peeking around as if I'm in a horror movie.

"Oh my . . . ," I breathe as I'm drawn inside to see more. The second my foot touches the marble floor, lights above the toilet and sink turn on. I turn slowly around, taking it all in. I cannot understand why Bert would ever want to leave this room. "It's heaven. Carrara marble–covered heaven."

His bathroom *does* have a steam shower big enough for two, even for a Bert-size two. The walls are a soothing gray, and there are miles and miles of creamy white marble—in the shower, on the countertop, on the floor. This is the kind of bathroom I'd hope to find in heaven.

Only two things stand out in the bathroom—one for how

wrong it is for Bert and the other because it sums Bert Floss up in a nutshell.

The toilet, a minimal throne of white, doesn't look like a toilet. At least none that I've ever been lucky enough to sit on. It's a slightly oblong shape, without a tank to ruin the lines. With just the slightest touch, the lid raises and lowers, and a press of the discreet foot pedal flushes it. Even for a toilet, it truly is a thing of beauty.

On the wall next to it, though, is a standard-issue truck stop urinal, complete with a sweetly antiseptic deodorizing cake. Even more disturbing is the mirror above it, set exactly to Bert's sight line.

I wander over to the sink to look at myself in the mirror. There's a little darkness under my eyes and red around my nose, but nothing a bit of concealer can't hide. But even makeup and great lighting can't hide the sour face that's staring back at me. I notice, for the first time, there's a distinct frown line in the making between my eyebrows.

"Lady"—I try to smile, but it makes me look like a slightly uncomfortable schoolmarm on parents' visiting day—"you look stressed out and then some."

I know enough not to give in to the temptation to open drawers or otherwise disturb the sanctity of Bert's bathroom any more than I already have. But the sleek digital scale in the corner is fair game. I slide off my shoes—no reasonable person ever wears shoes when she weighs herself—and then step on. The numbers blink a few times, as if it's not sure, before settling on 147.6.

"That can't be right," I gasp. "That can't be what I weigh."

I step on and off the scale a few times, but it always reads

147.6, except for the one time it rounds up to 148. Technically 147.6, even 148, falls within the acceptable range for my height of five foot eight, but it also designates me as obese for my zip code. I live in a part of town where a steady stream of size zeros parade up and down the streets as they make their way from their cars to Pilates classes to work off that last ounce of nonexistent fat.

The last time I weighed myself I distinctly remember clocking in at a respectable 133.3. The point three I wrote off as not having gone to the bathroom beforehand, but the rest I knew was all me. I remember feeling distinctly proud, maybe even smug. Despite my having given up any pretense of trying to fit working out into my life, my weight was still fine. That was a few months ago, or was it last year? Whenever it was, the fact remains that I don't weigh 133 pounds anymore.

I've gained fourteen pounds in the form of extra-cheese pizza (to stave off brittle bones) and double orders of Chinese chicken salad (for fiber) from the commissary. This doesn't take into account the containers of tom kha gai I pick up from my favorite Thai place on the way home, having convinced myself that the fragrant coconut soup is healthy because it's liquid. Liquid fat as it turns out.

"Oh, Raquel," I sigh down to my chipped toenail polish, "what have you done to yourself?"

Without letting myself think about what I'm doing, I strip off all my clothes and step toward the floor-to-ceiling mirror.

"No!" I scream and jump away from the sight, but there's no denying it. This is what I look like naked, and it ain't good. I minored in kinesiology, for Christ's sake! How could I have not noticed?

The obvious answer is because I haven't wanted to.

I've always been thin. When I was a child and teenager, a full roster of dance classes and cheerleading practice let me live off a diet of Cheetos and Sprite without suffering the consequences. When I was seventeen I practically lived in my Rollerblades, only taking them off when I discovered the joy that was Tae Bo. During college, I led step classes for my Alpha Theta Pi sisters. I did it because I liked the feeling of synchronizing a room full of women and because it got me out of some of the more hated sorority duties, like getting up early on weekend mornings to patrol the grounds for crushed beer cans and cast-off panties.

Daily exercise has, had, always been part of my life. I may have been a mediocre student, had a spotty record with boyfriends, but my abs had always been there for me. But once I got serious about my job at Belmore, the gym and just about everything else was pushed further and further down my to-do list. I've worked on building a career, but at the cost of something that was once very important to me—muscle tone.

Any I ever possessed has melted away like a generous pat of butter atop a stack of hot pancakes. What I've been left with is smooshy, gelatinized flesh that has been lurking just under the surface, waiting to take over my body.

"I have saddlebags," I say, my voice muffled by the silk-covered walls and heated marble floor. "*Fucking* saddlebags."

Damage Control . . .

"Where the hell have you been?" Frappa's voice booms over the speaker on Bert's desk.

I'm sitting on his chair, wrapped in a blanket-size towel after what has to have been one of the top five most sensational physical experiences of my life—a steam shower.

"Nowhere. I mean, I've been here the entire time." It's well past six, and I should be thinking about going home. "Why?"

"What the fuck, Raquel. I called your desk phone, your Belmore cell, and your other cell. No answer on any of them." Frappa delivers her sentences in a clipped, to-the-point tone. "In all the time that I've known you, you have never not answered at least one of your phones. Even when I called you and you were in the bathroom."

"Oh. Sorry." I feel my shoulders start to tense up. Maybe, once my skin deprunes, I'll take another shower before Bert's private cleaning guy shows up. There are so many knobs and showerheads in there, I only got to experience half of them. "I was . . . busy. I mean away from all my phones. Sorry. Really."

"Don't you 'sorry' me. I'm in the lobby and expect you to have your coat and hat on by the time I get there."

"Frappa!" Nothing. She's on her way. The fact that security doesn't let anyone who isn't on the visitor list past the check-in desk won't stop her. Frappa spends enough time at Belmore that she should have a satellite office here.

I dash into the bathroom and shove my still moist body back into my clothes. I ball up my panty hose and shove them in my pocket. Holding my shoes, I'm about to lock the door when I spot my unfinished gum ball task.

"Damn it!" I run on my tiptoes back to the coffee table and, like a toddler on a Chinese factory line, I start sorting gum balls, using both hands to double my productivity.

"What the fuck are you doing and why is your hair wet?"

Frappa looms over where I'm kneeling on the carpet. She's dressed in her usual Stevie Nicks best, a flowing skirt, bell-sleeved, low-cut top that barely contains her two heaping scoops of mammary heaven, and enough bangles on both her arms to set off metal detectors in a five-mile vicinity. Her abundant blond hair is piled on top of her head, held there by sparkly clips.

Frappa is in her early forties and has written off any ideas of entering another legally binding romantic relationship for the sake of her mental health and to preserve her personal assets. This vow freed her from a tortured life of constant dieting, and she proudly carries around the fifty extra pounds that come with not giving a damn and enjoying her life. Once a svelte Nordic snow bunny, she's morphed into a busty Brunhilde—minus the breastplate and horned Viking helmet. Whatever her weight, Frappa is just as commanding in person as she is on the phone.

"I'm taking all the blue ones out, and then I'll shove as many as I want into my mouth and chew until I dislocate my jaw." This is what I had actually planned to do with the rest of my evening. "What are you doing here?"

"What I'm doing here, sugar tits, is saving you from drowning in a stew of self-pity." She hauls me up from the floor.

"I'm fine, Frappa," I say without conviction. "I have to finish sorting these gum balls."

Frappa looks at me for a second before she pushes me aside, dumps both bowls into the machine, and screws on the top.

"Done," she says as she pops a stray gum ball into her

mouth. "From what I hear, the least of Bert's concerns should be blue balls."

"Oh, you heard." I slump down onto one of the couches, finally giving in to the depressive funk that's been hanging over my head since yesterday. "It's not as bad . . . Okay, maybe it is, but what am I supposed to do?"

"We're going out," she says. "That's the first thing you can do."

"I don't want to," I protest, knowing she'll win in the end. She always does. "I just want to go home, put on my flannel boxers, and tweeze ingrown hairs from my bikini line while I watch design shows on HGTV."

"Uh, no way, lady," she says. "We're going to stop by this cocktail thing I have to make an appearance at and then we're going to put our heads together and figure what your next move should be."

"I have no moves, Frappa. You of all people should know how it works. I'm Bert's assistant. If he goes, I go."

"You are coming with me to this party." Frappa pats my arm with heavily bejeweled fingers. "Because it's a party that you need."

"I'm not dressed for a party." It's my last lame attempt at staving off the inevitable.

"What you are dressed for is a funeral," Frappa says as she hauls me up by my armpits.

"Thank you for being so honest." I put my hand on Frappa's plump shoulder and squeeze.

"Honey, I'm fat, rich, don't give a fuck, and am holding enough cards so I can spare one for you." Frappa reaches into my pocket and pulls out my panty hose, considers them for a moment, and then stuffs them between the cushions of Bert's couch. "The least I can do is help out a friend who's too stupid to help herself."

"Again, thank you for your honesty," I say as I dig them out. "Now please shut the fuck up."

Occupational Hazards . . .

I'm stuffed into a strapless black pencil dress with an almost overflowing bodice Frappa talked me into and paid for during a frantic ten-minute stopover at Bebe. It's been a long time since I've shown so much of me, and there is a lot more me than there had been the last time I did.

"No, nuh-uh, Frappa. There's no way in hell that I'm getting out of this car," I say as she pulls into the long driveway of Walter Belmore's Brentwood estate. "Especially not dressed like this."

"What's wrong with how you're dressed?" She looks over at me, genuinely perplexed. "Did you forget you have a pair of tits under your nun suit? You look great. If I had half the ass that I do, we'd be dressed like twins."

"I can't, Frappa." All the same, when the valet opens up the door of Frappa's cherry red Jaguar, I get out. "There are people in there that I work with."

"Which is exactly why you're here." She stops at the foot of the stairs and considers which way to make the best entrance. "You are here to be seen. After my third husband left me for another man, did I stay home and cry?"

"Yeah, you kind of did," I remind her. She called me right

after he walked out, and that's when I knew we were really friends. She cried and took a pair of garden shears to his suits while I kept Kleenex and Ding Dongs close at hand.

"But I still made sure to go out to dinner at least four nights a week, and I never cried at the office," she says.

She entwines her arm in mine for support, and I press into her for some much needed body warmth. We march— well, she marches and I kind of am dragged along—up to the house.

"Bert can hide out in his mansion, but you need to show them that you're still a viable young, sexy woman who is not going to let herself get dragged under the bus because of someone else's very public fuckup."

"You have no idea how much I hate you right now." I sigh. "But I know you're doing this for my own good."

I make my first pass of the room right behind Frappa. I smile and nod and suffer through endless introductions with people who give me a look as if they know they should know me but can't quite place me. Frappa, who plays this game much better than I could ever hope to, doesn't mention Belmore or Bert. Tonight, in my tarty dress, bare legs, and high heels, I'm just Raquel, and it makes me feel even more naked.

Eventually, I find a quiet corner where I can sit and take in everything around me. Only the first floor of Walter Belmore's home is open to most guests. Stationed at the foot of the staircase that leads to the upper floor is a security guard whose job it is to make sure no one goes up the stairs who isn't supposed to. At regular intervals one of Mr. Belmore's assistants, who wear variations of the same suit, approaches with a guest or two, usually an exec and his spouse. The guard checks their names against a list, touches his hand to his ear and speaks into his shirt cuff, and then steps out of the way. As they make their way up the grand staircase, another couple makes their way down from their audience with the old man. I watch their faces carefully before they're swallowed up by the crowd. They have a certain glow that doesn't come from furtively snorted coke.

Face time, even a minute or two, with Walter Belmore is as coveted as an audience with the Pope, the President of the United States, and Oprah combined. At least it is for those who consider Hollywood to be the center of the universe.

I feel the beginnings of an anxiety attack coming on as the crowd and their phoniness suck the oxygen out of room, out of my very lungs. All I want to do is escape, but I can't make a scene. Instead, I quickly down two flutes of what must be very good champagne. The buzz hits me almost immediately.

I stand up, unsteady on my heels and with my head fuzzy from champagne. It would actually be kind of pleasant if I was at home in my pajamas and no one would care if I did a face plant on my secondhand Pottery Barn rug.

I carefully make my way over to where Frappa is talking the ear off a couple of Belmore execs and tug at the corner of her velvet scarf.

"Frappa," I say, sounding way more relaxed than I feel, "I'm going to make a circuit around the pool and then work my way back inside. Okay?"

"That's what I want to hear!" Frappa reaches down and gives me a pat on the behind. "When you're done with that, come find me."

My heels go from parquet floors to flagstone and dim

lighting soon enough. I stand in the shadows well away from the pool, watching as people mill about or stand in small clusters. I take deep breaths and close my eyes for a second, reaching out a hand to steady myself when a wave of dizziness sweeps over me.

"Hey! I know you." A guy around my age in an unremarkable suit ambles up to me. "Tell me where I know you!"

"Maybe it's me that knows you and not the other way around," I say, taking advantage of the fact that he's obviously loaded.

"Yeah . . . No! I know you. You work at Belmore." He digs his elbow into my side and whispers loudly, "Everyone here works at Belmore. Where do you work at Belmore?"

"I'm . . . I'm just a receptionist. Where do you work at Belmore?"

"Accounting. Big money. Big everything!" Again with an elbow to the ribs, this time, though, he purposely brushes the side of my breast. "My name is Mike. What's yours?"

"I'm Natasha," I lie. I know Mike, at least via e-mail. Maybe he'll figure out who I really am when he sobers up, but right now I have nothing to lose by not telling him.

"Here!" He thrusts a full glass of champagne at me. "It's free and it's good shit!"

"Why thank you, Mike from Accounting." I pretend to take a sip. "Do you know where I can find a bathroom?"

"I think there's one off the main hall," he slurs into my cleavage.

"Don't go anywhere. I'll be right back," I lie again.

I turn on my heel, ready to make a break for it, when I come face-to-face with Walter Belmore.

Walter Belmore, great-grandson of the founder, Horace Belmore, is somewhere between seventy-five and ancient, stooped over with a pale, liver-spotted complexion and an interstate of blue veins running just under the surface of his skin. It's well known, and documented, that Walter Belmore likes no one, including himself. He's gone as far as to have disowned all six of his children from his four failed marriages. He even sued his own mother after she suggested in a *Vanity Fair* profile that her son has a bit of a vindictive streak to him.

"Mr. Belmore. What a lovely party," I say, because it's the only thing I can think of that isn't "Holy shit, it's Walter Belmore!" I shake his hand and dip my head, stopping just short of a curtsy. Standing at a discreet distance are a half dozen guards and just as many assistants, keeping back the usual phalanx of toadies who hover around him like gnats.

"It's a lovely party," I repeat myself a little louder.

"Yes, yes," he says, looking at me closely. His blue eyes, sunken into his ancient face, are as bright and sharp as those of an MBA grad student on a double dose of Adderall.

"Are you having a nice time?" I ask.

"A nice time?" Walter Belmore echoes, looking at me as if I'm one of the aspiring actresses milling around his pool and drinking the champagne he's paid for.

"Thank you, Mr. Belmore, I am having a nice time. Your home is just . . . lovely." I stand with my sweating hands clasped in front of me, acutely aware of a stray thread on my hem, my dress tickling my knee. "Have a good night, Mr. Belmore."

"Very well, Raquel," he says and reaches out to shake my hand once again.

"Yes, thank you, Mr. Belmore." Heart pumping pure adrenaline, I scurry past the guards, assistants, and now fully sober Mike from Accounting.

I grab a couple of flutes off a passing tray, down them one right after the other, smile at yet another ogling exec, and go into the house to search for Frappa.

"Raquel!" Frappa waves at me, her pale arm like a beacon in a sea of Armani.

"I would tell you what just happened to me, but you wouldn't believe it," I say to her. "Actually, I don't even believe it. Maybe I'm drunk and it didn't even happen."

"Did you get lucky in the pool house?" she asks, eyeballing a hot waiter and the tray of mini–crab cake burgers he's carrying with equal amounts of lust.

"Kind of . . . I'm sorry, Frappa, but I really have no reason to be here," I say, hoping she won't launch into a lecture about self-esteem and networking.

"Honey, half these assholes have no reason to be here," she says, pulling me into a hug. "They just come out for these things because if they had to sit at home alone with their empty thoughts, they'd shoot themselves."

"When you put it that way, I guess I'm having a great time then." I laugh into her cleavage. She pats me on the back and then pinches me between the shoulder blades so that I'll stand up straight. "Frappa, I really need my jacket. I feel so exposed."

"Honey," she says, "people are staring because, as far as they know, real tits went extinct in this town along with woolly mammoths." Nevertheless, she fishes her valet ticket out of her purse and hands it to me. "You look great, Raquel.

Almost makes me want to stop eating altogether so I can be thin like you."

"I'm not thin," I say. "I feel like a chubby girl in skinny girl clothes."

"Poor baby." Frappa squeezes me around the waist. "If you really hate it, I can have someone drive you home."

"I'll be a grown-up, but you have to promise me we'll leave by eleven-thirty."

"Cross my heart," she says. "No later than midnight."

I weave my way through the crowd, avoiding unnecessary eye contact and making it clear by my pace that I'm going somewhere and I need to get there quickly. I'm not being paranoid when my ear catches snippets of conversation like "That's his assistant . . ." "As far as I know he's not coming back . . ." "That's her? What is she doing here?" "What do you mean she was talking to Walter Belmore?"

I'm within feet of the front door and the valet stand on the porch when I see him—Kyle Martin—at the foot of the stairs, where Walter Belmore is making his slow ascent back to the second floor.

"Raquel?" he says. "Raquel!"

I reach for a doorknob, the first I come to. Fortunately, it turns, and I duck inside, closing the door behind me. I lean against it, closing my eyes and breathing hard. When I open them, I realize that I've found the bathroom and that I'm not alone.

An overexercised blonde with that distinct L.A. plastic surgery look is sitting on the counter, trying to blow cigarette smoke out the open window while she stares at herself in the mirror.

"I'm sorry!" I say. "The door was unlocked."

"It's okay. Stay." She smiles at me, showing just the slightest edge of veneered teeth. "It's a little crazy out there."

"Yes . . . I mean it's a great party . . ." I wander over to the sink and wash my hands just to have something to do.

"I've had plenty of experience planning them." She smiles at me again and goes back to staring at herself in the mirror. "I'm Phoebe."

"Yes, I know," I admit.

Phoebe Belmore, Walter Belmore's niece, has acted as the official hostess for Belmore events since the old man divested himself of his last wife some years ago.

Phoebe burnished the dipshit party girl image of her teens and aimless years of her twenties by assiduously attaching her name to very PR-friendly humanitarian missions in her late thirties. (Really, who doesn't think third world children shouldn't have access to slightly irregular designer sneakers?) Of all the Belmores, and there are many, she's been able to craft the appearance that she actually does something with her life, even though all she's done is take her socializing to a more sophisticated level of socially conscious partying.

Her most significant feat, though, has been to worm her way into Walter Belmore's cold heart to become the only living relative he'll publicly acknowledge.

"You're Bert's assistant," Phoebe says as she takes a long drag on her cigarette.

"Yes." I stick my hand out, notice it's still soapy, and retract it again. I almost want to ask why the hell everyone seems to know who I am, but I don't. "Raquel Azorian."

"That's an interesting name," Phoebe says as she fluffs up her hair. "Is it Persian? If you don't mind me asking."

Since she'd already asked, I go ahead and answer.

"No . . . Maybe . . . Sometimes people think I am, depending on what part of town I'm in. As far as I know the Azorians are from Whittier." I can't seem to stop myself from prattling on like a fool. "My dad is an only child. Actually, he was raised in a boys' home, so he really doesn't know much about his family. I guess I should, you know, look into it, our genealogy. Family history is always interesting."

"Some more than others." She laughs but not unkindly. Phoebe's family history is also a corporate one.

The founder of Belmore Corporation, Horace Belmore, decreed that the company was to remain in family control and be head by a male descendant. The head cheese job has been passed down from one Belmore male heir to the next. Unfortunately for Walter Belmore, the current crop of Belmore males are nothing more than voracious teat suckers trading off the family name. Phoebe is the pick of the litter, but nothing short of a sex change and a legal amendment of her birth certificate will give her what she needs to sit in Uncle Walter's chair in the Big Conference Room.

I've always thought it was sad that my father doesn't know much about his family, even though he seems fine with it. Thinking about Phoebe's life, I realize that some people have it worse, even those who appear to have the world and an endless supply of irregular sneakers at their fingertips.

Phoebe looks at me with her overly wide, slightly bugged-out eyes which plastic surgery has just made more pronounced.

"How is it working for Bert?" she asks, moving on from the subject of the burden of one's last name.

"He's great. Everything I know about marketing, I've learned from him," I say, uncomfortable with the way she's looking at me even though I know she can't help it. Her eyelids are pulled so tight, it looks like she has to remind herself to blink. "He really is a genius."

"So he's not a hypercontrolling, paranoid micromanager?" she asks, a tinge annoyed that I'm not playing along with her bathroom gossip game.

"Bert is a great boss. It's a pleasure to work with him." I reach for a towel and dry off my hands. "It's a great party. Thank you for inviting me."

A smile curls her overplumped up lips so they roll unnaturally off her teeth. "Thank you for coming, Raquel."

I walk out of the bathroom, clutching Frappa's valet ticket, half tempted to accept the keys and drive off.

"Raquel." Kyle cuts me off at the front door.

"What is it with my life tonight!" I throw up my hands and feel my cleavage make a break for it. I yank up my dress and scowl at Kyle.

"Let's talk on the porch." He takes me by the elbow and leads me outside. "I was starting to think you shimmied out the window to avoid me."

"That's a good idea." I'm way too freaked out to be impressed that Kyle was waiting for me to come out of the bathroom. "I'm stuck here unless I want to call a cab or have some half-wasted high school dropout with a five-hundred-dollar haircut drive me home."

"I'd be happy to drive you home." Kyle puts a hand to the small of my back and steers me toward a quiet corner. "If that's what you want?"

"If you left now, it would result in a serious lack of ass to kiss," I say, taking out my bad mood on him. "And isn't that the whole point of these things?"

Kyle blinks and then lets out a loud, long laugh. "I knew there was something special about you. No wonder Bert wants to keep you all to himself."

"Yeah, lucky me," I mutter. "My fortunes are forever tied to Bert's, and he has a raging case of cooties."

"Listen, about that. Bert has stepped on a lot of toes over the years. Some people see this as payback, but you have my word—"

"Kyle?" Cris Fuller hurries over to us. He looks as if he expected to find Kyle with his pants around his ankles and me with my lips wrapped around his dick. "What are you doing here, Raquel?"

"Exactly!" I say, throwing up my hands. "Good night, Mr. Martin. Mr. Fuller. Now if you'll both excuse me, I'm going to go sit in my friend's car for the rest of the evening."

five | GUILT BY ASSOCIATION

Assuming the Position . . .

I ease my Honda Civic into my unofficially designated Belmore parking spot, level 5, twenty-two spaces from the elevator. I've gotten here right at eight, as usual, even though I don't expect Bert to come in. I'm on time not only to give the appearance that everything is as close to normal as possible on my end but also to ensure that no one takes my spot. It took me three years to work my way up from level 9, literally the lowest level on the Belmore ranking system. Level 9 is where the undistinguished interns and temps park. It's also where Security keeps the golf carts they use to patrol the grounds.

Even if my hopes of getting a promotion are in purgatory, it doesn't mean I have to give up my parking space.

Only Walter Belmore, who is driven to the office by his equally ancient chauffeur, has an assigned space. It's on level 1, right next to the fastest elevator. When he's not in, the space remains empty out of respect. Everyone else parks in accordance with rank and, more important, clout. To calculate clout, a convoluted formula takes into account title, base pay, bonuses, stock class shares, number of direct reports, and amount of invitations extended by Walter Belmore to join him for morning coffee in his private dining room in a four- to six-month period.

When there is a change in parking spots, all work comes to a standstill as people pause to parse out how and why it happened. Mostly they just want to know how it will affect them. The last big reorder in spaces was when Kyle Martin was named veep of Corporate. Kyle parks right next to Walter Belmore. Bert is three spots away, and Cris Fuller is on level 2 but a spot closer to the elevator than Bert is upstairs. Fuller would never dare usurp Bert's spot, but another vice president might. If that happens, I'll know by ten, when everyone, no matter how high ranking, is in the building. It's been two days since the incident, as I've come to think of Bert's flameout, and no one has made a move on his spot.

My own spot is decent and shows that I've risen, if not in title, in esteem with the whole company itself. My mention in the employee newsletter during my second year for my food drive efforts bumped me up an entire level. Considering my first days at Belmore, I think I've come a pretty long way. A level 5 parking space is nothing to sneeze at or take for granted.

I came to Belmore not as an assistant or even as a receptionist but as a mere temp. Without any connections to land an internship and not having gone to the right school to be hired on as a junior exec, I had to start from the bottom. My existence at Belmore was based solely on doing a job no one else wanted to do. Tasks so tedious and pointless not even interns could be forced to undertake them. Even so, when I got the call from my temp agency asking if I was interested in taking an open-ended assignment at Belmore, I said yes without a second's hesitation.

I fully admit I was dazzled by the idea of working at Belmore. They made the movies I paid to see and the sitcoms I grew up on. Belmore was not some second-rate mortgage company where I wouldn't have the time to learn the phone system and no one expected me to anyway. Things happened at Belmore, and I was convinced that I was going to be part of them. Even though all I ended up doing was sorting through health insurance claims for two months, I could answer with "Belmore" when someone asked me where I worked. The specifics I kept to myself as I bided my time for something better to open up.

Then one day, just like in a movie, I got the call. A receptionist had quit or had a breakdown (stories differed), and the marketing department needed someone to fill in. Looking to get out of a closet-size room with its incessantly flickering fluorescent light, I jumped at the chance to take over the desk, even though I was told it would be temporary. Qualifications for the job, besides not being an idiot, included impeccable penmanship and a pleasant speaking voice, both of which I had to demonstrate before I was let out of the closet.

From the second I sat down behind that semicircular desk, I started my campaign to prove myself indispensable. The custom is to pass the crappiest jobs down the line to the lowest person on the totem pole. And as Bert tries to keep his department free from interns, the junior execs are always looking for someone to foist their work on. It's that way now and was when I arrived on 17.

As a temp receptionist, not even a real Belmore employee, I became the person who was asked to lick envelopes, sort through spec scripts in the storage room, answer the phone, and greet guests. I spent three months watching how things worked and noting what didn't work. I read everything that wasn't sealed that passed my desk and charted the comings and goings of every person who set foot on 17. I knew who was lazy, who expensed lunches with their pot dealers, and who worked maybe three hours out of an eight-hour day. While I made their dentist's appointments and signed for dry cleaning, I kept tabs on everything important going on. All I needed was a chance to prove that I could do more than answer the phone and take down the occasional handwritten message.

"I've been watching you, Raquel," Bert said one day as he passed by the reception desk. "You'll go far in this company if you keep your head up and your knees together."

I'll admit to having gone through various scenarios in preparation for the moment Bert Floss deigned to acknowledge my existence. And I knew I'd get only one chance to make an impression, so I went for it. "Thank you, Mr. Floss. But from what I've seen, a lot of people around here don't know their heads from their knees."

Bert looked at me for a moment before he said, "True enough. Have HR send up someone to cover the phones. I have some work for you."

By the end of the day, I was an official Belmore employee with a salary of $42,789, full benefits, and the title of executive assistant. And I was in complete shock that it actually happened. People like me didn't become executive assistants. People like me temped until they figured things out, if they ever did. But here was my chance and, as Bert said in his own roundabout way, I was smart enough to take it.

Since then I've lived, breathed, and dreamed marketing, reading trade magazines and clunky books by supposed experts, filling notebooks with ideas, schemes, and nuggets of marketing wisdom from Bert. After so many years of half-hearted false starts (selling organic chakra balance cosmetics, two weeks in massage school, a rescinded offer to join the Peace Corps), I finally found my niche. This was supposed to be my very own corporate Cinderella story, and now I find, just moments before the ball, that I'm being relegated back to the kitchen without anyone to even cook for.

I dig through my bag, tucking my keys into the appropriate pocket, and pull out my Granny Smith apple. Before biting into it, I peel off a promo sticker for *Ducks!* that's stuck to its side.

Ducks! is an animated movie about a family of, yes, ducks, and it's Belmore's first foray into full-length animated movies. The Ward twins voice sister ducks, twins who couldn't be more different who have to come together to save the family pond. It's pretty standard fare, but the marketing has elevated it into a much anticipated event. And staring at the sticker, I know I have something to do with this.

A year and a half ago, I was surrounded by boxes of too small *Ducks!* stickers that were going to be trashed, eating my apple, and reading a memo regarding Belmore sponsorship of Governor Schwarzenegger's Healthy Kids program. Apple.

Stickers. Animated movie. Governor Schwarzenegger. The idea hit me so hard, it almost knocked me on my ass. I put together a memo with my idea and presented it to Bert along with his afternoon cup of coffee. After he read it, he peered at me over his glasses and said, "Looks like you won't be fetching my coffee for long, kid."

"If anything," I say to my apple, "we'll always have those memories."

I step out of the elevator feeling slightly less depressed by the prospect of spending my day hunched over a fax machine.

"I have no idea why you're smiling, Raquel," Cris Fuller, decked out in his usual too obvious designer suit and tie, says just as the doors slide closed behind me.

I know it's not some freak coincidence that we're running into each other. Fuller has been waiting for me. He never gets into the office before nine, and he's always one of the first to leave.

"Good morning, Mr. Fuller," I say, my hand curling around my apple. I have no problem with lobbing it at him if he gives me the slightest reason to do so.

"What's so good about it for you?" He leans in close to me but ends up taking a step back when I don't move. I focus on the peeling bridge of his nose and wait for him to say whatever it is he's so eager to eject all over me. "Must be pretty quiet in that office, all by yourself. Nothing to do, no one to see with a boss who won't show his face."

"Mr. Floss is working from home." There isn't much more I can say since he's right about everything. "We're in constant communication, Mr. Fuller. And I'll let him know you've been thoughtful enough to ask how I'm doing."

He straightens his tie and flicks his cuffs so they line up perfectly. His fingernails are nicely manicured, but the tops of his hands are as red as his face except for where his golf gloves shielded them from the sun. Not a good look, one that even French cuffs can't make up for.

"It's too bad, Raquel, that you haven't made more of an effort with me. But it's not too late. You don't have to throw yourself on Bert's funeral pyre," he says. "It's just a matter of time before this happens. You know that, right?"

"I bet you have your outfit already picked out, Cris, but until I see the memo, Bert is still my boss and yours, too." I have nothing to lose by being blunt with him. If anything, I think I'd disappoint Fuller if I didn't at least put up the pretense of a fight.

"You have a real problem with authority, Raquel," he says. He's livid that I've referred to him by his first name. Unfortunately for him, he can't tell on me to my boss, and he can't complain to anyone higher up without looking incredibly petty. "Normally, I like initiative, but I don't like it when it comes at my expense. My advice to you is to start sending out résumés. That's what happens when you mess with the big boys. You're just not . . ."

He trails off as the elevator doors open and out spill a group of junior execs. Seeing Fuller looming over me, they cease their conversations and scatter like startled geese.

"Thank you for the advice, Mr. Fuller. You have a very nice day," I say.

I walk away, calmly, never looking back. I duck into the women's bathroom, lock myself into the first empty stall, and eat the rest of my apple.

The Brush-off . . .

Human Resources is the only Belmore department headed by a woman, Dr. Clarissa T. Winterbourne, and is the unacknowledged finishing school of sorts for female employees who are coming into the company without a prestigious degree (like me) or are rough around the edges but have potential (again, like me). It's where I got my start and a floor I've avoided since then, not wanting to be reminded of my lowly beginnings.

"Hi, I'm Raquel Azorian. Bert Floss's assistant," I say to the receptionist. "I'm hoping I can speak to someone about an issue I'm having."

"I'll let Ms. Nicolson know you're here," she says with all the sincerity and efficiency of a call center support operator.

"Thanks," I say, feigning indifference I don't feel. I sit down and go through a stack of magazines without seeing a word or picture of what I'm looking at. When someone finally approaches me, I'm more than ready to spill my deepest secrets, even though I know this isn't the place for it. I just want someone to listen, sympathize, and tell me everything is going to be okay. Like Kyle did the other night, but this time on the record.

"Ms. Azorian? Hi, I'm Lisbeth," says a woman around my age but obviously new to Belmore. "Ms. Nicolson asked me to show you into a mediation room."

"Do you think she'll be long?" I have no desire to go back to my desk, but I've left the fax machine unattended for almost fifteen minutes.

"Maybe five minutes," she says, glancing down at her watch. "Do you want to come back later?"

"No, it's okay. I'll wait. Cute shoes," I say, bringing both our attention down to her red patent leather heels.

"Thanks! I can get away with wearing them once a week. Any more than that and . . ." She presses her lips together to keep herself from saying more. She looks like a girl, no, a woman who isn't afraid of her femininity. She certainly doesn't look like the sexless, hyperefficient droid I've become.

"I know what you're talking about," I say.

I used to be a cute dresser—never too trendy, but with my own twist to add personality to what I was wearing. When I got serious about my future at Belmore, I also got serious about what I wore, and that was the last of patterned skirts and quirky blouses. Women with any ambition to move up the Belmore ladder dress in slight variations of the same staid blue, gray, or black skirt suit over a jewel-tone silk blouse. Jackets are always worn in the hallways and to meetings, heavy perfume is frowned upon, as is too much makeup. We wear heels, but they are never too pointy or too high. Tights are always opaque but never patterned. Panty hose are nude but nowhere close to sheer. Bare legs are frowned upon except at the summer company picnic, where walking shorts with flats or sandals are acceptable.

We live with and, at times, enforce Belmore's rather parochial fashion rules of dress. A comment like "Oh, that's an interesting blouse" or "Did you get some sun over the weekend?" is enough to send a woman home to change or to the bathroom to wash off her bronzer. The last thing a serious Belmore woman wants is for someone to notice her for something other than her hard work.

There is, of course, a whole other class of Belmore women. What they wear is as far from my wardrobe as possible, even though their skirts still end at the knee and their arms are covered. They wear pencil skirts and clingy sweaters with three-quarter sleeves, bracelets that jangle and earrings that swing. Their perfume smells not like soap and water but like a field of flowers or a Japanese opium den. Their makeup plays up their features instead of obscuring them. They don't bother to hide the fact that they have curves or long hair, and they always seem to wear strapless dresses to the company holiday party. These women aren't looking to go any further, and they don't care who knows it.

Jessica, Mr. Cole's assistant, is one of these women, but the queen bee is Marisa, who is now Kyle's assistant. Her skirts are always the tightest and her sweaters the most clingy. There were other more qualified people for her job, but she made it known that whoever was dumb enough to apply for it would have to deal with her later. Not that these women, and a handful of men, are dumb. If anything they have to be twice as smart as someone like me because they have to play dumb while outthinking everyone else. Me, I took the easy way out and decided I'd let my looks go and my work speak for itself instead of trying to juggle both of them at the same time.

If I was relying on pretty, Cris Fuller would have been a lot nicer to me. He never would have seen me as a threat, but since I've made it clear I'm playing for keeps, he thinks I need to be dealt with before he can assume control of the department.

We come to a stop in front of a small room set up like a therapist's office. There is a small couch and armchair separated by a table with a box of tissues on it. From what I've been told, once the door is closed, the room is soundproof, and there's a hidden panic button near the armchair in case things don't go the Belmore way.

"Ms. Nicolson is on her way. Hope everything works out," Lisbeth says, lowering her voice.

For a moment I want to warn her to take her genuineness and run while she still can. Run far and fast before the overly air-conditioned halls of Belmore freeze her solid.

"Thanks," I say instead and step inside.

"Raquel?" A woman with a grown-out Victoria Beckham bob comes in just as I take a seat on one end of the couch. "Raquel Azorian?"

"Yes?" The way she says my name tells me I should know her. I have an excellent memory for names and faces, but for some reason I can't place her. "That's me."

"You don't remember me, do you?" She sits down, tugging her jacket closed to cover the pudge of tummy spilling over the waistband of her skirt.

"I'm sorry . . ." I trail off, giving her an I'm such an ass, please don't make this any more awkward than it already is smile.

"Of course. I changed my name when I got married. Vanessa Martinez? Eagle Rock High School?" Each word is full of meaning. This is all the information I need, and if I can't place her now, not only am I forgetful but I'm also a bitch.

"Oh, my God! Vanessa!" I don't remember her, and we both know it. "You've changed your hair!"

"I was into Goth then," she admits, "but, hey, high school is a time to experiment, right?"

"Yeah, those were the days," I say, because it would make me a total bitch if I didn't at least appear to agree with her.

I experimented with different looks but stayed far away from anything Goth except at Halloween. Vanessa, though, still has a heavy hand with black eyeliner, a fondness for too light face powder, and a penchant for shoe-polish-black hair dye.

"Wait . . ." Names and faces start to flicker across my mind until, finally, I figure out who she is. "Vee? You're that Vanessa?"

"No one has called me Vee in *years*. Oh, my God, this is so trippy!" She gives me an uncomfortable smile, and I can almost make out the woman behind the heavy makeup. "I was saying to the girls back there, I said, 'This can't be that Raquel Azorian. She was in the homecoming court and prom court at Eagle Rock High *and* voted best smile and best hair our senior year. That Raquel Azorian? Here? No!' But here you are! I had no idea you even worked here."

"Almost four years," I say, rounding up and not bothering to mention that I came here as a temp. Vanessa has access to my file and must already know this.

"Oh, my God!" Vanessa says, almost jumping out of her chair. "I just remembered what they used to call you in high school! The Rack. Remember?"

"Vaguely," I say, recalling not only the defining moment of my freshman year in high school but the event that set me on the path to popularity.

My mother attended a conference with my dad in London and promised to bring me back a souvenir because there's nothing that woman loves to do more than shop for crap. Instead of a small Big Ben replica for my desk or tea towels with the faces of royalty on them, she came home with a dozen Wonderbras. I wore them to their fullest advantage under concert T-shirts, tank tops, and my cheerleading uniform. It didn't matter that anyone could buy Wonderbra knockoffs at Kmart. Those bras vaulted me from obscurity to the primo spot under the shadiest tree in the quad. By the time my real breasts came in and the Wonderbras were nothing but faded scraps of nylon and elastic, I was well established as a popular girl. Still, I was kind of upset that I didn't win best personality along with best hair and smile. That would have given me the yearbook trifecta.

"I guess they still call you that, the Rack." Her eyes dip down to my chest, which is secured behind my three-button jacket.

"Not really." I shrug, feeling every ounce of those fourteen pounds that I've put on. "People grow up, right? Or at least you hope they do."

"God, this is so trippy," Vanessa says, her eyes theatrically wide. "Don't you think? What are the chances of us running into each other after all this time?"

"It's the kind of luck I've had lately," I say. If I've been able to avoid Vanessa in all the time I've been at Belmore, it has been through sheer luck, luck that has obviously run out on all fronts.

"So you went to Cal State L.A.?" she says as she glances down at my file. "For some reason I thought you went to UCLA?"

"I wish! Not to knock my alma mater. I was so busy with the social part of high school that my grades were decent but not spectacular." I chatter on as if I have all the time in the world. "I had a great time at Cal State. Made so many good friends, and I'm still active with my sorority. I mean, as active as I can be. Work keeps me busy."

"I went to Cal State L.A., too," Vanessa says, stubbornly reminding me how I've neglected our non-friendship. "Don't you think it's weird that we never ran into each other and, I don't know, had a coffee or something?"

"It's a pretty big campus," I say as innocently as possible. I'm almost sure I didn't actively avoid Vanessa, but I might have pretended not to see her at the student union a few times. "Huge, actually. I can't remember how many times I got lost just trying to find my classes."

"But we were incoming freshmen at the same time and graduated at the same time. I mean it's not like I avoided any of my old high school friends." She pauses for me to offer up a lame and patently false denial. When I don't, she shrugs. I've made my own bed, and Vanessa is going to make sure I lie in it. "So, anyway, what can I help you with?"

"I . . . I'm having an issue with . . . with the lack of vegan choices at the commissary," I say. Vanessa is not on my side, and now my only goal is to get out of here without her having anything to put into her report. "It really is something that has been on my mind for a while now."

"You're vegan?" she asks, glancing down at my file as if this information should be in there.

"I was considering giving it a try."

"Have you tried putting in a request for something vegan?" she asks. She may not give a flying rat's ass about me personally, but it's still her job to help me with my problem.

From the way Vanessa dresses, I know she wants to stay at Belmore but knows any move she makes will be lateral and that's fine with her. She'll never head her department, so it really doesn't matter if her suits don't fit as they should or that her roots show. Vanessa is comfortable, and for her that's enough, but it also means she's not going to let me louse up her situation by giving me a reason to complain she's not doing her best to help me.

"I should do that," I say, acting relieved. "I can't believe I didn't think about it. Thanks, Vanessa!"

"So is there anything else you need to talk about?" she asks. "Anything that has to do with your working conditions or who you're working with? I heard Mr. Floss is working from home . . . How is that going for you? Do you want to talk about that?"

"Umm . . ." I pretend to consider what she said, her offer to unburden myself and maybe make use of that fresh box of Kleenex on the table. "Everything is great up in Marketing. We're like one big happy family."

"All of Belmore is a family," she says automatically.

"We sure are, Vanessa." I smile. "It was really nice to chat with you."

"Yeah." Vanessa looks disappointed. There's nothing much she can put into her report.

We both stand up, and she holds open her arms to give me a hug. I step in and find myself crushed against her as she gives my back a few hard pats.

"Raquel, we're here for you," she says before she releases me. "Anything you say in here is completely confidential."

"That's really good to know." I blink and smile, and she blinks and smiles back. "Okay, I guess I'll be off then."

I head back upstairs to my desk and fax machine to stare down another day.

The Politics of Friendship . . .

There are only two faxes waiting for me when I get back to my desk. One is blank, and the other informs me in Bert's distinctive scrawl that he won't be coming in tomorrow. I look at my watch; it's not even noon and my day is already over.

"Who am I kidding—my day was over before it even started," I say to the silent fax machine.

Maybe I'll just go home and chip off the freezer burn from that log of cookie dough I've been ignoring. Not the best plan for dealing with my weight or career, but at least it'll save me from having to figure out what to do with myself during lunchtime. Lunch has become my most dreaded part of the day now that Bert isn't around to drag me to a meeting or keep me at a desk. Lunch is when I realize how alone I really am.

Senior executives rarely, if ever, set foot in the commissary, and they only do so when they want to be seen. Like execs, vice presidents eat out, in their offices, or in the executive dining room up on 24. Bert has never set foot in the commissary in all the time I've worked for him. His lunch— a chef salad exactly like the kind you can get in any decent Midwestern diner—arrives at my desk at 12:30 on days when he stays in. As I haven't put in an order, I can't even look forward to the few minutes of chatting with the guy who delivers the lunches. He always has the best gossip, but I can't justify having him bring me a shrimp salad with a side roll when my boss isn't here. Catering is not a delivery service for anyone lower than senior exec. It's just the way it is.

Groups of people, people who last week waited in line to

see me so they could speak to Bert, rush past my door, resuming their conversations a few feet away.

I set a Luna bar on my desk and am about to pop open a Diet Coke when I realize this is exactly what the Cris Fullers and Vanessas of the world want me to do. They want me to wither away in this office with only a fax machine to keep me company.

"I won't to do it," I say under my breath as another group scurries past my doorway. "I won't go down without a fight."

I swipe on the last of my lip gloss, neaten up my chignon, and then set off toward the elevators. I stride down the hallway, not giving any hint of the butterflies in my stomach. As far as anyone should be concerned, I have nothing to worry about. Still, I'm too chicken to risk riding in the elevator, so I trek down fifteen flights of stairs to the commissary.

I get to the second-floor mezzanine and pause before stepping into the commissary, not only to catch my breath but to ask myself if I really want to do this. There is no place to hide in there, with the floor-to-ceiling windows and open arrangement of round tables and chairs that seat two to six. Just like in the parking structure, where one sits to eat her Chinese chicken salad says a lot about her stock at Belmore.

Interns sit at the edges, closest to the main door and food service areas. The cool interns, those in Creative or Development and the alpha girls from PR, sit by the salad bar. The geeks and dweebs from Tech are relegated to the wet area—within arm's reach of the soda, coffee, and tea bar.

The rest of the room works into itself like a spiral. The closer to the center, the more concentrated the clout. A six-person table is the nexus of the Belmore commissary, where the elite of the interns (offspring of the very connected), high-level assistants, and rising junior execs sit. I once had a standing Tuesday and Thursday seat at the nexus, but it's been a few months since I last made the time to come down here. I was too busy working toward my now nonexistent promotion to bother.

I grab a tray and head for the salad counter before I realize I can't risk a piece of spinach lodging itself in my teeth. I move toward sandwiches, my stomach flipping over itself at the thought of trying to choke down bread, meat, and mayonnaise. Soup won't work because my hands shake when I'm nervous. I settle on a carton of yogurt and a can of ice-cold Diet Coke. I carry my tray carefully, edging my way closer and closer to the center of the room. When no one tries to stop me, I set it down and take a seat next to Jessica, who lucky for me is not having lunch at her desk outside Mr. Cole's office.

"Hi," I say as nonchalantly as possible.

"Oh, hello, Raquel," Marisa, Kyle's assistant and reigning queen of the nexus, says. As if on cue, everyone else offers up a greeting, but they keep their eye on Marisa to see what the next move should be. "Aren't you hungry?"

"I have a dinner thing tonight, so I'm saving some room." I tap my spoon against the carton of yogurt. Eyes flicker down, buying me a few seconds to work up my courage. "But tomorrow is sushi Thursday. I'll definitely be here for that."

"How are things on seventeen?" Marisa asks, neither denying me nor confirming that I'll be welcome back to her table. "I've heard some pretty crazy stories. Is it true that Floss tried to choke Fuller?"

"No," I snap. Marisa is trying to bait me. "It wasn't anything like that."

"Okay." Marisa's eyes narrow for a second before she moves in for the kill. "So why is your boss calling in sick?"

"He's not calling in anything. He's working from home," I say, fully realizing how lame this makes me sound. I'm defending a man who up until Monday was a major player in the Belmore game. And the thing is, I can't even defend him because anything I say will be too close to the truth, and that will just make him look weak.

"Whatever you say, Raquel." Marisa dismisses me with a flick of her hair. "So, Angie, what's going on in Legal? I heard that there was a huge mix-up with the Ward twins' contracts?"

I force myself to sit there, eat my yogurt at a leisurely pace, and take sips of my Diet Coke. No one, not even Jessica, tries to engage me in a side conversation or draw me into the main one. It's the longest ten minutes of my life, but I make it through most of my carton of yogurt without gagging or drawing any more attention to myself.

"Well," I say as if I've just had one of the most satisfying meals of my life, "I'm heading back upstairs."

"Bye, Raquel," Marisa says without looking up. The other women wave but are careful not to make prolonged eye contact.

I pick up my tray and walk away, knowing that I'll never sit at the nexus again. I make it outside and lean against a wall, breathing heavily through the beginnings of an anxiety attack.

"Raquel?" Jessica hurries up to me and pulls me behind a large potted plant. "I'm really sorry about what happened in there."

"Thanks, really," I say, feeling a spark of hope.

Jessica doesn't have as much pull as Marisa, but people still follow her example. I might not get invited out for after-work drinks anytime soon, but there's still a chance I might get asked to pitch in on a baby shower or engagement gift. Sushi Thursdays might be out of the question for now, but I'm willing to make the effort.

"I just wanted you to know Cris Fuller is really pushing to have Bert fired. He's meeting with everyone. He's even saying . . ." She trails off when a group passes us on their way out.

I want to tell her it's okay, she doesn't have to say anything that might come back and bite her in the butt. But instead I wait. I need to hear something, anything that will tell me I'm going to be fine.

"Just watch your back," she says.

She gives me a quick hug and hurries back inside the commissary. I vomit into the potted plant and climb the fifteen floors back to my desk.

six | HOME AND WORK

The Hot Spot . . .

I drive away from Belmore not unlike an escaped convict in a getaway car—glancing over my shoulder every few seconds expecting to see a security golf cart in hot pursuit. It's just after one, and I've never just up and left work. I know plenty of people who run errands during the day, but I always put in my ten hours at my desk. The only times I step away from my desk are when Bert sends me off to do some task, like visiting wholesalers to find out how cheaply plastic figurines can be made.

I need to gather my thoughts and figure things out. There's no one I can talk to at Belmore, and Frappa is under the impression that I'm formulating some sort of big-picture plan, but it's pretty clear to me that I haven't a clue as to what I should be doing with myself.

Sitting at my desk and guarding Bert's office isn't doing me, or him, much good other than putting me square in the middle of Cris Fuller's radar. Who knows? Maybe he's right. Maybe what I should be doing is figuring where I'm going to go next instead of hoping that Bert will come back and save my promotion. And I know of no better place to undertake this endeavor than at the mall. Not for the shopping but to go to the bookstore. Books are full of answers and guidance I will never get from my mother, are less haranguing than Frappa and, if I pay cash, they won't leave an electronic record like an Internet search will. The last thing I want anyone to find out is that I've accepted the fact that I might have to look for another job.

When I was considering the pros and cons of renting my current apartment, I took into account the attached garage, the almost new stacked washer-dryer, functioning dishwasher, and a sweet twenty-minute commute to work that would keep me off the freeways. These were all definite pros, pros that almost outweighed the cons of the lack of a second bedroom, a small kitchen that opened into an equally small dining area and living room, and drafty single-pane windows. What really convinced me to up my budget by an extra $180, give up on a second bedroom, and accept the constant traffic noise was much more practical. Mayfair Manors, as my four-unit building is known, is sandwiched between two of Los Angeles's most famous shopping meccas: the Beverly Center and The Grove.

Of course, my dreams of spending leisurely weekends or evenings after work wandering in and out of stores have turned out to be just that, dreams. The closest I come to either place is when I'm stuck behind cars that are trying to get into the parking lots. Around holiday times, I avoid the streets around both altogether. (I do all my gift shopping online and months in advance.)

As I wait for the light to turn in to The Grove's parking lot, I avoid making eye contact with people in the car next to mine. I can almost guess what they're thinking: "Another wannabe actress on her way to work at Banana Republic" or "Look, some spoiled kept girlfriend off to spend her sugar daddy's money." At least it's what I always think when I see anyone not working at one in the afternoon doing something remotely enjoyable.

"When did you become so judgmental?" I ask myself. "That's an easy one, Raquel. Around the time you put on your first pair of Belmore-sanctioned panty hose."

What I need to do is get a boyfriend, but I haven't gone out on a date in over a year. I feel my eyes tear up behind my sunglasses.

"No," I say over the sappy song playing on my car radio, "I will not waste time crying about my lack of a love life. I need to figure out what the hell I'm going to do about my job, Bert, and Belmore."

I walk out of the parking lot with my shoulders back, head up, looking like I have something more going on in my life than just an early afternoon of aimless shopping. Of course, no one could care less. They're all too busy strolling along and enjoying the mild weather while keeping an eye out for celebrities.

Inside Barnes & Noble I head straight for the Business and Career section upstairs and scan the spines of books for titles that look interesting. I pull a few out, then look at the covers and flip to random pages. More than a few are rejected because I don't like the cover image or the smarmy tone. I already know I need help, but I don't need someone to yell at me (too may capitalized and boldface words) or appeal to my spiritual side (it's not like I can use Jesus as a reference).

After a solid hour of looking, I finally settle on two: *The Résumé Resuscitation Kit: Spinning Your Professional Disasters into a Career Revival* and *Do What You Do Only Better: How to Take Your Career to the Next Level,* both by a Julia Law, Ph.D., who looks to be infinitely more in control of her life than I am of mine. The core ideas of her books appeal to me—I might have screwed up, but that doesn't necessarily mean I'm completely screwed—the cover images aren't too cutesy, and the tone is confident but not smug.

I tuck them under my arm and grab a copy of *The 7 Habits of Highly Effective People* to learn which of these I'm lacking. I add copies of *Moby-Dick, Crime and Punishment,* and *Great Expectations* from the buy two, get the third free table, making them an intellectual bargain. I carry my books to the checkout counter and set them down, wondering what the person behind me would make of my selections. They're all over the place, I know that, but at least I'm not buying a copy of *Twilight* and an issue of *Cosmo.* That would label me as desperate and crazy.

"Do you need a bag?" asks the clerk, a slight girl with a nose ring and a bad haircut.

I scan the display of canvas tote bags and grab one printed with interlocking hearts. "I'll take this, too."

"Cool," she says, ringing it up as a separate purchase. "Plastic bags suck for the environment."

"They really do." I have to agree with her, even though I

only got the bag because I thought it was cute. Maybe some-day I might even use it to tote my gym gear because, after I get my career in order, my plan is to start working out again.

As I walk away from the counter, my stomach gives a ferocious growl and I realize I'm hungry. I sling the tote bag over my shoulder and make my way into the in-store café, where I immediately zero in on the comforting sight of the pastry case.

"Hi," says a cute guy with bravado that belies the fact he's wearing an apron and a name tag.

He's very cute, good-looking actually, but this is a city of pretty faces and great bodies. His sandy blond hair is just floppy enough, his eyes very blue with dark lashes, and he's tall and lean. Much too good-looking to be working at a book-store café, but I'm guessing this job isn't his life's ambition. Whatever his deal, it'll be a treat to have someone so tasty looking pour me a cup of coffee even if I'm not in the mood for any harmless flirting.

"Hey," I say, looking down at the croissants I know I won't be ordering. Just because I've blown off half a day of work doesn't mean layer upon layer of flaky, buttery pastry is some-thing I can indulge in.

He puts both hands on the case and does a modified push-up. "Are you meeting someone for coffee?"

"No, I'm . . ." I cast about for the perfect L.A. phrase. "I'm taking a day off of work for some me time."

If there's one thing people on the west side of Los Ange-les understand, it's "me time."

"I dig that." He reaches over and offers his hand. It's cool, smooth, and smells of antiseptic soap. "I'm Rory."

"Nice to meet you, Rory. I'm Raquel." I give it three firm pumps and then resume my internal debate between a zucchini muffin and a slice of banana bread. Both probably have the same amount of fat and calories as a croissant, but one has fruit and the other vegetables. "I'll have a medium decaf coffee, room for cream, and a . . ."

"Where do you work? Here at The Grove?" Rory asks, taking advantage of my pastry indecision.

"Why would I spend my day off at the place where I work?" I ask with a half smile. I know my answer is borderline bitchy, but he's asking for it.

"Beautiful and sarcastic, I'm a dead man." Rory grins and flashes the dimples on each of his cheeks.

"Yeah," I say, openly staring at him. I know that smile, and I've seen it recently.

"Is someone actually working here?" asks a jittery looking woman around my mom's age. She's wearing an expensive tracksuit with flip-flops and looks royally pissed off.

Rory rolls his eyes at me. "Don't go anywhere."

"I want a large nonfat latte with four shots with this much"—she holds her fingers about half an inch apart—"foam. But the foam has to be two percent milk. Understand?"

I rock back and forth on my heels, trying to remember where I've seen Rory and his dimples before. He's around my age, maybe a couple of years younger, but there's no chance we went to school together. Dimples like that would surely get voted best smile. I know I don't know him from Cal State, where I mainly stuck to frat boys because it was just easier to date them.

If I have seen those dimples before, it has to be because of something Belmore related. I think back to all the premieres and after parties I've been to, but I can't picture him at any of them. Still, the more I stare at him, the more I'm sure I know him and I know him from Belmore.

"Hey, beautiful, where'd the smile go?" Rory says as he hands me a large cup of coffee instead of the medium I asked for.

"Sorry," I apologize for some reason. "I've got work on the brain."

"Know that feeling and I got the cure. You want to know what it is?" Rory smiles at me and folds his arms on top of the pastry case.

"I'm almost afraid to ask," I say. I should just ask him "Do I know you from somewhere?" but that sounds cheesy even within the confines of my mind. He would assume I'm trying to pick him up. And if he does assume that, I'm more than tempted to see where it goes.

"Anything you want, Raquel," he says as he gestures to the pastry case, "is on the house."

The tracksuited woman snorts in disgust as she pops the lid off her drink to inspect the cup's contents.

"My parents taught me to never accept gifts from strangers," I flirt back, mostly for the benefit of tracksuit woman. "But I'll take a slice of banana bread."

"I'm not a stranger." He hands me the bread. "I'm Rory and you're Raquel and this is the best slice of banana bread ever made."

"Hold on there, Rory," I say, trying to keep myself from giggling at his sincere act of shallow kindness.

"Too fast, eh?" he asks with a grin, and again how I know him tickles the back of my mind.

"Rory?" I can't take it. If I walk out of here now, I'll never figure it out and it'll just torture me. "This is going to sound really cheesy, but—"

"This is not enough foam and it's whole milk!" the woman yells, putting a stop to everything going on in the vicinity of her voice. "This is absolutely ridiculous! I can't believe this! Who's in charge around here? Hello!"

A woman wearing a once white dress shirt and faded black slacks hurries over to her. "I'm the manager, ma'am. What's the problem?"

"He got my order completely wrong. I come here at least three times a week. I order the same thing every time. I don't understand why this happened. Oh wait, I do. Your employee"—she jabs a finger in Rory's direction—"is too busy trying to pick up women to pay attention to his job."

"Ma'am? I can have Rory—" the manager begins.

"This is the worst customer service I've ever, ever experienced, and I want to know what you're going to do about it!"

"Rory? Please get over here," the manager says in a tight voice.

"I gotta deal with this," Rory says, genuinely unconcerned. "So can I see you again? Or are you just going to use me for free coffee and muffins."

"You should really go," I say. I don't need this much drama in my life and sort of feel embarrassed about the whole thing. Plus, Rory is not my type. After I turned twenty-five, I vowed never to date anyone who wasn't at least three years older than I am. "I need to, um, get back to work."

"But you're taking the day off. Remember?" Rory says, leaning in close so he doesn't have to raise his voice. He pulls a pen out of his apron pocket. "If you leave now, I'm going to spend the rest of the day hoping you come back."

"Rory," his manager says. "Now."

"I'll say this for you, Rory," I tell him as I take the napkin where he's scribbled his phone number, "you do have an effect on women."

Renesting . . .

I make the short drive home after deciding it's a safer place to enjoy my free coffee and banana bread and read my books. As I pull up to my street, I see a whole other way of life I'm not privy to as I'm usually at work during this time of the day. I pass overexercised and neglected wives and girlfriends as they speed-walk in pairs or jog alone with only their iPods for company. Sharing the leafy sidewalks with them are a steady flow of nannies pushing high-end strollers. A few of them are also walking dogs along with their overdressed charges.

This is the kind of life my mother wants me to have, but only because it's the life she thinks she wants for herself. To me it looks boring and pointless. Sure, I want to get married and maybe have a kid or two one day, but not now. I don't want live like I'm on permanent spring break, and I don't want to tie myself down with human responsibilities. Either way, an on her way to being unemployed almost twenty-six-year-old who's carrying an extra fourteen pounds isn't exactly a hot commodity around these parts of L.A.

"Don't fool yourself, Raquel," I say out loud as I wait for a group of strollers and speed walkers to cross the street in front of me. "It's not like you've had the chance to turn down any proposals of the work or marriage variety."

When I pull up to my apartment, I'm more than ready to bury my head under the covers. I click on the garage door opener and, instead of opening, it makes a mournful grinding sound. "Damn it," I say. "Another thing to add to my list."

I can park in front of my place, blocking the driveway, but then my neighbors will know I'm home. This wouldn't be such a big issue if my neighbors, the Kashinis, weren't also my landlords. The last thing I need right now is either of them making polite inquiries about my job security. Mr. Kashini, who spends his days watching CNBC, is particularly in tune with how crappy the global economy is. When I told him I worked at Belmore, he added it to his stock watch list. More than once he's greeted me with the news that it's dipped a quarter of a percent or gone up two points. It's news I always greet with a smile, as I have no idea what he's talking about.

I get out and heave the garage door open, pulling something in my back in the process, but at least my car is tucked away and out of sight. I come in through the kitchen and run right smack into the open refrigerator door.

"Holy crap!" I scream, sloshing coffee all over my hand, tote bag, and floor.

"Raquel! You scared me!" My mother stands in front of my fridge, clutching her heart with one hand and the TV remote with the other. "What are you doing here?"

"I live here." I set what's left of my coffee on the table

next to her jumbo-size makeup carrying case. "Why are you here, Mom?"

"I thought you were going out of town, Raquel," my mother says with enough reproach in her voice that for a moment I consider the possibility that I'm in the wrong. "Why are you home?"

I'm going to answer with the obvious "Because I live here." I knew when I gave my mom a key she would be stopping over whenever she wanted, but she usually comes when I'm not here. She's dressed in slacks, a turtleneck, and loafers—her usual window-shopping outfit—so my first guess would be that she just dropped by on her way to the mall. The presence of luggage, though, hints that this visit might be a bit longer than an afternoon.

"My boss has the flu, and so I took a half day," I lie. She raises an eyebrow at me, so I have to add some truth to my reason for being in my own home. We both know that I never take time off from work—even when I'm sick I work from my kitchen table. "So, uh . . . I went shopping and ran some, you know, errands and stuff."

"Did you get fired?" she asks without an ounce of bedside manner.

"No! And please don't start in on my job," I say.

"Raquel, what kind of parent would I be if I didn't want the best for you?" She gives up on the fridge, with its pathetic offerings of old Chinese food and moldy cheese, opens the freezer, and closes it just as quickly.

"I think it's what's called toxic parenting nowadays," I scoff. "But thank you again for your efforts, Marlene."

"If you were married, I'd have a lot less to worry about,"

she says. My mother lives for things to worry about. She'll bounce from obsessing about the stock market to worrying about the plunge in real estate values or that her Botox is wearing off too fast. If she doesn't have something to worry about, she'll find it. "I could finally sleep at night."

"Sorry, Mom, but no one has asked me to marry him today." I pour what's left of my coffee in the sink but decide not to check if my books got wet. When she isn't looking, I toss the tote bag underneath the sink. The last thing I need is to give my mother solid evidence that there is something wrong with my job. "It's only Wednesday. I might be able to rustle up a fiancé by the weekend."

"Don't be cute, Raquel." My mother reaches over to tuck a strand of hair behind my ear. She continues to fuss with it until I pull away. "It would be a shame for you to miss out on being a wife and a mother because of your career."

"I hardly think my job is going to keep me from getting married and procreating," I say, not bothering to remind her that she already has two grandchildren and maybe another one in the works. "Plenty of women manage to be mothers and wives and have careers that they enjoy."

"From what I read in magazines, more women have discovered that they can't have it all," she says, countering the perfectly valid point I just made with one of her own. "You should freeze your eggs."

"Why would I want to freeze my eggs?" I ask, aghast at her suggestion. "I'm nowhere near my expiration date."

"Because of all that's out there"—she wrinkles her nose—"so many diseases and germs, all floating around."

"That may be true, Mom, but I'm not going around letting

all that's floating around out there in here," I say, pointing at my crotch.

"You should ask your father for the money he's set aside for your wedding. You're obviously not interested in finding a husband," she says as she gestures to my skirt suit.

"What are you talking about? What money?" I ask.

Despite my dad's brain, my parents aren't rich. He's a great thinker, but instead of thinking about how to make money, he focused on academics. My mother used to think he could invent something, but he was too busy reading his journals and books to take the time to do it. Even though they're comfortable, JPL didn't exactly pay him in peanuts. I think my mom expected to be rich. She certainly made it known how disappointed she was with living in Eagle Rock instead of a few miles over in Pasadena.

"Your father may want to live like a professor, but he has some money tucked away." She sighs with exasperation. "It's not much, but he's not as pure as he'd like you to think. He made some money while he was doing his great and noble work."

"Is this enough money for a down payment on a house?" I ask, not giving in to her baiting. If she has an issue with my dad and money, that's for them to sort out. "I'd rather have a house than a wedding. And how come you're mentioning this stash of cash now? I could have used it when I had to get new tires for my Honda."

"Stop joking around, Raquel. It's the least your father can do for you," she says. "You can't help it that you didn't turn out to be a genius like Steve."

"So what's with the suitcase?" I ask, knowing I have a less than 50 percent chance of getting a straight answer out of her. My mother has never been one to consider logic an important part of any conversation.

"It's so hard for girls now, I almost feel sorry for them," my mother continues on, with a healthy dose of self-pity more for herself than for us girls. "You have to be smart, funny, look fantastic all the time, and you have all these choices. When I was your age, we thought it was fine to just be a wife and mother. Now, you girls think you have to have it all. But you can't, Raquel."

"What's going on, Mom?" I ask. She's all over the place, and she's giving me a headache. It hasn't been enough time between visits for me to have built up the reserve of strength I need to deal with her.

She twists her wedding ring around her finger for a few moments before she answers in a heavy voice. "I've left your father."

"Left him where?" I ask.

"Don't be a smart-ass, Raquel," my mother says through the beginning of tears.

"I'm sorry, Mom, but are you trying to tell me that you and Dad have had a fight or what?" My parents always fight—it's their means of communication.

"I've left him," she declares with a finality that makes my stomach sink. This is no tiff between two people who should have figured things out a long time ago. She's really left him.

"Why?" I ask. What I really want to say is, "Why are you doing this to me?"

"He knows why," she says. Her eyes begin to tear up.

"Does he?" I ask. If I draw it out of her in bits and pieces, I'm more likely to get a truer version of the truth. My mother's a champion at stonewalling. She won't tell me why she's left him because it's perfectly obvious to her why she has. If I can't see her reason, or more likely reasons, it makes me just as culpable as my father for her situation.

"Mom? Did you and Dad talk about this?" I ask.

"You want me to go?" she asks, looking unsure for the first time. "You don't want me here either."

"No, of course you can stay, Mom."

My response is automatic and instantly regretted. She assumes that if she walks out on her husband she can stay with me. And I guess if I was to lose my job, I'd pretty much assume I could move back home, so I really can't tell her she's not welcome in my tiny one-bedroom apartment.

"Of course you can stay while you and Dad figure things out." I try to backtrack without actually rescinding my offer. "Have you told Steve about this?"

I haven't checked my personal cell phone since yesterday, and I know I have a few messages. I'd assumed they were from Cricket, so I felt justified in ignoring them.

It's understandable why my mother wouldn't go to Steve's. He has a family and his own life, one that includes Cricket and babies. I have a pullout couch and no life besides Belmore and worrying about the quality of my eggs.

"Steve knows," my mother says, by which she means that she hadn't confided in me first because I'm a bad daughter. I hand her a roll of paper towels from the counter as she lets loose with the tears.

"What is it he knows that I don't?" I ask, trying to keep my voice level. My mother wants me to ask, but if I come off pushy, she'll shut down to punish me. "What did Steve say?"

"He's upset with your father, of course," she says, letting me know I'm also expected to be upset. "He knows how your father is. You know how he is, Raquel, even if you are a daddy's girl."

"What did Dad say about you guys separating?"

My mother continues to cry into her fist, having rejected the scratchy paper towels. I hand her a clean dishrag, and she shakes her head. The closest box of Kleenex is by the couch, but I know if I break off my gentle interrogation, I'll never find out what I need to know.

"Mom?" I ask, trying to sound patient and understanding even though I'm on the verge of getting annoyed. Like with Steve, it'll take some finessing to get the whole story out of her. "What did Dad say about this?"

"Nothing, as usual," she says with disgust. She's not happy about my hesitation in donning a Team Mom T-shirt but, like my dad, I need more facts. "He's too busy with his damn flowers."

"Mom?" I put my hand on her arm, hoping to stave off another flood of tears. "Did you tell Dad you were leaving him or did you just leave?"

"I can see that my life falling apart is happening at a bad time for you, Raquel." She brushes past me and takes up residence on my couch.

"I'll make you some coffee," I say, acting as if this is something like a normal visit.

Which in a way it is, except for the crying and me being here. Sometimes during the week my mother drives over from Eagle Rock, parks her car in my garage, and makes the nominally aerobic walk over to either The Grove or the Beverly Center. She spends hours wandering from store to store, taking mental notes about what catches her eye, and is gone before I get home. The following day she'll drive into Down-town L.A. and scour the most remote corners of Santee Alley for knockoffs of what she's seen but could never bring herself to pay retail or even sale price for.

I put on a kettle of water and take out the large coffee cup she gave me when I turned twenty-five. It's a bright pink ceramic mug inscribed with statements like "I'm beautiful," "People like me," and "I'm smart and talented." It is, yes, a big cup of self-esteem. I set it on a tray, along with a napkin and a plate of Lorna Doone cookies, her favorites.

In my pantry I keep a tin of International Coffee sugar-free decaf Café Vienna, also her favorite. I add two heaping tablespoons to the cup before drowning the powder in boiling water. I pour it straight, instead of slowly from the side, and it puffs up, asphyxiating me in a cloud of overly sweetened faux-coffee dust.

"Do you have any Baileys?" she asks.

It's another favorite of hers. I pull the sticky, almost full bottle from the fridge and add a generous pour to her steam-ing cup of self-esteem. I've been fixing her this drink for years, since I was old enough to boil water, but back then the coffee was full of real sugar and caffeine. The Baileys was always Baileys.

"Tell me what's really going on, Mom," I ask, hoping the prospect of boozy fake coffee and slightly stale shortbread cookies will soften the blow.

"I've decided it's time to have my own life. I've raised my children. Steve's married and successful, and you are . . ." My mother gives up and returns to the central theme of her life, but this time feeling completely justified stating it out loud.

"It's time for me to be happy before I'm too old to be able to enjoy my life. It's me time."

"Couldn't you join a book club or take a pottery class, Mom? Why this? Why now?" I'm appealing to her sense of duty even though I know my mother has no problem with putting herself first.

"Why not now? And you should know why," my mother says in a wounded voice.

"I guess," I mumble, reluctant to concede she has a point. I can't fault her completely.

My father has always been a party pooper, and life with my mother has been one overlong party. My mother is a difficult person, but she has a great sense of humor. My dad isn't the best at communicating his feelings, but he never lets a special event pass without at least a phone call. Despite these good qualities, I've known since I was three that they were mismatched. I'm actually surprised it's taken this long for something like her walking out on him to happen.

"I just want to make sure you guys at least talked about this," I say. They've been married almost forty years, and a person doesn't just give up on that because she wakes up feeling peevish.

"There's no point in talking to your father. It's like talking to a brick wall," she says. The same can be said of her, but now is not the time to bring it up.

"True enough, but still you should give him a chance," I say. "I'm sure if you told him how you feel, he'd try to be . . . not so much like he is."

The last thing I want is for my parents to get a divorce. It will be messy, with my mother trotting out the emotions and my father the facts. I want them to continue on with the way things are. Why bring up all these issues? What good will it do any of us? Why can't they pretend to be happy? They've being doing it for years.

"Maybe you guys just need a few days apart? Or maybe you can go see a marriage counselor?" I say.

"He probably hasn't even noticed that I'm not at home." My mother starts to cry. She's not interested in finding a solution to her problems, much less working toward one. My mother's cries quickly ratchet down to sniffles as she waits for me to agree that my father is an obtuse emotional ogre.

"Of course he'll notice, Marlene." It's what she wants to hear, but I can't keep myself from adding, "He'll be wondering why lunch is so late."

My mother hiccups and glares at me. I tuck a blanket around her, kiss the top of her carefully colored hair.

"I'll go see how he's suffering without you."

"If your father asks for me, tell him I said he can go fuck himself and his fucking flowers, too." Her eyes are still teary, but I can tell she's feeling better now that I've offered to drive down to the house to check up on him. "Tell that selfish bastard the only way he'll ever see me in that house again is if he begs me to come back on his hands and knees."

"I will, Mommy," I say as I hand her the remote and a box of Kleenex.

Father Time . . .

I sit behind the wheel of my car, stuck in predictably hellish freeway traffic. I've no desire to get in the middle of my parents' marital issues and know there's no way I can undo almost four decades of messed up interpersonal dynamics. This is a job for a therapist, Oprah, maybe Steve, but certainly not me. What do I know about healthy relationships? The healthiest and longest one I've had so far is with my job, and that's not going so great.

Even with traffic, I still haven't come up with any sort of plan on how to get my parents together by the time I pull opposite the tidy bungalow I grew up in. My father's out in the yard tending to his roses, probably exactly where he was when my mother drove away, leaving him. I walk across the wide street, shaded by impressive oak and maple trees, and stop on the other side of the fence.

"Hey, Daddy, how are things looking?"

"This is going to be a good year, Raquel." He leans over and gives me a pat on the shoulder, then brushes the dirt left there from his well-worn garden glove. "I'm hoping my hybrid comes in this season."

I look down at the dead leaves he's stripped off to give the blooms more space to breathe and suddenly feel a pang. I know my father lives in his own little world, where logic and facts reign supreme. Sometimes his gestures to reach out to others, like his wife, are so subtle they are ignored or misinterpreted by people, again like my mother, who can't fathom how his brain works.

My mother's jealous of the retirement hobby that has turned into somewhat of an obsession for my dad. To her it's yet another reminder that he prefers something else to her company. He grows these roses for her, but it's never occurred to him to tell her that. Instead he snips the blooms at their peak, sticks them in a vase, and sets them on the table, where my mother glares at them as if they are unwelcome guests and throws them out at the first hint of wilting.

"How's work?" he asks.

He takes off his gloves and tucks them into the monogrammed garden canvas tote full of tools. It was my gift to him, along with a copy of *The Complete Idiot's Guide to Gardening,* at his retirement party. So in a roundabout but very concrete way, this is my entire fault. If my father didn't have his flowers to pay attention to, he might have given some of his attention to my mother. I know this makes no sense, my parents' issues run a lot deeper than roses, but I can't help but blame myself.

"Work sucks, Dad," I say, and it feels good to tell the truth. Work does suck. Even though I won't go into the details of why it sucks, letting myself admit it to someone who I know won't judge me is a relief.

"Sometimes work does suck, but it will get better," he says. My father wipes the sweat off his brow, shoving back the floppy khaki fisherman hat on his head. "Your mother will be home soon."

"She's left you. She's at my place," I say. I've always had a hard time lying to my father. Either we discuss something or we don't. This is something we have to discuss, and there's no other way but the direct one to approach it.

My father looks up but then goes back to pruning his rosebushes. I watch him, giving him time to work through this in his own way. I don't have high hopes for him jumping in his car and racing down to make amends with his wife. That kind of grand gesture just isn't in his nature, but I do know he's thinking about it. I wait for him to process it, relieved to know someone else is sharing the burden of their marriage with me.

Finally he puts down his clippers and says, "I have to respect her reasons, whatever they might be."

I say nothing but notice he doesn't ask me if I know what her reasons for leaving are. That's just not my father. He figures if my mother wanted him to know, she would have told him before she left. This leaves me in the exact same spot, stuck between them, acting as messenger and reluctant interpreter.

"Okay." I turn to go. My mother will want to hear about his every reaction, and my father has revealed precious little about his feelings, as usual.

"Tell your mother I'm here when she is ready to discuss matters," he says so I don't have to go back empty-handed. He still doesn't understand one of my mother's many reasons for leaving him is that she doesn't want to discuss matters with him. She wants her husband to talk to her.

"Can I get that in writing?" I say. It's not much, but at least it's something. "I guess she'll be staying at my place for a few days then."

He rocks back and forth on his heels for a moment, thinking this over before he answers. "I'm sorry about that, Raquel."

"No sweat, Dad. It'll be fun," I lie. Unlike my mom, I know he'll be fine on his own. He won't need me to hold his hand through this.

He walks me across the street to my car. Before I get in, I give him the usual good-bye peck on his cheek. He shuts my car door with a secure thunk, and I start the motor.

"Raquel?" He taps the window and waits for it to come down before continuing. "Everything will be fine."

"Thanks, Dad," I say as I turn the key in the ignition. "I'll call you later, Daddy."

I appreciate the effort. He's tried to say something soothing yet innocuous so it doesn't make things worse. Too bad he's saying it to the wrong person. It's my mother who needs to hear there's still hope that everything will turn out fine. When I glance back in my rearview mirror, my father is standing in the middle of the street and considering how his roses look from there.

seven | DESPERATE MEASURES

Dressing the Part . . .

My mother chatters on about everything and nothing as I get dressed for work. I go through the well-practiced motions of putting on panty hose, snipping the tags off a new bra, and steaming imaginary wrinkles out of my suit. She keeps talking, and I catch the beginnings or tail ends of phrases. "Mid-fifties is the new thirty, Raquel . . . a woman doesn't know what she wants in bed until she's at least . . . liposuction and a face-lift . . . never implants, way too tacky . . ."

I find some small comfort in the fact that I can fake normalcy well enough to fool my mother. The last thing I need is for her to use my problems at work as a reason to start in on the Baileys and International Coffee before *Good Morning America* is over. If I were to even hint of something going on in my life that would compete with the drama in hers, it would only add to the copious burdens she's already laying on me.

I listen with one ear as she goes on and on about her dashed hopes and unfulfilled dreams. I make noncommittal noises when she presses me to agree that everything wrong in her life is my father's fault. Right now all I want is to get out of my own home before she starts on the next chapter of her woeful saga.

I step out of my almost walk-in closet wearing my favorite charcoal suit and an emerald-colored silk shell. Shoe wise, I've gone with my usual pair of sensible black leather, round-toe pumps. There's nothing different about this outfit from what I usually wear, but it's my lucky suit. I was wearing it when Bert plucked me from the reception desk and sat me behind the one outside his office. The waistband of the skirt is a little tight, even though I'm wearing control-top panty hose, and I'll have to leave the jacket open because it pulls when I button it, but it's not like I'm going to be invited to a company fashion parade. It's just going to be me and my fax machine boss all day long.

"So what do you think?" I ask, knowing I'm not going to like her response.

My mother is perched on my bed, where she slept while I tossed and turned on the pullout in the living room. She rubs her temples against the intrusion of early morning sun, since I deliberately raised the blinds in the hope that some natural light would alleviate her black mood.

"You're never going to attract a husband if you dress like that, Raquel," she says, her voice full of reproach as she takes a good long look at my outfit. "I gave you such a sexy name, and you go and waste it on something a woman twice your age and with half your body would wear."

"Thanks for the fashion advice, Mom, but I'm going to work, not out on a date," I say as I debate my watch choices.

I have two, a Cartier Tank knockoff from one of my mother's Santee Alley excursions and the complicated Swiss Army watch Steve gave me when I got hired on at Belmore. I usually alternate between the two, but I decide to nix both. Last thing I need is a reminder that time isn't on my side.

"Just because you're going to work, it doesn't mean you have to dress like a prison matron," she continues, warming up to the subject of how I'm wasting the best years of my working life by not working it. "You don't go out, Raquel, where else are you going to meet a husband?"

I'm smart enough not to share with my mother that I've dated a few guys from work, always making sure they were from different departments. Dating someone from Marketing would be like fooling around with a cousin, way too close for comfort. Of course, office romances are not encouraged by the company, but they're inevitable when social life and work life start to revolve solely around work. There have been more than a few marriages in the years that I've been with the company and just as many divorces and breakups.

My own social life outside of work got smaller and smaller until it finally disappeared sometime around year two. I used to hang out with my sorority sisters, taking weekend trips to Vegas or up to Lake Tahoe. I was a dependable bridesmaid, but as I got more into Belmore, I started sending my regrets along with something very nice from the gift registry. Nowadays I delete Evites unopened from my in-box as a matter of course. Not that I've been getting very many lately.

"When was the last time you went out on a date?" my mother asks.

"Years ago. I think it was junior prom." I put in my hoop earrings, staring up at the ceiling so I don't have to meet her eyes.

My last Belmore boyfriend, Kurt from Legal, was serious enough about us to bring up the "love contract" issue. Belmore asks that employees involved in personal relationships make the trek down to Human Resources to sign one so that the company can't be held liable for any messiness that might result. Kurt, being from Legal, knew what kind of murky waters we were treading and wanted to make sure everything was aboveboard. Our romance amicably fizzled out when we both decided we'd rather focus on our careers. We both loved our jobs too much to let something as trivial as liking each other get in the way of things.

"Don't you want to get married, Raquel?" This from the woman who has spent the last half hour telling me of the many ways marriage ruined her life.

"What good would a husband do me?" I say with more indifference than she deserves. "Even if one showed up at my door with a bucket of chicken and a six-pack of Diet Coke, I don't exactly have room for him to sleep over."

"I'm just trying to be helpful, Raquel," my mother says as she eases herself off the bed and out the door.

I go into the bathroom to do my hair, listening for either the teakettle to whistle or the microwave to beep to gauge how her day is going to go. If she has enough patience to let water boil, it might not be such a bad day. If she's heating water in the microwave, spending my day in my crypt of an office suddenly sounds like a whole lot of fun. All I hear is a chipper voice prattling on about what's coming up in the next hour. I go into the living room to see what's up even though my hair is only half done, and I'm relieved to see my mother filling the kettle. I gather my hair in its usual bun as I wander into the kitchen to keep an eye on her.

"Is your boss going to let you leave early today?" she asks as she adds a heaping tablespoon of flavored coffee powder to what is now her big cup of self-esteem.

"I don't have much food in the house," I say in an attempt to make conversation. "There's lots of microwave popcorn and a box of Progresso soup Cricket gave me."

"Hmmm," my mother says as she watches the kettle. "Soup and popcorn. Is that what girls are eating nowadays to stay skinny?"

"I have to work late to make up for yesterday." It's a bad lie, so transparent, but my mother has other things on her mind.

"Raquel, do you have any more?" She points at the empty bottle of Baileys, letting the gesture finish the sentence for her.

"I think there's another one in the garage." I wait for her to tell me not to bother, that's she's going to be proactive and do something with her day. Instead, she pours lukewarm water from the kettle into the cup and sticks it in the microwave. "I guess I'll go get it and that soup, too."

My mother smiles and says. "That's a pretty blouse, Raquel. You should wear that color more often."

"I can leave work early if you want," I offer with well-practiced reluctance I know she'll ignore. "You can take me shopping for something slutty."

"You don't have to, Raquel. I know how important your job is to you. I'll just stay here and catch up on my soaps." She looks over at her cell, which is set square in the middle of the coffee table. "Maybe I'll call Steve later."

"I'll try not to stay too late. I'll tell Bert I'm not feeling well," I say, feeling guilty for not wanting to be around my mother.

"Sure, sure." She pulls her cup out of the microwave and carries it over to the couch. "When you get back you can set me up with one of those Facebook accounts."

"You want me to what?" I ask. I know my mother will not only expect me to set up a profile for her but want to "friend" me. "How do you know about Facebook?"

"I need to meet men, Raquel." She sighs as if this is yet another burden she has to endure. "I'm not getting any younger, and neither are the men I'm interested in. I have to get out there as soon as possible, before the ones that are left are taken."

"If anything, Marlene, I should be the one trolling for a man. And oh, by the way, you're married."

"It doesn't mean I can't look. And what's a little healthy competition between single women?" she asks. "It'll keep us both on our toes."

"I don't think there's anything healthy about a mother and daughter competing for guys, Mom. It sounds like a scary Lifetime movie to me." I'm trying for levity but end up suppressing a shiver. "What if Dad finds out?"

"If you talk to your father today, tell him I'm having the time of my life." Her face, reflected on the TV screen, is sad. "And go out and find me a son-in-law before it's too late."

"Numbers one and two on my list of things to do today, Marlene." I blow her a kiss, and she blows one back.

"Raquel?" she calls out just as I'm about to escape. "Did you forget to get me the . . ."

"Oh. Right," I say, trying to keep any judgment out of my voice. I reach way back into my pathetic pantry and pull out a fresh bottle of Baileys where I'd been halfheartedly trying to hide it. "Here you go, Mom."

She smiles at me and goes back to watching TV. As I walk out, I pick up her car keys and shove them into my coffee-stained tote bag.

Mutual Interests . . .

The first thing I do when I get in to the office, even before I stow away my purse and tote bag, is check the fax machine. There's a lone sheet of paper, facedown on the tray. I flip it over and read what Bert has to say for himself this morning. There's a typed address and a string of five numbers. That's it.

I'm about to sit down to google the address when another fax comes in, written in Bert's familiar scrawl. "Take a cab. Don't let anyone see you leave."

"Gee, Bert, paranoid much?" I say, even as my eyes dart around to make sure no one is spying on me.

I fold the fax up, shove it into my purse. Before I leave, I make sure Bert's door is still locked and I set a hot cup of coffee on my desk. I doubt I'll be back before it gets cold, but it will buy me some time before anyone notices I'm not in the building. Even though no one is talking to me, I know Fuller has his minions checking up on me.

I walk to Fuller's office, not surprised to see Matthias's desk is still empty, and try the door. It's unlocked. I hesitate for a second before opening it, but no one comes in or passes outside to keep me from going in. I let myself into Fuller's office, taking as few steps as I can to get to his bathroom. The door is ajar so, instead of opening it, I slip through, bumping my boobs, but it's better to risk a bruise than leave any unnecessary fingerprints. It's just a few more steps to his secret door, and I use the hem of my jacket to turn the handle to let myself into the stairwell.

I head down the seventeen flights of steps, making sure not to hurry so that if anyone walks in on me they won't get the idea that I'm trying to sneak out of work. When I get down to the first level, I'm out of breath more from anxiety than from the effort. There are two doors—one leads into the lobby and is right behind the security guard desk, and I'm banking on the other one leading outside.

"Please, please, please, door." I close my eyes and call in all my good deeds to whatever force in the universe governs this particular part of my reality. "Please lead to somewhere out of here and don't sound an alarm when I open you."

I count to three, turn the handle, push the door open in one smooth motion, and find myself blinking into sunlight. There's a small service path that leads down to the sidewalk. Acting as if I'm taking an early morning stroll, I walk along, making sure to avoid the industrial-grade plants on either side. When I get to the sidewalk, I glance behind me before I jaywalk across the street to the Century Plaza Hotel. I ask for a cab, tip the doorman, and give the driver Bert's address. This, from fax to finish, takes under ten minutes, but I'm panting like I just sprinted a mile.

I've never been to Bert's house. He's not the type of boss

who asks about my weekend or gives me tips on where to vacation. Even though I know everything from his cholesterol level to how many hours he spends in therapy each week and to never approach him with an idea until it's fully thought out if not put into a memo, Bert has always kept our relationship distant. I work for him, therefore I know these things because they're part of my job. They're no more intimate than knowing how he takes his coffee.

I've never taken his seeming lack of interest in me outside the confines of the office personally because I know he likes me. He's told me as much. "I like you, Raquel. You're not a fuckup like my kids are." Or "I like you, Raquel. You kiss ass but you don't bend over to do it." How could I not see him as my office father figure when he says things like that?

"What's that?" the driver asks. He's an older guy, heavyset with a mustache. All he needs is a tweed cap and an unlit cigar and he could play a cabdriver in a movie.

"I'm sorry, I guess I was thinking out loud," I say. Without being obvious, I try to adjust the top of my panty hose to keep them from digging into my waist.

"It happens." He shrugs and goes back to his driving. A few minutes later he drives up to the security gates that lead into the exclusive community of Bel Air, where Bert lives. He slows down even though the guard station is just there for show. The cabbie creeps along as he searches for Bert's address. The houses are set well back from the street, hidden behind gates and carefully tended hedges. I'm too busy gawping at ornate gates, wondering what and who is behind them, to pay attention and am startled when the car comes to a stop.

"Okay, kid, this looks like it's it. You want me to drive you up to the house and wait?"

"No, thank you," I say, knowing the last thing Bert wants is a shabby yellow cab idling in his driveway. "I'm fine here."

I pay him, climb out, and then punch the series of numbers into the pin pad that's set into the stone pillar by the gate, a simple iron and wood design. The gate swings open and I start up the drive, stopping for a second to make sure it swings closed again. The cabdriver is still there, watching. I give him a perky wave to let him know this kid is okay and then walk up the rest of the way at a brisk pace.

Bert's house is old enough to not seem faux anything even though it reminds me of a Merchant Ivory movie set. There are large, shady trees that are just slightly overgrown and a rambling English garden that's the size of a small park. The house is a three-story stone structure with a much-peaked, slate-tiled roof. Ivy, so green and glossy I want to reach out and touch it to make sure it's not plastic, climbs up the gray stone façade. The windows are large and many paned with fresh white trim. The overall feeling is one of quaint dilapidation, and I'm sure it costs Bert a chunk of change to keep things looking the way they do.

I know Bert loves this house as much as he can love anything. He has a small replica of it sitting on the credenza in his office that I sometimes find him running a handkerchief over to keep it free from imaginary dust. Otherwise his office is devoid of anything to do with his life outside Belmore. He doesn't even have the requisite family photos on his desk.

I knock on the door, my knuckles meeting solid wood that muffles the effort. I press the bell once and stand back. I'm

not sure who I expect to answer the door and am surprised
I've gotten this far without running into a gardener or pool
boy.

Before the bell finishes chiming, the door opens, and it's
opened by Bert himself. He's wearing a terry-cloth bathrobe, a
Belmore cap pulled down to his ears, flip-flops, and sunglasses.

"Hi," I say, taken a bit aback by the sight of him.

I've never seen Bert in anything but a suit, usually a
three-piece one. For the annual Belmore Halloween party, he
always goes as James Bond. The joke is that his costume is
the same tux he wears to every Belmore event. Seeing him,
I realize I assumed Bert slept in a suit or at least in proper
pajamas.

"Don't just stand there," he says with his usual gruffness,
"come inside."

"Hello. Sorry," I say.

I step around Bert and into the foyer. There's art everywhere, all modern and in contrast to the largely traditional
furnishings. I've always known Bert was well off, but this
looks downright rich to me—rich enough to not have to care
about working for a living.

"Let's talk in my office," he says. I follow a step or two
behind, trying to keep my heels from clicking on the polished
wood floor. The house is eerily quiet and feels empty even
though it's full of really nice stuff.

Bert's home office overlooks the garden and drive. He
must have been watching me from the second I stepped out
of the cab, which is why he answered the door so quickly.

Instead of taking a seat behind his desk, he goes over to
one of the armchairs in front of the fireplace.

"You eat breakfast yet?" he asks. I shake my head, even though I'm sure Bert knows I haven't. He's as familiar with my eating schedule as I am with his. We both don't eat breakfast until well after nine.

I watch as he picks up a phone and barks some orders into it. Above him is an Andy Warhol portrait of his first wife, Maude Adler. As Miss Maude, she hosted a kids' television show that Steve was practically raised on and I watched in repeats. After it was canceled, she went on to a decent career in movies and TV, but she gave it up to be Bert's wife. From what I know, that got boring for her, and she tried to get back in the game but realized the game had moved on without her. She died of complications from a face-lift my first week of junior high.

Steve picked me up from school that day and burst into tears as soon as I got in the car. He was so upset I assumed that either Mom or Dad had been killed in a car wreck, and I was a little pissed off at him when I found out he was crying over a woman he'd never met. He'd been carrying quite a torch for Miss Maude, and her death sent him into a long funk; he ended up moving back into his old room for a while. Even my mother felt bad for him, and she'd always been jealous of Steve's TV bond with Miss Maude.

When Steve found out who my boss had been married to, he was decidedly chilly toward me, until he worked through his unrequited love for Miss Maude. All the same, while Steve will listen to me talk about Belmore, he'll shut down if I slip and mention Bert directly.

Bert sits opposite me, fixing his robe so it stays closed around his knees. "So how's it going?"

"It's not going, Mr. Floss," I say. "The phones aren't ring-ing and everyone is avoiding me."

"Yeah, I figured as much. That prick Fuller." Bert rubs the bridge of his nose as if he's trying to stave off a headache. "He's probably strutting around like he owns the place."

"Pretty much," I say. "He's calling meetings, handing out projects. Basically, Mr. Floss, he's doing your job."

"That red-faced fucker has been gunning for me for a while." Bert sighs. I don't bother to add that it was Bert himself who gave Fuller the bullets to shoot him down with. "He's a sneaky rat fuck, but he's good at what he does. And he knows how to play the political game."

I sit and say nothing. Bert's not telling me anything I haven't seen or experienced firsthand.

"Is he giving you a hard time?" Bert asks. I look at my boss, exasperated that he even has to ask. "Yeah, of course he is."

A young guy in a polo shirt and khakis comes in with a tray and sets it on the table, whispers something in Bert's ear, and then leaves. I don't make a move, so Bert is forced to pour me a cup of coffee. Technically, I'm a guest, a pissed-off one, and I'm not about to pour my own cup of coffee.

He sets it on the saucer along with a croissant. I take a cursory sip and set the cup on the table. "Are you coming into the office anytime soon, Mr. Floss?"

"Why bother?" Bert says, heaving his big shoulders. The robe opens a bit, and I catch sight of the gray hair on his chest. "I think this old dog is done at Belmore."

"I don't think so," I say, shaking my head. I would never have thought Bert would give up and roll over so easily, and because of someone like Fuller? It's even more insulting. "You're a very important part of Belmore, Mr. Floss. I'm sure . . ."

I'm sure what? Really, what do I know about Bert's relationship with Walter Belmore or even Kyle Martin? Just because I haven't been handed a pink slip and escorted out of the building doesn't mean they're backing my boss. If anything, his official ouster could be in the works right now and they're just waiting for the right time to announce Bert's "retirement."

"The only thing that's sure in this business, Raquel," he says wearily, as if it's costing him whatever energy he has left to form the words, "is that there's always somebody younger, faster, and better at bullshitting who wants your job."

"I don't think anyone wants my job." I take a few more sips of my coffee and then set it down for good. "I should be getting back, Mr. Floss."

"You might as well take the day off, but I know you won't. That's why I like you, Raquel. You're not lazy like the rest of them," he says, watching me from under his bushy eyebrows. I suppose keeping them tidy is the least of his concerns nowadays. "I'll have Xavier drive you back."

He gets up, and I follow suit. We walk in silence to the front door, where Xavier is already waiting.

"If there's anything I can do for you . . ." Bert trails off.

"I'll be sure to send you a fax, Mr. Floss," I say. I don't even feel better when I see Bert crack a smile. "Good-bye, Mr. Floss."

"Good-bye, Raquel," he says.

Once in the car, I look back and see Bert's in his office window. He doesn't wave, and neither do I.

Interpersonal Skills . . .

I have Xavier drop me at the Century City Hotel. It's a bit before 10:00, and I've missed the usual 9:30 meeting that Fuller has taken over running now that Bert isn't coming in. Not that Fuller expected me to attend—he left me off the memo list. At least I've made his day. Instead of crossing the street to Belmore, I wander into the hotel lobby and sit on one of the couches by the door.

I watch people check in and out, and how the employees keep things moving and calm. Their blue blazers, worn with either skirts or slacks, on both the women and the men, are nice enough and not too far off from my own uniform. Maybe they're hiring. I worked at the mall throughout high school and more than a few conventions as a temp; I'm sure my customer service muscle isn't completely atrophied. Even better, maybe they have a nice desk job where I won't have to deal with anyone. Nah, I couldn't work here. Way too close to Belmore. I'd end up running into—

"Raquel?" Kyle Martin is standing over me with an amused expression on his face. "What are you doing here?"

"I'm just sitting here," I admit.

"I can see that." He sits down next to me, close enough so I have to scoot over to make room for him.

"What are you doing here?" I ask. He smells good, a mixture of not too heavy cologne, soap, and expensive suit.

"My condo is being remodeled, so I'm staying here for a while." He shrugs as he looks around. It's a nice hotel, but I'm sure he's stayed in better. "It's convenient, close to work, but I still manage to be late."

"I doubt anyone is going to write you up, Mr. Martin."

"Call me Kyle. Seems silly this Mr. this and Ms. that." He laughs, and I realize he's nervous. A subdued thrill passes through me; I'm making Kyle Martin nervous. "Other than Walter, we're all about the same age. Right?"

"It's just tradition." I actually don't mind it. It's what makes Belmore Belmore. "I could never imagine calling Bert by his first name. At least not to his face."

"How are you holding up?" he asks. He eases his arm onto the backrest so his hand is near my shoulder. "Cris is really spreading his wings with Bert out of the office."

"He's taking over the whole damn department," I say, not bothering to hide my bitterness. "And he's an ass. I really don't care if you tell him, because I'm seriously considering a career change. I think they're hiring here."

"Don't say that, Raquel." Kyle reaches over and tucks a strand of hair behind my ear. "It wouldn't be worth going into the office if there wasn't a chance of running into you."

Kyle's sunburn has faded into a nice tan, and we're sitting so close I can see a small scar on his chin. He's looking at me like a guy looks at a girl he's interested in. Without thinking, I lean in and kiss him. Long and hard. When we pull apart, we're both breathing heavily.

"I'm so glad you did that, Raquel." I open my mouth to answer him, but he stops me with a finger to my lips. "And if you call me Mr. Martin, you'll ruin the fucking moment, so don't."

"Are you willing to be a little later to work?" I ask.

What do I have to lose? My job? My reputation? None of it matters, it's over. Bert in his sad bathrobe said as much. I may as well do the one thing I said I'd never do—sleep with someone from Belmore whom I'm genuinely attracted to.

"Are you serious? Because if you're kidding, I'll fire you," he says, looking as happy as a puppy dog who's found his first bone.

"You have no idea how serious I am, Kyle." I reach out my hand and pull him up with a little tug.

eight | FUTURE PERFECT

After the Glow . . .

After a couple of showers, one with and another without Kyle, I'm back at my desk. We staggered our exits, with me leaving first and him a few minutes after. Right now, as far as I know, he's up in his office on 24 going on with his day as if he didn't start it by going down on me.

"Holy crap, lady, what did you do and why didn't you do it sooner?" I say, channeling Frappa. Of course I'm going to tell her, but not over the phone and definitely not here, where private news doesn't stay private for long. Frappa is the only person I trust with information like this. Sleeping with someone like Kyle Martin is not just a booze-fueled make-out session with a Mike from Accounting or a semiserious thing with a Kurt from Legal. This is big stuff and, with the way my life is going, I'm betting that it'll go majorly wrong instead of in the Barbie and Ken dream house direction. But I don't regret it, not for a second.

It was fun, okay, more than that. It was sweet and sexy. While we waited for the concierge to send up condoms, Kyle asked me if I really wanted to go through with this. That I was straddling him at the time, my skirt bunched around my waist, and had one shoe off just made me want to tear into him all the more. And not only because it's been a while since I slept with anything that didn't require batteries. Kyle, it turns out, is a very considerate and capable lover with a good sense of humor. As he said after he got my bra off, "Thank God your tits are real, Raquel. You have no idea how awful it is out there." He was even into my heavy-duty panty hose and made taking them off part of our foreplay.

I giggle and look down at my desk, where I've been sitting for a solid fifteen minutes replaying everything in my head. Thinking about what he said after he made sure I was taken care of makes me want to burst out laughing again. "I just came like a fire hose," he said. The laugh I had was just as good as the orgasm. Like a *fire hose* . . .

"Fire hose," I yelp. I dive for my purse. "Fire hose!"

I scramble through my bag, tossing things aside until I find the key to Bert's office. I let myself in and lock the door behind me. Making myself at home in Bert's palatial en suite is one thing, I was really upset that day, but what I'm going to do now is grounds for being escorted out of the building by the scruff of my neck.

I take a slow turn around, not touching anything until I absolutely have to, trying to think where Bert would store potential projects. His office is surgically clean, free from dust and clutter, and largely foreign to me. Besides coming in here when invited, I don't really spend any time inside Bert's office.

I don't replenish his supply of pens or keep his files tidy. Bert takes care of these things for himself. Bert has never said he doesn't trust me, and I've never given him a reason not to. That he didn't ask for his key when I saw him this morning must be a sign that he knows I'd never do anything I shouldn't do.

"Right? Whatever," I say. "I'm here and here for a good reason. It's not like I'm going to take a shower . . . again."

I snicker as I survey his desk from a distance. I'll stay away from it, since I know all the drawers are locked. I'm not sure what he keeps in them, and at this point I think that's a good thing.

"It has to be here," I say as I move toward the credenza, where the media equipment is stored. Normally it would be my first place to look, but I wouldn't be surprised to find it free from anything but blinking electronics. I slide the door open, and there it is. Still in the case with my handwritten label and propped against the DVD player is *Fire House Hero*.

"Thank you, thank you, thank you." Kneeling on the carpet, I do a few bows of gratitude. I put the disk in the player and, still on my knees, make my way over to the sitting area.

I settle myself down on Bert's viewing chair and punch the sequence of buttons that brings down the shades, drops the screen, and starts up the player. I speed through the credits until I find what I'm looking for and freeze the screen on a pair of dimples that are attached to the face of Rory, the flirty coffee jockey.

"I knew it! I knew I'd seen that smile before," I say, almost crying with relief. Taking deep breaths, I force myself to go back to the beginning of the movie. I have to be objective here, or as objective as I can be under the situation. "Be a marketer, Raquel. Don't force yourself to see something that's not there."

Fire House Hero had been destined to join the hundreds of other straight to DVD efforts that are churned out by obscure studios and small production companies every year. It, and other assets, had been acquired in a mercenary takeover of the floundering independent production company by Belmore a few months before. Most of what they had was junk, but the company had enough cachet with the tween to perpetual teen set and a specialization in campy movies featuring attractive unknowns that it was worth the effort to take a look at their *entire* library to see what had some marketing value. Bert had given me the job of wading through *American Pie* and *A Walk to Remember* rip-offs. I spent an entire weekend speed-watching movies until my thumb was sore from fast-forwarding and my eyes were crossed from the stupidity of it all.

I'd been in hour sixteen of my crap movie marathon when I pushed *Fire House Hero* into my overheated DVD player. Even through my exhaustion, I realized what was penetrating my fried brain and taking place before my bloodshot eyes was a cut far above the rest of the dreck I'd willingly subjected myself to.

As I rewatch it, my initial thoughts are confirmed. The movie itself is pleasant enough, if tragically formulaic, but the real diamond in the muck is Rory Tilley. A toothy pretty boy with, as it turns out, abs galore. Rory has been endowed by the genetic gods with perfect hair, wide blue-green eyes, pouty mouth, and a square jaw that looks good in person but is downright panty creaming on-screen. That his parents were smart enough to give him a movie star name is just a bonus.

What the movie needs is more Rory, through either recutting or doing additional shoots. At the very least there should be a montage of Rory with his shirt off, laughing, holding a hose, set to a jaunty Belmore music artist's tune. This would be something my marketing report could suggest, but I'd have to have some solid numbers to justify the added expense.

Rory pulsates on the screen, elevating *Fire House Hero* from jalopy to luxury midsize sedan. His natural ease in front of the camera is obvious and overcomes clunky dialogue like "Fire scares me. It haunts my dreams and my days. But I can't let fire or my fear of fire get the best of me. I'll fight fires until I die . . . It'll probably be in a fire."

What's better is he looks good while saying it. He's a natural actor, his great looks backed up by enough talent so that he can someday look back at *Fire House Hero* as being his Leo DiCaprio guest starring on a couple of episodes of *Growing Pains* moment. This guy, giver of free coffee and slices of banana bread, is the real deal. Or, at least, real enough to maybe save my promotion and Bert's job.

I walk over to Bert's desk and dial one of Frappa's many numbers. I skip through the menu and hit the button that will take me directly to voice mail. "Hey, Frap, it's me. I'm hoping we can talk. Things are getting weird at Belmore, but I think I might have something here that will help. By the way, this is Raquel."

I hang up, use a tissue to wipe away any smudges on the phone, and for a few moments take the time to enjoy the truly spectacular view outside Bert's window.

The Rat King . . .

With studied calm, I go back to my desk. I have the *Fire House Hero* DVD tucked under my jacket, and all I want to do is transfer it from my armpit into my purse. Technically, I'm not stealing the movie, just borrowing it. Though if Cris Fuller finds out, he could say I was. But he's not going to find out because—

"Crap," I say.

"Raquel." Fuller is standing in the doorway. His fake tan is a shade lighter, so he looks almost normal, but he's whitened his teeth so they are almost glowing. Maybe one of these days, he'll get it right. "Nice to see you finally got around to showing up for work."

"Good morning, Mr. Fuller." I freeze in place, my arm clenched to my side.

"It's lunchtime, Raquel. Where have you been?" he asks, looking around suspiciously at my stuff strewn across the floor and desk.

"Here," I lie. I haven't even started up my computer, and the cup of coffee on my desk is stone-cold. I sit down, move some papers around, and grab both my cell phones. "Mr. Floss asked me to take care of some filing."

"And are you done with that?" he asks, his well-groomed brows arching as much as his forehead full of Botox will let them.

"Yes," I say, knowing that if I make things too difficult, he'll just pay more attention to me.

"I have some things for you to take care of," he says, flicking imaginary lint off his suit cuffs. "I spoke with Human Resources, and they've given their okay, so you can't go running to them to complain."

"Of course," I say. As I stand up, I let the DVD drop to the floor and edge it under the CPU cabinet with my foot.

"You can leave those here," he says of my cell phones.

"Of course, Mr. Fuller." I set them on the desk and follow him out.

I'm not going to get in a pissing match with Cris Fuller. Not now, when I'm on the verge of something. He wants me to give him attitude so he has a reason to frog-march me down to HR. That he's wasting his time on me tips his hand. Even though I'm walking two steps behind him, I'm the one in the power position. Fuller's a petty man, and I can use that to my advantage. I'm only mildly surprised when we stop at the empty reception desk.

"You're going to be covering the phones until further notice," he says with obvious joy, and then he waits for me to react.

"Of course, Mr. Fuller." I won't bother to ask what's happened to the receptionist. She was a temp, and the last time I saw her she was crying in the bathroom. I circle around the desk and take a seat. The phone rings, and I answer it. "Thank you for calling Belmore. This is the marketing department. How may I direct your call?" I punch in the extension, put the phone down, and wait for the next call.

"Is there anything else, Mr. Fuller?" My voice is perfectly pleasant and doesn't give any hint that my hands are curled into fists underneath the desk.

"No," he snaps. I'm ruining his day by not bursting into tears over his grand scheme to bring me to my knees.

The phone rings, and I smile at him as I say, "Thank you for calling Belmore. This is the marketing department. How may I direct your call?"

He stands there, seething, waiting for me to make a mistake, but I don't. I'm like an affable robot, precise and unemotional. Out of the corner of my eye I see a mass of gray and navy blue descend down the hall and stop a few feet away from us.

"Mr. Fuller?" One of the more confident of the junior execs speaks for the group. "We're expected in Development."

Fuller reaches out, and another junior exec puts a file into his hand. "You know what's expected of you, Raquel."

Fuller gives me one last glare before they walk, as a unit, into the elevator and disappear. He doesn't need to worry about me. I'm not going to do anything but what I'm supposed to do. For the next hour I answer calls, sign for packages and interoffice mail, and don't indulge in any unnecessary small talk. I smile when people who used to wish me good morning or ask me about my weekend hurry past without making eye contact.

Only Matthias is human, or dumb, enough to stop and acknowledge that I've been put into the corporate stocks. He hangs back as most of the marketing department heads down to the commissary for the monthly birthday cake break. No one asks if I'm coming. Even though it's my birthday month, they're not willing to spare me a piece of cake. Not when Fuller has made it clear I have the plague.

"Oh, my God, Raquel, this is just unbelievable," he says in a shocked whisper as soon as they're gone. "I can't believe Cris would do something like this to you."

"I can believe it, Matthias. Pardon my bluntness, but your boss is a jerk of the first order," I say, and it feels good to say it. "And if this is the worst he has planned for me, I think I'm getting off pretty easy."

I appreciate his concern, but I don't need any more melo-drama. I refuse to be a victim of my circumstances. Fuller might think he's put me in my place, but in between answering phone calls, I'm planning my next move.

First thing I need to do for any of what's swirling around in my mind to matter is get back to my true desk, grab my purse and tote bag, and shove the DVD inside. If I have time, I'll start up my computer and print out a copy of the *Fire House Hero* memo I wrote for Bert. It's sitting in a folder on my desktop. There's no marketing report, not yet. Bert signed off on my memo, saying he thought it had promise and he'd get back to me. *Fire House Hero* was on his radar, but not a priority for either of us. Now, I'm convinced, it's both of our salvation.

"This is just not fair," Matthias says. I'm not sure if he's upset about what's happened to me specifically or if he's worried that a precedent has been set so that it can happen to anyone. "You're an executive assistant. He shouldn't be able to do this to you. It's humiliating!"

"He can and he has." I shrug, not wanting to make this any more of a big deal than it is.

Sure, I'm humiliated, but knowing this is what Fuller wants me to be helps take the edge off. I can't waste the energy to get angry about it, not now. As long as Cris Fuller doesn't fire me, I'm okay. I just need a few days to make something happen, and then he won't be able to touch me. Of course, what I'm planning to do could get me fired, but I'll worry about that later.

"I just have to make the best of it," I say, hoping Matthias will get the point and move on.

"It's just so . . ."

Matthias trails off as the elevator pings and the doors slide open to reveal not Floss and his evil entourage but a delivery guy carrying an impressive bouquet of pink tulips.

"Who are they for?" Matthias asks as I sign for them. "No one ever gets flowers on this floor. I heard some girls from HR saying that most of the good stuff goes to . . ."

I tune Matthias out as my focus goes to the name scrawled on the cream-colored envelope: R. Azorian. I snatch it out from where it's tucked between the blooms and shove it into my pocket. An orgasm and flowers? Is this guy for real?

"Raquel? Are you okay? Are you going to pass out?" Matthias asks. "Should I get you a Diet Coke?"

"No, it's okay. I just realized . . . something," I say as I fan myself with a notepad. "You should go back to your desk before someone sees you talking to me."

"I don't care. I hate this place." He pouts. "Maybe I'll ask for a transfer up to Creative. I hear it's way more fun up there."

"It is," I say, wanting Matthias to move along, but craving his company at the same time. "I'd offer to talk to Jessica about it for you, but it would probably kill any chances you have."

"I'll talk to her later." He leans into the bouquet, looking for the card I have in my pocket. "So who are they for?"

"You," I say. "Someone sent them to Bert, but since he's not coming in today, you take them."

"Who would send Bert pink tulips?" Matthias asks. "That's kind of weird. These are the kind of flowers a guy sends to a girl he's into. And I know for a fact that no one is in love on this floor. I've asked. So who sent them?"

"Someone who doesn't know Bert very well but wants to," I say as I heave up the vase and hand it over to him. "Maybe I can come visit them later?"

"Sure, just not when Cris is around. You understand," he adds quickly with an apologetic look.

"I totally do, Matthias," I say. "And I promise not to hold it against you for having to ignore me when other people are around."

"You don't deserve this, Raquel." Matthias gives me a quick hug over the desk. "No one does."

"Please, I'm fine. Take the flowers and enjoy them for me . . . I mean for Bert."

As soon as Matthias is well enough away, I reach into my pocket and carefully open the envelope to slide out the card. It reads, "To R, who has the prettiest pink two lips I've ever kissed. K."

The Bigger Picture . . .

Besides a couple of bathroom breaks and the state-mandated fifteen minutes to grab an apple out of the break room, Fuller makes sure I stay at reception. Every so often he has a junior exec trot over with a menial task for me to do. This is bad enough, but they're under orders to stand there while I complete it.

For the most part, though, I don't let it get to me, and when it does I force myself to think about what really matters—*Fire House Hero* and Rory Tilley. I go through the motions of sealing envelopes, sorting through clippings that have already been sorted, and pulling staples out of documents only to have to restaple them an hour later when another junior exec comes back with them with a smile on my face.

At six on the dot, I switch the phones over to the automatic system and hurry back to my office. Fuller is waiting for me right inside.

"Mr. Fuller, is there something you need?" I ask, edging toward my desk, where I can see a corner of the DVD case poking out from underneath.

"The key to Bert's office," he says. He already knows I'm going to say no, but I guess he wants to cap off his day with one last pissing match. "I know you have it."

"I'm sorry, Mr. Fuller, but Mr. Floss has expressly forbidden me from giving that key to anyone but himself," I say.

I'll lick his envelopes, sign for his muffin baskets, but I'm not giving him the key. Not just because it's Bert's key and he has no right to ask for it but for the sheer principle of it. Jerks are a dime a dozen in this industry, and I've dealt with enough of them to know that, if I give in, things will just go from bad to worse. Fuller is trying to bully me, and if there's one thing I don't like it's a bully.

"I don't care what Bert says. He's not here." There's a rise of color that starts from his collar and works its way up Fuller's neck. He's getting way too mad much too fast.

"I'm sorry, Mr. Fuller, but I'm sure you understand why I can't. If you'd like me to call Mr. Floss and clear this up, I'd be happy to." I pick up the phone and start to dial even though I have no intention of putting Bert on the phone.

"Who the fuck do you think you are?" Fuller spits, his

face now fully red. "You work for me, and you're very lucky to still have a job. This is *my* department."

"I'm sorry, Mr. Fuller, was there a memo I didn't get?" I say. "Maybe an announcement that I missed while I was stapling documents?"

"You little bitch—"

"Hey there, Cris." Kyle walks over to my desk, putting himself between me and Fuller. "Is everything okay here?"

For a second I feel my eyes tear up, but I quickly blink them away. Kyle is not my boyfriend just because we slept together and he sent me flowers. And I don't need him to fight my battles. I can handle Fuller.

"Mr. Fuller was just wishing me a good night," I say, my voice sounding steady enough. I gather up my phones, shut off the fax machine, and slip the *Fire House Hero* DVD into my tote bag. "I hope you have a nice night, too, Mr. Fuller. Good night, Mr. Martin."

I walk out and quicken my pace when the yelling starts. People slow down to listen; others poke their heads out of their offices and cubicles.

Matthias darts out of his office, almost running me over. "What's going on? Is that Kyle Martin?"

"I have no idea. Hey, Matthias?" I wave my hands in front of his face to get his attention. "Is your computer still on?"

"Did Mr. Martin just call Cris an asshole?" Matthias asks, wide eyed and loving every second of the drama I just want to flee from. "Someone talked to Defamer and Deadline Hollywood about Bert. Do you think it was Cris?"

He puts his hands to his cheeks, and for a second I can see why he gets away with murder. He is beyond adorable—

even his gossipmongering is cute. I'll compliment him later; right now I need his computer for something.

"Focus, Matthias." I grab his shoulder and turn him to face me. "Is your computer still on?"

"Yes, why?" he asks, reluctantly tearing himself away from the action.

I yank on his arm, dragging him back into his office. The tulips are set on the desk, where everyone can see them.

"I need to access something from the server," I say, sitting down while he hovers in the doorway. "I'd do it from my desk, but Mr. Martin and your boss are having a, uh, meeting."

"A meeting? They're having an argument! A really good one, and I'm missing it," Matthias complains. "The only exciting thing to happen here since Bert ate it on Monday, and I'm at my desk. Sorry, Raquel. It's not your fault Bert ate it. I mean you didn't . . ."

I wave him off as I enter passwords, navigate servers, and finally pull up the folder where all department memos are kept. I always save a copy here as a matter of course, even though I know some execs horde their memos on their desktops until they're ready to unveil them. A few quick clicks, and the printer beside Matthias's desk starts to hum.

Not wanting to waste any time, I type Rory's name into IMDb.com. All that comes up is a bare-bones page for *Fire House Hero*. I'm relieved to see that Rory doesn't have any other credits to his name. I give Defamer and Deadline Hollywood a quick glance, and see that, yes, someone unnamed has told both blogs that Bert is off on medical leave. It was bound to come out, but I know Belmore didn't want it to get out this way. I can't worry about it now, though. The printer unspools the single sheet of paper that makes up the memo I wrote.

"What's that?" Matthias asks, more attentive to what I'm doing since the yelling has stopped.

"Nothing. Just a memo Bert wants me to fax over to him." I fold it in half and hold it loosely in my hand. Trying to play casual, I ask, "You doing anything tonight?"

"Yeah, some of us are going out for drinks. Jessica and Marisa are starting this group for assistants," Matthias says. As he realizes that I haven't been invited, his cheeks go pink. "I mean, I probably won't go. *Survivor* is on tonight."

I can't help but laugh. "Please, Matthias. When was the last time you stayed in to watch TV?"

"Never," he admits. "I don't even have a TV. I feel so bad about how everyone is treating you."

"Don't. And I don't expect you to join me in martyrdom. Go out for drinks and tell me all about it tomorrow. I'll meet you in the stairwell at ten."

I peek out the door and duck back in. Kyle is stalking toward the elevators, and Fuller is heading this way.

"Jesus, can't I catch a break?" I say. For a second I want to stamp my feet, pound on the door, and scream at the top of my lungs. Who says a twenty-five-year-old isn't entitled to a tantrum once in a while? "And I didn't even get a fucking slice of birthday cake."

"Go out through the secret door," Matthias says, pulling me into Fuller's office and pushing me into the bathroom. "Hurry!"

"You're a saint," I say, giving him a quick kiss. Matthias is putting himself on the line, not just by talking to me but by unwittingly helping me out in my scheme to bring down his boss and bring back my own. I owe him big time. "You're saving me every which way from Tuesday."

"It's the least I could do. By the way, cute bag," Matthias says as he shuts the door, "too bad it has coffee all over it."

I stand there in the murky light of the stairwell, even though I should be moving as fast as I can down the seventeen floors to freedom. Not daring to look, I reach into my tote, feel around, and let out a breath when my hand touches the napkin Rory wrote his phone number on. I pull it out and look at it. There, a little smudged but clear as can be, are ten little numerals that might add up to something major.

"Yes," I say, quietly knowing I'm this much closer to never having to call Cris Fuller "Mr." again. "Yes!"

nine | IN BETWEEN LIVES

Multitasking . . .

Once I get to the safety of my car, I dial the numbers from the napkin on my Belmore cell phone. My hands are shaking so bad with all the adrenaline coursing through me, it takes me two tries to get it right.

"Yeah?" a male voice says. Whoever this guy is, he needs to hock up some major phlegm. I just hope he doesn't do it in my ear.

"Hi? I'm looking for Rory? My name is Raquel. We met the other day at . . . where he works." I cross my fingers hard. My feelings would only be slightly hurt if he gave me a dummy number, but only because he was the instigator. I came into the café just because I wanted a coffee and baked goods fix. He was the one who started the flirting. "Is this Rory's number?"

"Rory?" he asks, sounding completely at a loss as to who Rory is. It causes my heart to sink somewhere near the vicinity of my Nine West pumps. Of course it wouldn't be this easy. I pull out of my space, knowing I'll be heading directly to The Grove. "He's not around. He's out."

"Does he have a cell phone number where I could reach him?" I ask.

"This is it," Rory's phlegmy friend says. "But I can take a message and make sure he gets it."

"Great! I mean, cool. No, what I really mean is great!" I bounce up and down on my seat, causing my car to rock slightly. Behind me a conga line of slow-moving Belmore employees snake their way toward the exits. "Can you do me a huge favor? Can you have him call me back the second he gets back from wherever he is?"

I rattle off numbers but stop short of asking him for directions to where Rory lives. I can tell from his tone that he thinks I'm some scary stalker.

"You got them?" I ask, unable to keep myself from micro-managing him. "Three, one, zero—"

"Yeah," he says and hangs up.

Next I call my mother, who's left a dozen messages, which I don't bother to listen to on my personal cell. She answers on the second ring. "Hello?"

"Hi, Mom! I'm sorry I didn't call you back. I was in meetings all day and I forgot my phone at my desk. So do you want to go out to grab something to eat?" I'm hoping if I mix light-heartedness and apologetic along with a firm plan of action, it will curtail any sort of reaction that will keep me on the phone with her the whole drive over.

"Raquel?" she asks, clearly confused, which I will blame on the Baileys. It's the Baileys's fault that my mother called me twelve times while sitting on my couch and watching my TV. "It that you?"

"Yeah, hi, it's me. Raquel. Everything okay?" I have to ask. I know, of course, that nothing is okay, but I'm hoping she's not suffering from some fast-acting dementia that started up around lunchtime.

"Where are you?" she asks.

"I'm on my way home." I'm getting close to the garage exit and don't want to bother to switch over to my hands-free device, which is somewhere in my bag. With my luck I'll find it right away, but it'll turn out to be the one for my Belmore BlackBerry.

"Oh, okay. Did you talk to your father?" she asks. A stab of guilt mixed with annoyance hits me in the belly. The likelihood that she's been waiting around all day for me to call her so she could tell me to call him is very high. "Raquel?"

"No. Do you want me to? I can if you want," I offer.

At least a phone call to my father will be short. Since there's nothing I can tell him about my mother that he probably doesn't already know, we'll stick to the facts. Yes, she's still in my apartment. Yes, she's still upset. No, she's not ready to be logical. No, it doesn't look like she'll be coming home anytime soon. Good night and take care. End of conversation.

My mother is silent for a moment before she answers. "Make sure to tell him that I never loved him."

She sounds like a person who is miserably in love. Or maybe she wants love and that's what's making her miserable. I don't know which is worse and don't want to have to figure it out for her. I have enough on my mind. My own personal life has gotten a bit more complicated than it was this morning. Meaning I now have a personal life, whereas before I had none. At least I took having sex with Kyle personally. I'm not sure what he thinks about it, but I hope it at least means—

"Raquel? Are you still there? Did we get cut off?"

"I'm here, Mom. I'll call him when I get home. I need to hang up now, pulling into traffic. I'll see you soon," I say as I catch sight of the sea of red taillights ahead of me. Santa Monica Boulevard is backed up in both directions. "Gotta hang up, bye!"

As I inch forward I scroll through my BlackBerry to see if I missed a call from Frappa. There is an unfamiliar 212 number, and it's the only call I've gotten on that phone all day even though I forwarded my desk phone to it. Bert must be deep in his funk; he didn't send a single fax after the two from this morning. Another problem for another day. Right now I need to be proactive with my Save Bert plan and tell the one person I can trust what I did and who I did it with this morning. I hit call return and pray that it leads to Frappa.

"Hello?" asks a slightly raspy voice that doesn't belong to Frappa.

I swallow my disappointment that it's not her, but I'm not willing to give up just yet. "Hello, I'm trying to reach Frappa Ivanhoe. This is Raquel Azorian at Belmore."

As I see what's backed up traffic, a multicar fender bender, I reach for my bag to find my earpiece. Last thing I need is to get slapped with a ticket for talking on my cell phone while driving.

"Frappa isn't here. She's like out. You want me to tell her to call you?" A heavy sigh fills my ear.

I know that sigh. It's been immortalized in countless You-Tube parodies, sampled for a dance hit, and even popped up in a cheeky TV commercial for stain remover. It's the sigh that belongs to either Cat or Cara Ward. Not only do they look exactly alike but they sigh the same as well.

I have to ease myself out of the conversation as quickly and carefully as possible. I can't give the impression that I don't want to talk to either Cat or Cara, Frappa's prized clients. To hurt whichever Ward twin's feelings not only would lessen the likelihood that my message would ever get to Frappa but could have professional repercussions. Those two rich bitches are notorious for holding grudges. It's their full-time hobby after partying, wearing designer clothes, and occasionally acting in derivative movies and television specials. They've run more than a few people out of town, and I doubt they'd have trouble freezing me out of the whole of Westside L.A. and the cooler parts of the rest of the city as well. Or maybe I'm just flattering myself.

"I'll just try her cell." I go for straightforward, hoping it won't be warped into something like a mortal snub. "Sorry to bother you."

"You can't. She got like mugged. She was like standing outside our like hotel and some guy like mugged her. She got like blood all over my brand-new Balenciagas. But she's like my agent so it's fine. I guess."

"Is she okay?" My phone beeps in my ear, and I pull it away to see a blocked number is trying to reach me. I ignore it. "Was she hurt?"

"Well, yeah. He like smacked her after she like cussed him out for mugging her. And then she hit him back and he ran off." Another sigh followed by an indifferent giggle. "It was kind of like funny until the blood like got on me."

"That's like horrible," I say. My personal cell goes off. "Please have her call Raquel as soon as she can."

"Okay. Sure. Whatever," says Cat or Cara and hangs up.

"Hi? Hello?" I'm now holding two phones, but in my defense I'm at a complete stop.

"Hi, Raquel!" It's Cricket. Damn me for answering without checking. I need to assign her a ring tone. Maybe the snippet from the shower scene in *Psycho*. "I don't want to take up any of your time because I know you're incredibly busy."

I wait until I realize she's waiting for me to tell her that it's okay for her to take up even more of my time and for me to tell her I'm not incredibly busy. Or maybe that would be rude? Maybe I should tell her I am busy, but I have time for her. I don't understand Southern manners. Maybe the way she is has nothing to do with manners and she's just passive-aggressive. I know my mom is beyond passive-aggressive, but these mental moves of my sister-in-law's are new to me. Or maybe I'm just tired.

"Are you there?" she asks.

"What's up, Cricket?" I ask, moving the conversation forward even as traffic refuses to budge an inch. I dig around for an earpiece as I get closer to the cluster of police cars, fire trucks, and ambulances.

"I just heard from Steve that Marlene is staying over at your place. And I said to Steve, no, that can't be! It's no secret that your parents were having issues, but for her to move out? It's so unexpected! How could we have not noticed that things were this bad?"

"I'm sorry, is this what you said to Steve or are you asking me?" I'm definitely getting a ring tone for Cricket and feel stupid for not having done it sooner.

"In times like this, Raquel, family needs to come together," Cricket snaps.

"Cricket?" I look in my rearview mirror and see that it's filled with flashing lights. "I'm being pulled over and . . . I'll talk to you later."

It takes me ten minutes to edge my car over to the curb. In that time I miss another call from my mother, three from Cricket, one from the 212 number, and one from a blocked number that I'm pretty sure belongs to Kyle. The cop knocks on my window, and I roll it down.

"Hi, Officer," I say as I hand over my license, registration, and proof of insurance. I keep both hands where he can see them and smile. "I'm sorry. I know I'm not supposed to be on my cell while I'm driving."

"You're almost making this too easy," he says as he starts writing up the ticket. "People aren't normally this nice about getting a ticket."

"Officer," I say with nothing but true sincerity, "this is the most normal thing that's happened to me all day."

Mother's Helper . . .

After heaving the garage door open to park my car inside, I backtrack to the front of my apartment instead of going in through the kitchen. I stand at the mailbox, buying myself a few more seconds of solitude as I go through every single piece of mail. Even the sight of my ton of magazines, everything from *National Geographic* and *The Economist* to *Cosmo* and *People,* both *Teen* and regular *People,* doesn't make me happy. There are a few bills and one hand-addressed, oversize envelope with way too many stamps on it.

I put the rest of my mail between my knees. It's a lot, so I really have to squeeze them together, and slit the envelope open with my car key. I pull out a card, a close-up shot of some kind of flower. Inside there's a handwritten message in loopy script. My eyes immediately go to the signature—Nicolette Meyers.

"Isn't that sweet." I take a breath and read the card aloud. " 'Rachel' . . . okay, close enough . . . 'Thank you so much for helping me out at the premiere of *Risk Management III,* number one movie in the country. All my love, Nicolette Meyers' . . . Well, that's a first."

"Raquel?" My mother peeks through the blinds. "Is that you?"

"Yeah, it's me. Don't call the cops." I hurry inside, dumping my mail on the table by the door and taking a look around at the same time. My mother isn't the neatest person in the world, but things don't look too bad. If I have some time before bed, I'll tidy up so I don't have to wake up to a messy house. "Sorry it took me so long. There was a dumb accident . . . What are you wearing?"

My mother, all fiftysomething years and uncombed hair of her, is wearing one of my Victoria's Secret Pink sweat suits. I lived in those during college, along with one pair of Ugg boots after another. The sweats, but not the boots, were in the sealed boxes I was this close to calling Out of the Closet to come by and pick up.

"You have no food or water in your house, and I can't find my keys." My mother flounces over to the couch and picks up the remote.

"Water comes out of the tap, and I told you there was soup. I can order something or run to the supermarket if you want." I pick up my keys, only too eager to have an excuse to leave. "Or I could go pick something up? There's a Thai place that's great, but they don't deliver. How does Thai sound?"

"Someone called here and hung up twice," my mother says. "You should get a security system. Or put some men's boots on the porch."

"Sorry?" I drop the keys on top of my stack of magazines. "Boots on the porch?"

"A rapist will think there's a man in the house. Or maybe you can get a dog." She holds up an old issue of *InStyle*. "These puggles look to be very popular. It would give you an excuse to meet some nice men when you go out and walk it."

"No dog, but I'll think about the boots." Why she hasn't shared this safety tip with me before is a question for another day. "I think I have a Lean Cuisine in the freezer. Grilled chicken primavera. Very yummy. Okay, not very, but if you're hungry enough, it's really almost delicious."

"Let's order pizza," she says, a spark of life coming into her eyes. "And drink beer and watch *Pretty Woman*."

"Whoa, those sweats are working their sorority house magic." I sit down next to her and give her a pat on the leg. "Why don't we go out? Nowhere fancy. You can keep the sweats on."

On hearing my words, she snuggles deeper into the couch and pulls a blanket over her lap. She's not planning on going anywhere and, when I think about it, I realize that's probably a good thing for both of us. She fits into my old sweats well enough, but they just look wrong. I'm going to have to get up in the middle of the night and get rid of those boxes of clothes.

"Okay, I'll order us a pizza, but we're going to have to make do with what's on cable. I don't own *Pretty Woman*. It'll be fun."

"Your father hasn't even bothered to call me," she says, going from giddy to tears in a minute flat. "Or do you think he's the one who called and hung up?"

"I only use that line to update my TiVo and screen phone calls. It was probably just a telemarketer who lost his nerve, Mom," I say, giving her another series of what I hope are morale-boosting leg pats. "Dad never calls me, and if he was going to, he'd call my cell. I don't even think he knows my home number."

I don't want to burst her bubble, but I'm not going to let my mom string herself along, waiting for a phone call that isn't going to come. At least not until I physically dial the phone for my father.

"So should I order a pizza?" I ask. My mother flips channels, settles on a rerun of *Friends,* and then turns up the volume. "Okay then."

I get up and lock myself in the bathroom. Even in here I can't get away from her. She's taken over my countertop with her creams and lotions. She's also brought along a hair dryer, curling iron, straightening iron, and hot rollers.

"So why does she have her hair in the fucking scrunchie I use when I give myself a face mask?" I ask my bathrobe. I hear my landline ring in the living room, and I dart out to pick it up. "Hello?"

"Raquel?" It's Kyle. Toe-curling, orgasm-inducing Kyle.

"Oh . . . Hey." I walk toward the bedroom, trying to act as casual as possible even though my stomach is doing flip-flops. My bed is still unmade, and I throw the back of my mom's head an annoyed glare. "Hi."

"I've been trying to reach you. Are you okay?" he asks.

"Sure. I'm great. I mean, not great, but pretty okay," I say. I head back into the bathroom and shut the door.

"For the time being, Cris is in charge of the department," Kyle says. "I just wanted you to hear it from me first."

"Is that official?" I ask. My mind is racing, trying to figure what the different scenarios might be, what they mean for me, and how I can work them to my advantage.

"Things are in a holding pattern for now. Walter wants to keep this within the company. Unofficially, Bert is on vacation and Cris is under my direct supervision until this is resolved. He shouldn't be bothering you, but if he does I want you to tell me," he says. "Can I see you? Tonight?"

"I wish I could." I open the door and peek out at my mother. She's still sulking. She throws a dirty look toward the bathroom, and I duck back in, banging my elbow on the towel rack. "Listen, Kyle, I'm not trying to be coy but—"

"I promise not to do anything to you that you don't want me to," he says. "And I'll buy you dinner. The room service at the Century is decent, but more important, fast."

"Tempting," I say. "But I should really—"

"Raquel!" my mother yells. "That's an awful long phone call with a telemarketer."

I close my eyes for a second and come to a decision. "Kyle? I'll see you in forty-five minutes."

"Great. I'll order up a case of Diet Coke and strawberry Pop-Tarts."

I open the door, march out and put the handset back on the charger, grab my family cell phone, and then go straight back into the bathroom. I dig through the cabinet under the sink until I find my GiGi wax warmer and the Ziploc bag where I keep the muslin strips and applicators. It's been a while since I've waxed myself, and things don't look too bad, but I want to make an effort.

"What are you doing?" my mother asks from the other side of the door.

"I'm ordering you a pizza. I have to go back to the office. Bert needs me to finish up a big project before tomorrow. I might be gone awhile." While the wax is melting, I tweeze any stray hairs from my eyebrows. "What do you want on your pizza? The usual?"

"Just cheese. I'm on a diet. Let me in, Raquel." She jiggles the knob.

"Give me a minute, Mom." I put a little extra whine in my voice. "I'm busy in here."

I run a brush through my hair and leave it loose so it falls around my shoulders. I text in the order to my usual pizza place with one hand and focus on getting my makeup done with the other. One of the joys of being ambidextrous. Only snag I hit is forgetting to brush my teeth first, so I have to do my lips twice.

"What's that smell?" she asks, her voice sounding like it's coming from the vicinity of the couch.

"I lit a candle. You know I can't go unless I'm relaxed," I say. The wax is lavender scented and almost ready. I strip to the waist and tuck my blouse into the underside of my bra to keep it out of the way.

"You should see a doctor about that. Or get more fiber into your diet," my mother says over the TV.

She's changing channels again. I don't have any beer in my apartment, but I do have a bottle of wine in the closet from a goody bag. Red or white, I'm not sure, but I'm confident my mother won't quibble once she sees it.

I smooth some wax over the top of my tiny triangle, starting with the spot I know will smart the least. Despite the calming scent of the wax, I feel beads of sweat break out across my forehead. I lay the muslin strip across, pull my skin taut, and then yank.

"Holy nut balls," I pant. "Now I remember why I don't do this myself."

"What was that?" my mother asks, muting the TV.

"Pizza is on the way, Mom. There's a bottle of wine in the closet by the door. Why don't you open it or stick it in the fridge?" I do another strip, trying to stay true to the shape that's already there. "Wineglasses are in the cabinet over the microwave."

A few more yanks and I'm done. I check out my handiwork in the mirror, having to stand on my tippy toes to do so, and am impressed. Sure there are some strays I'll have to tweeze and maybe my triangle is a little wonky, but I just saved myself fifty dollars. I bunch up my panty hose and underwear, shove them into the hamper, and put my skirt back on. A little translucent powder across my forehead, nose, and chin, and I'm done.

"Mom, I'll call you if I think I'm going to be out really late," I say, slipping on a pair of suede, pointy T-strap heels I've been saving for a special occasion. "But I can already tell you, I think I am."

Pillow Talk . . .

I open the hotel-provided toothbrush and add a dab of Kyle's Crest toothpaste. I'm wearing the hotel robe and hotel slippers, and just finished eating hotel food after having sex in the hotel bed.

I watch my face in the mirror as I brush. I'm flushed and my hair is a mess and I look exactly like a woman who has just had some of the best sex of her life. Who knew coming over in my lady suit sans panties would have such an effect on a man? Kyle seemed even more into me this time than he did in the morning.

"Do you want to go out for dessert? We can go to Pinkberry," Kyle says from where he's lounging on the bed. He has his arms folded under his head and a sheet very minimally covering his goods.

I spit and rinse. "Sorry, but I hate Pinkberry. I'm more of a Dairy Queen or McFlurry type of person. Plus, you're buck naked, and I kind of want to keep you that way for as long as possible."

I snuggle up next to him, and Kyle tucks my head under his chin and plays with my hair. This feels good. I could get used to it, whatever it is.

"So can I ask you how you like Belmore?" I run my hand down his smooth chest. "I don't want to ruin the mood, but I'm really wondering."

Kyle takes a deep breath, my head rising and falling with it, before he answers. "You know, no one besides my shrink has asked me that."

"Great. If you tell me that you also sleep with your shrink, I'm going to feel really weird." I nudge him in the ribs. "I'm just wondering because Belmore must be very different from owning and running your own company."

"I'm not totally used to it, but Belmore is a cornerstone of the industry. They've been around since hand-cranked cameras. There's a lot of history, and much of it is really good," he says, giving me a rather practiced answer.

"But do you actually like the place?" I ask. I know he has the title, the office, class A shares, and a secure enough position in the industry, but all that doesn't mean he can't hate his job.

"No bullshitting you, huh?" Kyle laughs, kissing the top of my head. "I think Belmore is a great company that can be better. We have to look to make history, not just rely on the past to carry us forward."

"True enough, but being that the company lives and dies by the Belmore name, I'm not sure what's going to happen once Walter Belmore, you know, retires."

"That man will outlive us all, Raquel." Kyle tilts up my chin and kisses the tip of my nose. "Can I tell you something and know that it won't leave this room?"

"If you haven't noticed, I'm sort of a pariah at work." I lean up on my elbow to look into his face. "And you bitch slapping Cris Fuller isn't going to help. People are going to wonder about why you care if he bullies Bert Floss's assistant."

"Don't worry about him. He overstepped and needed to be put in his place. I got the okay from Walter before doing it." He works his hand into the robe and starts stroking my bare back.

"Oh," I say, momentarily distracted by his touch and reminded at the same time of my precarious position at Belmore. "Okay."

"Hey," he says, kissing me on the lips, "I did it for you, but . . . you know. This? Us. I want to keep separate from work. Is that okay?"

"No. I mean yes." My conflicting feelings about what he said can wait until later to be sorted out. Right now I just want to stay in the present. "Work is the last place I want to have my private life aired out. So what's your big secret? And it better be good."

Kyle turns on his side so we're face-to-face. "I had lunch with Walter today. You know he looks old and kind of frail, but he's completely there, thinking ten steps ahead of everyone else. It's amazing to see how his brain works. Anyway, we're having lunch and he says to me that he's very happy with the job I'm doing and that if he could have it his way, I'd take over the company when the time comes."

I roll over onto my back and stare up at the ceiling. "That's intense. What's he going to do? Adopt you?"

Kyle laughs, opens the robe I'm wearing, and runs his fingers in between my breasts. "It was just talk. I'm sure he's just disappointed with whatever latest fuckup his male progeny have gotten themselves into. I'm happy where I am and, like I said, Walter Belmore isn't going anywhere."

"Still," I say as I push Kyle onto his back and straddle him. "It must be nice to know he likes you that much."

Kyle reaches up and pushes the robe off my shoulders. "What's nice to know is that you like me."

"I never said I liked you, Kyle." As his hands reach for my hips, we both know I don't have to say that I do.

ten | OUTSOURCING

Afternoon Delights . . .

I had very little sleep the night before and am wearing yes-terday's outfit, but there's a spring in my step, and not just because it's Friday. Kyle bought me a pair of panties and sheer panty hose from the hotel boutique, and he also sent me off with a can of Diet Coke and a Pop-Tart tucked into my purse. As he promised, Cris Fuller has been a largely absent pain in my ass, even though he did have a willing underling make a comment about my leg wear.

Other than that, I haven't given him the chance to even set eyes on me. I spared myself a reminder of where I am on the pecking order by staying far away from the commissary. And Fuller did me a favor by keeping Matthias on a short leash and not giving me an opportunity to gush about why I look so happy when I should be just plain miserable. Not that I would ever tell Matthias who it is I'm sleeping with—gossip is his trade and currency—but it would be nice to share hints of my delicious secret with someone who has the capacity to feel happy for me.

Other than boffing and getting boffed by the second most important person at Belmore, I'm very careful to do everything by the book. I stay out of Bert's office, don't take any extra breaks, forgo reading gossip blogs, I don't take or make personal phone calls at my desk, and I especially don't work on my side project. I keep myself busy dragging out whatever work I can conjure up for as long as possible. Bert has been no help whatsoever. Other than a fax letting me know it's okay to hang on to his key for the weekend, he hasn't been in touch.

By four o'clock I'm left with nothing to do but untangle a mass of paper clips and rubber bands from the bottom of my desk drawer. I'm bored, and the fact that life at Belmore is going on without me doesn't help. Every so often my e-mail pings with messages from Cris Fuller—it seems besides doing away with my boss, he's also done away with memos. The first thing he did was reverse all of Bert's changes to the *Extracurricular Activities* logo, and it's one minor nitpick after another. Nothing major, besides killing the paper memos, but I know these little things will add up.

"Not much I can do about that, right, Bert?" I ask the silent fax machine. "Looks like I can take another bathroom break. Don't go anywhere, I'll be right back."

I take my time walking down the hall to see what other people are up to. As I pass doors and desks, people look up, some smile and quickly look down, and a few stare at me outright. None of the senior execs have come out in open support of what Fuller is doing, but they haven't protested either. It doesn't matter. Right now Fuller has enough eager junior execs doing his bidding to give him some genuine clout in the department, so no one is going to say boo to him.

I let myself into a stall and force myself to pee even though I don't need to. As I am pulling my panty hose up, I snag them with my fingernail.

"And I was so close to having an almost not so crappy day," I moan.

I pull them up, hoping the snag will stop before it reaches the hem of my skirt, but no such luck. It's traveled well below my knee. Disgusted, I wad them up and stick them in my suit coat pocket. I slip into my shoes and prepare to emerge bare legged at Belmore for the first time ever. I have an extra pair in my desk, but I know they're going to be too small because they've been in there for three years. I'll have to barricade myself behind my desk until six.

"So what did he say?" someone says as they push open the bathroom door. "Did he say he'd call you or that you should call him?"

"Right now I don't care," snaps her companion. "I have cramps and I want to go home."

"You can't," the first woman answers. "Cris expects to go out for drinks."

"Again? We've been out for drinks or to lunch every day since he ran Bert off. I have a life, you know. Just because he doesn't."

"Sssh!" Toilets flush, and water runs in the sink. "So, uh, yeah. The Ward twins are booked for studio time tomorrow morning at nine. Mr. Fuller has confirmed it with their agent."

"That's wonderful. I'll have to congratulate Mr. Fuller," says the one with cramps.

"Yes, he's asked me to tell you that you're going to get to sit in on the session."

"What the fuck! I have cramps and it's the weekend," crampy gals wails. "If I go, I'm going to show up when I want to."

"Sssh," says her friend as she ushers her out.

I sit back down, letting the news wash over me—Frappa is back in town. She hasn't called and is the one person on the face of the earth (besides Bert) who hates to e-mail. I rush back to my desk, knowing I have to do something and I'm going to have to do it on company time. I search for the number of the bookstore café and then pick up my desk phone and dial.

"Café. Jill speaking."

"Hi. Hello. I'm hoping I can talk to Rory for a second." I take a deep breath and keep my eyes on the door, ready to hang up the second someone approaches.

"Rory isn't scheduled to come in until tomorrow afternoon. You want to leave a message?"

"No thanks, I'll just try back then. Bye."

I hang up and stare at my desktop, trying to put pieces of the puzzle of my career together in my head. I don't want to write anything down, because Fuller would be well within his rights to ask me what I'm working on. My plan was to use my weekend to cobble a marketing report together. I can't very well put in the request for the research even though I can sign Bert's signature better than he can. Not only would it cost a few thousand dollars but it would take too long. On my laptop at home I have about a dozen marketing reports that I can cut, paste, mix, and match to come up with a feasible report that will relate to *Fire House Hero*. This is not at all ideal, but I'm banking my memo and PowerPoint presentation will be enough to get me to the next stage, a movie screening where audience members will fill out comment cards. I'll need Bert's help for my plan to get to that stage, but I'm hoping he'll see the possibility in *Fire House Hero*. He has to.

One of my cells rings, and I crack open the drawer where I keep my purse to see who it might be. It's my BlackBerry and a 626 number I don't recognize. I crouch down low, ducking under my desk to answer it.

"Hello?" I can't help noticing there's a lot of dust under here. "This is Raquel."

"Hey, Raquel. It's me, Rory, calling you back." He says this in such a laid-back manner, for a moment I'm transported to a place where life is good, the beer cold, and women are always eager.

"Thanks for calling me back, Rory." Oh, yes! So worth hiding underneath my desk, but I need to play it cool. I sit up, trying to find a more comfortable position. I put yoga on my list of things to rediscover.

"So what can I do for you?" he asks. "Raquel Azorian."

I realize he has no idea who I am, but this is not the time to let my ego get bruised. I'm just one of the many women he's given his number out to, but I'm more persistent than the rest, which should make me desperate in his eyes. I'm surprised he's bothered to call me back. I guess it's a slow Friday for him.

"Yeah, we met at the bookstore café a few days ago," I say, hoping this is enough to jog his memory. Other than re-creating our encounter minute by minute, this is the best I can do without props and a couple of other people to play his manager and the irate 2 percent foam lady.

"Oh, yeah! Hey, how are you doing?" He still doesn't remember me, but whatever. I'm not calling him for a date or even a booty call, this is all about business.

"I might have mentioned when we met the other day that I work at Belmore—" I edge myself up and back into my seat as I see Fuller and his lackeys pass my door on their way to the elevators.

"Belmore as in *Belmore*?" Now I have his attention.

"Yes, I do, and I just saw *Fire House Hero*. We thought you were beyond great in it." I sound cool, detached, and professional. *We* sounds so much better, because *we* can mean anyone. Even Bert pulls out a *we* now and then when he needs a little extra muscle to get what he wants done. "We just had a screening for it the other day and, Rory, people are excited."

This is all about stroking Rory's ego. He makes lattes for a living, but he's still an actor, and actors are unshakable in their belief that they are special. It's their very specialness that sets them apart even when they're foaming milk, taking lunch orders, or sitting around waiting for someone to notice them. Rory must know that I know *Fire House Hero* is the only credit to his name. He's not signed with an agent and probably doesn't even have a decent head shot, but what he does have is me on the other end of the phone.

"I've been taking some classes," he says. "Working on character development and refining my craft."

"Good to hear, Rory. What I want to know is if you'd be interested in meeting with my friend Frappa Ivanhoe." I stop talking and wait. If Rory is anything more than halfway serious about being an actor, at least the kind who cares about being a household name and making tons of money, he will know her name.

"Oh yeah," he says. He's my bitch, totally and completely, but he's going to have to play it cool. "I've heard of her."

"Let's do this. I'll call her up and see if she'd like to meet you," I say.

I can't make any outright promises to Rory, but I do know Frappa's type well enough. She likes to find them early in their careers (in the case of the Ward twins it was even before birth—their parents had been clients of hers), they have to have some modicum of talent, be very good-looking, and willing to turn their careers—lives really—over to her. If she sees what I see in Rory, she'll make him a star. And I need him to become one as soon as possible. One way to do that is for him to be seen with the right people . . . like Cat and Cara Ward.

"That would be awesome," Rory says, his cool leaving him completely. "I know this might not turn out to be anything, but do you think I can quit my job?"

"Wait until Monday," I say with a laugh. "By then we'll all have a better idea of what's going to happen."

"Okay. So you'll call me?" he asks as my desk phone goes off.

"Can you hold on for a second?" I ask, already reaching over to pick up the handset. I press my finger over the speaker of my BlackBerry and hope Rory doesn't hang up. "Bert Floss's office. This is Raquel."

"Raquel?" It's my mom, and she sounds more agitated than usual. She must have run out of Baileys and microwave popcorn. I should have made a quick trip to the supermarket during my lunch hour and resupplied.

"Hi, Mom. I can't talk right now. I'm at work." I look at my watch. I can't leave until six without giving Fuller something real to write me up for.

"You need to go talk to Steve," she says. "He sounds very upset."

"Upset about what?" I ask. If she thinks Steve is upset, chances are something is bothering him. It might be very minor, but my mother is as in tune with Steve's moods as the tides are with the moon. She once knew he had jock itch after a thirty-second phone conversation when he was in the tenth grade. "Did you talk to him?"

"He won't talk to me. He's not returning any of my calls. I think that Cricket is screening and deleting my messages."

"Well . . ." I trail off.

She might be right about Cricket, but there's a good chance that her angel Steve is just not picking up the phone or checking messages. My brother has never been one to rock the boat or even acknowledge that there is a boat, especially when it comes to our mom. His way of coping has always been avoidance. Still, I wouldn't put it past Cricket to "edit" what's on the answering machine.

"Just give him some time to call you back. I'm sure he's very busy with something," I say.

"He is so unhappy, Raquel. You have to go talk to him. I would, but I'm busy with my divorce," she says.

"Divorce? I thought you guys were spending just a few days apart," I say. I'm not going to panic. This is just more crazy talk from my mother. She doesn't want to divorce my dad. They might not love each other as they once (maybe) did, but their mutually assured dissatisfaction with each other is what's kept their marriage together.

"I need to take control of my life, Raquel." My mother has been reading self-help books again. "I'm in charge of my destiny."

"I'll talk to Steve. Go to the mall, get some fresh air. We'll talk when I get home."

"You'll talk to Steve. Today." My mother has spoken, and she'll make my life a living hell until I acknowledge that I hear her.

"Yes. I promise." I hang up on her and go back to my cell. "Rory? Sorry about that. Minor emergency. So can we meet tonight?"

"Sure. Sure. My buddy is playing a gig in Silver Lake. I'll text you the details and we can meet before," he says.

"Sounds great. See you tonight." I hang up on him and shove my paper clip and rubber band project into the drawer.

Shoptalk . . .

The Belmore Tower is nothing but a speck in my rearview mirror by 6:05. On the seat next to me are printed directions to where I'm meeting Rory at 7:00. Even though Silver Lake is near where I was born and raised, it's a part of the city I never spent much time in. Honestly, I never even knew it was there until I went to a high school party that got broken up by cops. At the time the neighborhood was considered sketchy, but I wasn't worried. I was too busy running from the cops to care.

Nowadays, it's chock-full of writers, musicians, actors,

and the very cool, who consider themselves even cooler for not living on the west side of Los Angeles. They get off on living in a neighborhood that's eclectic (meaning everyone's not white and rich) without having to actually deal with anyone who isn't like them. Their little piece of northeast L.A. has higher property values and even a decent neighborhood elementary school (hipsters have the money and, more important, the time to get involved) along with cafés, boutiques, and art galleries that appeal only to them. In other words, it's a grungier version of what's on the west side.

I grew up in Eagle Rock, and aside from regular trips to the Glendale Galleria, a few miles and one bus ride away, I stayed within my bubble. In two years of temping after college, I saw more of Los Angeles than I had in the entire twenty-one years that I'd lived there. When I decided to move to the west side, I felt like I was moving to an entirely different city.

By some miracle I make it from Century City to Silver Lake in forty minutes while still braving the Hollywood Freeway for a portion of the trip. I nudge my Honda through the winding streets of Silver Lake, looking for a parking space within the vicinity of Fraulein Freddie's, where I'm meeting Rory. After ten minutes of circling, I find one across from a renovated split-level home. It's all bare windows and cool people enjoying each other's company behind them. Maybe they're playing a card game like SET and smoking really good weed while their hostess whips up a locally sourced organic meal in her sleek kitchen.

"Whatever," I say. "I'm so very happy for you and your knockoff Eames furniture."

I have a few minutes to kill, so I pick up the latest issue of *B,* Belmore's in-house slick magazine. I flip the pages and stop when I come to the story on the party I crashed with Frappa at Walter Belmore's. It's mainly pictures, and I see Kyle is in a good many of them. In one he's standing next to Phoebe Belmore, who looks positively skeletal. Even her big fake boobs look undernourished. If I could give her the fourteen pounds I plan to lose, she'd look almost human.

My phone rings, and I grab it when I see Frappa's number come up.

"Are you okay?" I say as soon as I accept the call. "What happened?"

"Oh, you heard about that." She laughs. "I got popped in the lip, but the cops found my inept mugger trying to use my credit card to buy designer jeans on Rodeo. You gotta love L.A."

"So everything is good?" I ask. "You're fine?"

"Everything is under control. I have both Cat and Cara under house arrest for the night and will personally be escorting them to the studio tomorrow morning," she says. "Don't worry, Raquel, they'll be there."

"No, I mean with you, are you okay?" I look at my watch. It's already seven, but I know I'm expected to be a few minutes late.

"I'm a tough broad, Raquel. You don't need to worry about me. So am I going to get to see you tomorrow? I know Cris Fuller is taking credit for convincing Cat and Cara to come in, but I'm not going to dignify that bullshit story. I won't let them set foot in the studio unless I see you there."

"I'll be there," I say. "And I might be bringing someone. His name is Rory."

"Bring whoever you want," she says, generous as always. "Any friend of yours was to be a step up from the leeches Cat and Cara surround themselves with."

"Great. See you tomorrow."

I hang up on Frappa and check in with my mother, who makes me promise again to talk to Steve. Just after seven, I lock my car and make my way down to the better-lit street where Fraulein Freddie's is. As soon as I step inside, I can see I'm lucky to have found parking as close as I did. The place is packed. A band plays with unbridled enthusiasm onstage to a perfectly disheveled crowd in their skinny jeans and oversize plaid shirts. Most of them are drinking out of huge glasses of beer, and none of them look like Rory Tilley.

"I'm here," I text Rory. "Where r u?"

A few seconds later he texts back with "Where is here?"

"Oh, crap," I mutter, thinking they've blown what looked to be a lively joint for someplace even louder and hipper.

"Frau. Freddy @ front door," I text. I let out a whoop that's lost in the noise when he texts back, "Don't move. Coming to get you."

"You Rachel?" asks a lanky and bored-looking guy wearing sunglasses.

"Nope," I say and then, thinking twice about dismissing him, ask, "Are you perhaps looking for a Raquel?"

"Yeah, sure. We're over here." He walks into the crowd without apologizing for getting my name wrong or looking back to make sure I'm following.

"Raquel!" Rory slides out from the booth where he's sitting. He gives me a long hug and a kiss on each cheek. "So glad you found it. Isn't this place killer?"

We sit back down, me in the middle of the horseshoe-shaped booth with Rory on my left and his friend who's bad with names on my right.

"Hi. I'm Raquel Azorian. I'm handling the marketing proposal for *Fire House Hero*," I say to the table in general. "Nice to meet you guys."

I don't need to meet and get to know them to know what type of people Rory's friends are. L.A. is full of people who don't seem to work even though they claim to be employed, usually in a nebulously creative field that doesn't have set hours. They are always passionate about what they want to do (write, act, direct, compose), but they never seem to work at doing it. What they are is always free for lunch but in the bathroom when the check comes.

"Kevin, he's got my back. You guys talked on the phone," Rory says, pointing toward the guy in sunglasses. "Next to you is Chaz, he's an awesome screenwriter, and somewhere around here is Jordon. He's an actor, too."

"He's supposed to be getting us beer," Kevin says, lifting his shades to facilitate his ability to see. "We're celebrating Rory's big break."

"That's nice," I say. There's way too much studied irony for me to handle.

"True that," Rory drawls. "My homeboys are giving me a hard time about selling out. They didn't want me to do *Fire House Hero* in the first place."

"That producer totally screwed you over, Rory," says Kevin, looking at me like he expects me to do the same.

"I totally understand," I say. I have to make nice with the friends, even though this is all business. And for them to understand that, I have to pull out my best industry speak. "But at the same time, *Fire House Hero* is a great vehicle to launch your career, and it will open up all sorts of opportunities for you, Rory."

"He could be the next DiCaprio," Kevin says. "He has skills."

"Or Pitt," counters Chaz, who adjusts his skullcap so it sit on his head just so. "Pitt's the man. Fucking brilliant in *Twelve Monkeys*. No fear, man, none. That's what Rory should do next. A *Twelve Monkeys*. I'm working on something in that genre."

"Of course," I say, being noncommittal. "He should do something edgy to show his range."

What Rory's going to do is commit to doing whatever he can to making *Fire House Hero* his calling card. If Chaz wants to write his screenplays full-time, Kevin go from answering Rory's phone to managing his career, and the still missing Jordon do more with his life than fetch beers, they all need Rory to sell out. We all know that, but delusions have to be indulged.

"Rory has options and won't miss out on any of them. Definitely," I say, leaning away from Chaz, who I'm almost sure just farted.

"You won't turn into another Tobey Maguire, right? Or that dude from the *Lord of the Rings* . . . what's that dude's name?" Kevin asks, even though he very well knows his name.

"We just want to make sure Rory isn't turned into some product." Chaz puts enough twist on the word so his distaste of the Hollywood machine is evident to all.

"Guys, come on. This is good for me," Rory says, trying

to placate them. "I need to crack the commercial market, establish my name, and then I can do edgier films. Like your script, Chaz. Right, Raquel?"

"Exactly. It's all a matter of building up momentum." I take a deep breath, wishing I had a mug of beer, but now's the time to launch into my pitch. "*Fire House Hero* is a genre vehicle with tremendous crossover appeal. It'll get the attention of top directors and producers. That kind of leverage gives actors the freedom to pick and choose future projects *after* they establish themselves as names who can open movies. Once you're established, there's really nothing you can't do. And to do that you need an entrée, a calling card. Something people in the industry can reference, and that's *Fire House Hero.*"

This is stretching it, but it's what Rory and his friends want to hear. They want to believe that Rory, and they, will have some say in how things go even if they don't. It's in my best interest to get everyone behind the marketing of Rory Tilley, star of *Fire House Hero.*

"What do you say, guys?" Rory asks. He'll still go on without them, but right now he needs their okay to take the next step.

"You're going to take care of my bud, right?" Chaz looks deep into my eyes. "You're not going to sell him out?"

"Yeah," Kevin chimes in, quick to claim his seat on the gravy train. "You're not going to turn him into a douchebag? Or some action figure?"

I look at them, biting back my retort that it's probably the dream of most actors in Hollywood to become an action figure.

"That would actually be kinda cool," Chaz admits. I give him a big smile.

"Yeah," Rory says with a grin. "It would."

"Guys, come on, focus," killjoy Kevin says, flexing his puny managerial muscle. "You're on the level, right, Raquel?"

"Trust me," I say with such sincerity that it almost brings tears to my eyes. "You have no idea how much I want *Fire House Hero* to work for all of us."

Brother's Keeper . . .

I turn left onto Colorado and take it all the way to Steve and Cricket's house. I'm hoping Cricket won't be there even though it's almost nine and I can't think of her being anywhere else but ensconced in her dream house. I drive by and am surprised to see her car isn't tucked in next to Steve's. I park behind a large RV a few houses down.

I walk up to the front door and ring the doorbell and wait. I haven't been given a key to the Craftsman, and it's not because Cricket has been too busy to remind Steve to get a copy made for me. I've always had a key to every dumpy apartment Steve lived in, and Steve has a copy of my apartment key, but I guess this is different. Steve has his own family now, and my not having a key to his house just proves it. After a couple of minutes of inspecting my cuticles, I ring the bell again and press my ear to the solid oak door, trying to make out the sounds of muffled footsteps.

Nothing. I gave Steve a pair of noise-canceling earphones (snagged from the Belmore communal swag closet) as a welcome to fatherhood gift, and they're good enough to keep out most noise, like complaining, crying, and doorbells. Cricket hadn't appreciated the joke, but made sure to let me know that my brother practically lives in them in the thank-you card she sent.

I go around the side of the house, my shoes crunching over the uneven layer of gravel on the driveway until I hit the powdery dirt of the backyard. When I reach the window of the converted sunroom, I stand up on my tiptoes and tap the glass with my car key. When my tapping doesn't elicit the desired result of him poking his face in the window, I take a few tentative leaps, holding securely on to my knockers, so most of my face will clear the sill.

Hop and hold. "Steve!" Hop and hold. "Steve!"

Nothing again.

"Fuck it," I say and try the door off the kitchen. The knob turns in my hand. "Steve? It's me. Your sister. Raquel. Are you in the bathroom?"

I stand very still just inside the kitchen and listen for the toilet flushing and footsteps. The house sounds empty.

"So I'm assuming that no one is here," I say loudly. "So I'm leaving now . . ."

I reach inside my purse for a pen to jot down a note for Steve on the fridge memo pad just as the front door opens. I scamper into my brother's office to hide. My plan is to jump out and scare the bejesus out of him.

"Steve, honey? You home? I'm ovulating . . . ," Cricket calls as she walks toward the kitchen. "My girlfriend Lindsey is watching the twins, so we have a couple of hours. Steve?"

"Fuckity fuck fuck fuck," I mutter under my breath. I

leave my hiding place, take a seat in front of Steve's computer monitor, and pray Cricket won't Mace me when she finds me in her house.

I try to arrange myself in the most nonthreatening posture possible. For me that means a typing position. I put my fingers on Steve's grubby wireless keyboard and glance up at the instant message window that pops onto the monitor. My hands fly to my eyes in an attempt to shield them from the text on the screen, but I peek through my fingers and read anyway.

"Steve? When I say we have two hours, that means we only have one . . ." Cricket sounds annoyed, her voice coming from the front staircase, where she's waiting for my brother and his penis.

"Super fuckity fuck fuck fuck!" I say as I scroll through the conversation my brother was having with someone who went by SweetPiece_69 until a few minutes before I arrived. It ends with my brother, SeñorLongSchlong, having typed in "c u in 10."

"Steve!" Cricket shouts.

I reach for the mouse and click the window closed just as my sister-in-law steps into the office.

"Hi!" I leap up from the seat, not giving Cricket a chance to be startled or scream "Intruder!" at the top of her lungs. "Steve stepped out. He'll be right back."

"Where did he go?" she asks, clutching at the neck of her sweatshirt.

"Um, not really sure. He was gone when I got here," I admit. I figure my brother will do better facing Cricket's ovulating wrath if I don't add any lies of my own to those that he's already probably telling her.

"How did you get in?" Cricket says in a much more accusatory tone than is necessary. We are, after all, family.

"The back door was unlocked," I say, in what I hope is a breezy manner. "That's a bad habit of Steve's. When we were kids he once . . . Well, that's a story for another time. I just wanted to ask Steve about my tax stuff. I'll come back later. Not this weekend, though. I'm working on a big project."

I rush over to Cricket, give her a stiff hug, and make a break for the front door.

"Raquel?" she calls right behind me.

My hand on the handle, I turn to acknowledge her when I'm suddenly shoved back by the opening door.

"Raquel?" Steve pokes his head around the door, looking and sounding surprised as well as a tad guilty. "What are you doing here?"

"I'm leaving. Stopped by just to say hi and . . . Cricket's here and . . . I'll . . . Bye!" I give my brother a kiss on the cheek and flee.

eleven | FUTURE PERFECT

White Lies . . .

My mother isn't buying that I really do have to go into work on a Saturday. According to Marlene, I'm seeing someone and I don't want to introduce him to her. Which is sort of true, but I'm not sure where I stand with Kyle or if I should even be entertaining thoughts of inflicting my family on him. I've given him the number to my personal cell, but he has yet to use it. Even though I wouldn't mind seeing him, my priority is Rory and *Fire House Hero*. First work and then maybe some play.

"No one can possibly work the hours you do, Raquel," my mother says from the comfort of my bed. "I know something is up."

"Mom. Please." It's all I can say, because she isn't too far off the mark. I'm not sure if I told her what was going on that she'd even be happy for me. I don't know if I should be happy for me. I've never done anything or anyone like Kyle before.

"Hang-up phone calls, staying out all night, not answering

your phone." She ticks off the clues one by one. "I know what you're up to."

"I talked to Steve last night." I'll leave out what I saw and heard, but I know the mere mention of his name will shake her off the topic of my nefarious love life. "I think he's taking up jogging again, and you know how he is when he gets into something. He forgets about everything else."

"It's symbolic. He's trying to run away from Cricket," my mother says, pulling down her eyeshade. "And can you blame him?"

I don't answer her as I try to take a look with my hand mirror at the outfit I've put together. The jeans are a bit too snug, but my wrap sweater camouflages the parts of my waist I want to hide, and my never worn until today red flats remind me of Lisbeth from Human Resources. I've kept my makeup simple and my hair loose but pinned away from my face. I think I look, well, cute, but it can't hurt to get a second and very honest opinion.

"So? Do I look okay?" I ask my mother. I stand there as she lifts the eyeshade and checks me out, starting from my shoes and working her way up. "Hurry, Mom, I have to go."

"You look fine." She sighs as she settles back into bed. It's a quarter after eight, but still much too early for her to be up. "You're going into work on a Saturday, Raquel. Who's going to see you?"

There she goes again. My mother is going to needle me until I spring a leak and confess everything to her.

"There's the bald security guard who works weekends. And no, I'm not having a torrid affair with him. He's married." I walk over and give her a quick kiss. "You're going to be okay, right?"

When I got home last night she was already asleep, a half-eaten pizza on the kitchen counter next to an almost empty bottle of wine. I'm hoping she can make it through the day without hitting the Baileys.

"I'm going to the mall later," she mumbles, clearly ready to get back to sleeping. "Maybe I'll call Steve later to meet me for lunch. Without Cricket."

"Yeah, do that. I'm sure he'll be answering his phone from now on."

I head out through the kitchen door, figuring it's easier to push open the garage door than pull it. It takes a kick as well as a push, but I get it open. I'm tucking my underwear back into my jeans when I realize I have an audience—my nosy landlord, Mr. Kashini. When he showed me the apartment two years ago, he made sure to ask in his very particular, roundabout way if I smoked, stayed up late, threw lots of parties, or was involved with anyone who would be over a lot.

"Hi, Mr. Kashini. I didn't see you there." I immediately pull my hands out of the back of my pants.

"Miss. Raquel. Hello and good morning." This is how Mr. Kashini always greets me except he switches out the *morning* for *afternoon* or *evening*, depending on what time of day we happen to run into each other.

"How is your wife?" I ask. Mrs. Kashini is an awesome cook. It's almost worth having to deal with him just to eat her leftovers once or twice a week.

"My wife is very much good. We are expecting our daughter and her husband for a visit. He now works in South Carolina as a researcher. You perhaps also have a guest?"

"Oh, no, not a guest. My mother is staying with me while my father paints the house. She's very sensitive to smells, so she's going to be here for a few days," I say. "Mr. Kashini, it's good I ran into you. The garage door—"

"Ah, Raquel, I think my wife is calling me in for breakfast." Mr. Kashini is also very cheap. There's no way he wants to hear about my issue with the garage door since then he'll have to do something about it. "Please tell your mother not to play the TV so loud at the nighttime. My wife is also very sensitive."

"Of course. You have a good day, Mr. Kashini," I call after him.

I get into my car and drive over to the studio, where I'm hoping Rory (and just Rory) will be waiting for me. I need to prep him for his meeting with Frappa, introduce him, and then I need to disappear before Cris Fuller's toady gets there.

Rory needs to make a great impression on Frappa, but he also needs to charm Cat and Cara Ward. This, of course, is all machination on my part. If the three of them hit it off, they'll go out tonight and Rory will get his picture taken by the paparazzi. Those pictures will end up on blogs and maybe even, please God, in *Us Weekly,* and then my cobbled-together marketing report for *Fire House Hero* will be all the tastier because I can claim Rory's star is on the rise.

I pull up to the recording studio, a nondescript one-story off of La Cienega Boulevard, and not seeing Rory waiting out front like I asked him to, I drive around the block, hoping he's just a bit late. On my third pass around the building, I reflexively look into the window of a beat-up Saab that's parked in front of it. I hit my brakes with a screech, double-park, and run to bang on the window.

"Rory!" He's in there with his lame posse, smoking out. "Rory, can I talk to you please? Now."

"Yeah, hey, Raquel." Rory hops out and tries to close the door before a waft of pot smoke bowls me over. "You're early."

"No, Rory, I was on time, you're late and getting wasted, and now we're both late."

How can he afford pot anyway? It isn't cheap, and he and his friends barely have two nickels to rub together. At least this is what they hinted when they let me pick up the bill for their beer and pretzels last night.

"Now we only have"—I check my watch—"five minutes before Frappa gets here."

"Don't get mad, Raquel. I just needed to take the edge off. I'm pretty nervous." He comes in for a hug, but I hold him back. "Aaw, don't be that way."

"I am that way. Do us both a favor, say good-bye to your friends and air yourself out. I don't want Frappa to see your ramshackle entourage and get spooked by your baggage."

"Okay, fine, fine. Be cool. We're cool," he says, trying very hard to sound not stoned.

I'm ruining his buzz. Good. If anyone should be stoned out of their mind, it should be me. I'm used to stress, but living like this is starting to get to me. Last night I had a dream that Cris Fuller and his phalanx of toadies were chasing me down the halls of Belmore and chucking wadded-up memos at me.

I park my car, keeping one eye on Rory in the rearview mirror. By the time I reach him on the sidewalk, his friends are driving away. Immediately I start to fuss with his hair and tug at his clothes. He's kept it safe with jeans, a white V-neck T under a grandpa cardigan, and Chucks. Despite being pissed at him, I can't deny that he looks tasty. Frappa will eat him up like he's a warm butterscotch brownie topped with a scoop of vanilla ice cream. I can only hope the Ward twins are also in the mood for dessert.

"This is how it's going to go down. You're going to be charming and honest. Do not try to bullshit Frappa Ivanhoe about the work you've done. If there's anything—pictures, home videos, you name it—that can come back and bite you in the butt, you tell her. You tell her the name of every agent or producer you've met with. She'll find out anyway. Frappa appreciates people who are up-front with her. If you lie to her, she'll not only stop taking your phone calls but make sure you never do anything else with your life than make lattes. Understand?"

Rory nods, looking slightly more sober. I don't want to scare him, but he needs to be sharp. I give his hair one last tousle as a gleaming SUV pulls up to the curb. A bodyguard gets out and stands between us and the door.

"Ready?" I ask Rory. He nods mutely.

Frappa comes out first and is followed by the stick figures of Cat and Cara Ward. Already I can see them peering at him over their huge sunglasses. Even Frappa does a double take. This is good. Very good.

"Fuck me," Rory breathes.

"If you're lucky, they might both fuck you at the same time. It's been known to happen," I tell him. "And if they do, you tell Frappa, not your friends. She'll figure it out for you.

"You ready to meet your future?" I ask as I give Rory a slight push forward while I reach into my purse for the *Fire House Hero* DVD. All I need is for Frappa to watch fifteen minutes of it. "Hi, Frappa, Cat, Cara."

"Hi," the Ward twins say in unison, their sunglasses pointed squarely at Rory.

"Frappa, this is Rory Tilley, who I mentioned on the phone yesterday."

"Umm-hmm," Frappa says, already aware of the sparks that are flying between her clients and Rory. "So this is your friend?"

"Yeah." I step away from Rory, who immediately finds himself with a twin on each arm. I take a deep breath, ready to launch into my spiel about his potential. "He's—"

"I can see what he's got," Frappa says as she watches Rory light cigarettes for Cat and Cara with a lighter he pulled from his pocket. When he's offered one, he waves them off, saying, "I don't smoke. Nicotine is some heavy-duty shit, man."

"Totally," say Cat and Cara, who keep puffing away.

"Girls, what did I say about smoking in public?" Frappa asks, looking around for paparazzi.

"After this we promise to be good. Very good," says either Cat or Cara.

"Yeah, Rory is going to make sure we don't smoke more than half a pack," says the other twin. "Right, Rory?"

"Absolutely," Rory says, working his dimples.

"Okay. You have five minutes," Frappa says to me. "What's his deal?"

"It's this," I say, holding up the DVD. "Belmore bought a production company, and *Fire House Hero* was part of the booty. It hasn't been released, and no one knows about it. Marketing wise, it's a winner in key demographic areas and so is he. You can't deny that he has something."

"What I hope he doesn't have is crabs or mono." Frappa

holds out her hand for the DVD. "Is this something you're working on for Bert?"

"Yes, definitely," I say, bending the truth to fit my needs. I don't even have his signature on the memo I need to have taken things this far. "I'm doing this for Bert."

Frappa gives me a hard look, making me wish I'd put on my sunglasses. "I know you're lying, but you've got balls and instinct. Plus, I know Bert has taught you everything he knows, and that's worth a lot. I'll watch this and get back to you by tonight."

Before I can stop myself, I rush in to hug her, making her wobble on her sky-high gypsy boots. "Thank you, Frappa. You're saving my ass."

"Don't kid yourself, Raquel, you're saving yourself." She hugs me hard and then pulls away to look into my eyes again. "Just don't lie to me again."

"Promise," I say, knowing I truly mean it.

Like Father, Like Daughter . . .

I sit at my parents' kitchen table, my purse in my lap, telling myself I won't stay long. I watch as my dad sorts through seed packets, putting them into precise stacks. He's come up with a complicated color-coded planting chart that he's trying to explain to me, but I'm only listening with half an ear.

Aside from the light on over the table, the rest of the house is dark, and all of it is quiet. If my mom were here, at least two TVs and the radio in the laundry room would be on and she'd be talking over each of them. No wonder my dad hasn't made any real efforts to get his wife back—he finally has the peace and quiet he's always wanted.

"Hey, Dad. Can I ask you something?" I interrupt him before he can get too deep into the topic of succulents and soil drainage. It's a conversation I know from past experience that he can keep up for hours. "Do you miss JPL?"

"No, I did what I wanted to do there. It was time for me to go and make room for some fresh blood." My father shrugs his shoulders. He's sixty-four, but a life indoors has shielded his skin from the sun, so he could pass for his early fifties. "I was thinking of maybe getting my accreditation to teach junior high science."

I'm not at all surprised he'd want to do this. My father has always wanted to be in the world of academics. Finding himself married within a couple of months of meeting my mother derailed all his plans for a life as an austere professor.

"Dad? Mom mentioned something about money you'd set aside for me. For my wedding? I was wondering if I could sort of borrow it?" I ask in a rush. "Not all of it, just a portion."

If this money does indeed exist, I need it now for something real and not for a wedding I'm not sure I'll ever have. I mean, sure, I hope to get married, but I'm not actively pursuing it as a goal in the next few years.

"What do you need money for?" There's no judgment in his voice, he just wants to know, and he's well within his rights to ask.

"Well . . ." Where to start? Not with the truth. I don't want to worry my father, and my chances of getting reimbursed are fifty-fifty at best. "I want to buy a new car. Something cute and zippy."

"What's wrong with the Honda?" he asks, finally looking up at me. My father is very attached to my car for some reason. "Is it giving you trouble?"

"No, nothing like that," I sigh, hating the fact that I have to lie to him. Frappa called me just before I arrived to tell me she was taking Rory on as a client. But her offer is contingent on Belmore backing *Fire House Hero*. For that to happen I need to take my plan to the next step, and that's going to require cash. "I just want a new car. Is that okay? I have some money saved up, but I'd like to pay cash for it. I just need five thousand dollars."

My father is silent for a long time as he thinks what I've said over. I feel bad lying to him, but to tell him why I really need the money would be to invite him into the mess that's become my life. A mess I'm creating for myself. I could just sit back and wait for them to ax me. I would probably get a nice, fat buh-bye check out of it. But I can't give up that easy, even if it means asking my father for money he's saved for years to see his little girl have the princess wedding of her mother's dreams.

"I can transfer it to your account on Monday," he says. And just like that it's done. No grilling or second guessing. The only thing my father expects me to do is show up with a new car. That particular issue, I'll deal with next week.

I wonder just how much he's set aside. Really, it's kind of silly for my father to think he has to pay for my wedding. Like I told my mom, I'd rather have a down payment for a house. A wedding lasts a day, but a house is an investment.

"Why haven't you asked me about your wife?" I'm ready to move on to the rest of my uncomfortable agenda.

"How's your mother?" he asks reflexively, not looking up from his work.

This is not a cold or dismissive gesture on his part, it's just the way he is. If he missed my mother, he'd say so. If he never wanted to see her again, he'd have no problem with telling me that. Right now he has his seeds, his charts, and blissfully uninterrupted time to focus on them.

"She's still at my place. Do you need the address?" Unlike with Mom, I can joke about this with Dad.

Instead of answering, my father gives a short, dry laugh and pats my shoulder. I get up and take a turn around the house, curious to check out his living conditions. Everything looks to be in order. There are no dirty dishes in the sink or mixed color laundry in the dryer. The fridge is stocked with his favorite foods—yogurt, milk, apples—and fresh towels hang in the bathroom.

My mother has always played up how Dad would never know what to do without her. Looking around the house, I can't help but notice that it's tidier than my mother ever kept it and she had a cleaning woman come in once a week. My father is doing just fine. If anything, he's doing better without her.

"Marlene is not going to like this," I say under my breath as I pour myself a glass of water. "She's going to freak out."

I go into my old bedroom and sit on the edge of my princess bed, feeling as droopy as the canopy overhead. The phone rings, and the various extensions in the house go off one after another. I wasn't allowed to keep a phone in my room, so I dash into the kitchen to answer it, pure reflex on my part.

"Hello? Azorian residence."

"Raquel?" My mother sounds well past tipsy and on her way to drunk. I guess it turned out to be one of those days after all.

"Hey, Mom! How was the mall? Did you buy anything?" I talk fast, hoping to take advantage of her alcohol-induced confusion. "Make sure to keep the receipts. You always end up returning stuff anyways."

"Where are you?" She's skipped confused and veers right into being annoyed.

"I'm at work, Mom," I say with the right amount of exasperation in my voice so she'll believe me. "Remember? I had to come in to finish a project? I mean, write memos. Anyway, I'm almost done, so I should be home in a couple of hours. You want to go out to the movies?"

"Raquel?" my father calls from the front of the house. "Where are your keys? I need to move your car."

"Is that your father?" she asks. "Are you at your father's house?"

"It's your house, too, Mom." I toss my father my keys and go back to my room.

"Is the place a wreck?" she asks, sounding more like her old self.

"It doesn't look like when you're here, that's for sure." The truth but phrased in such a way as to make my mother feel better without actually having to lie to her.

"Good. Maybe he'll finally see what it means to be without me."

"Yeah, that's what I'm afraid of," I mumble. "Listen, I'm just going to make sure he's okay and then I'll come home."

I look out the window, the one I used to sneak in and out of when I was in high school. It's dark outside, and I wonder what Kyle is doing right now. I'm also wondering why he hasn't called me.

"Tell him I'm seeing someone and that I've never been happier." Her words are getting more slurred. "Tell him I just got home from a date and I'm getting ready to go meet another man for drinks."

"I will, Mom. Bye."

I replace the phone on the base in the kitchen and hear my father call something out followed by the screen door squeaking open. There are voices in the living room, and one of them belongs to a woman.

"Dad?" I charge into the room and come upon the neighbor lady pressing her impressive bosoms into my dad's chest as she hugs him. "Hi! Dad, you have company."

"Raquel," Jerri from across the street says. "I had no idea you were here!"

Jerri is my parents' busty and much divorced neighbor. She's also my mother's Nellie Oleson—the woman my mother always competes against and openly dislikes even when smiling into her face.

"Hello, Jerri," I say, knowing my father will be annoyed with me if I'm rude.

"Not there, Robert, it'll leave a ring on the table," she clucks as he's about to set a plastic-wrapped dish on the coffee table. "You're just as helpless as a child! You need to be looked after."

"Dad," I say with enough alarm in my voice to startle myself along with him. We both know exactly how this will play out when I'm forced to recount it in exact detail for my mother. Jerri, on the other hand, is as cool as the cucumber salad she's holding.

"Jerri was just dropping off some leftovers," my father says in his own defense.

"Not leftovers, Bobby." Jerri puts her hand on his bicep even though there's no reason for her to be touching my dad. "All freshly made by yours truly."

"Much appreciated. Thank you," he says.

My father shuffles his feet and runs his hand through his freshly cut hair. He's busted and he knows it, even though I'm pretty sure he has no interest in Jerri, not even in her salad.

"Why don't we sit down for a little something to eat?" Jerri asks, heading into the kitchen. "Your father has been skipping meals these days, Raquel. Last night he told me he was going to order pizza! A man his age shouldn't be having pizza for dinner."

"It's from the place on Eagle Rock Boulevard," my father says to no one in particular. "It's very good."

"I made him some *penne arrabbiata,* my own grand-mother's recipe. Bobby, where do you . . . Never mind! I think there's just enough for the three of us. That is if you're stay-ing, Raquel?" She pokes her head into the living room. "I'm sure you have a hot date to get to, right?"

"Thanks, Jerri, but I'm heading home." I can't tell her to leave my father alone, that's my mother's job. I'll just have to trust that he's smart enough not to sample more of Jerri than what she's offering up on her plates.

"Robert, do you want to have some wine?" Jerri asks as if I had already left.

"Bye, Dad, and good luck." I kiss him on the cheek and snatch my keys out of his shirt pocket at the same time.

Other People's Problems . . .

I lean into the kitchen sink as I scrub out the pot my mother burnt trying to heat a can of soup. My head is still fuzzy from the couple of Tylenol PMs I downed around three, when I got desperate for my eyes to stay closed. Between having visions of my father and Jerri making out on my princess bed and looking over to see if I'd missed a call from Kyle, I wasn't able to sleep.

My front door opens and closes, and Steve, bearing a carrier tray of fragrant coffee balanced on top of a foil-covered glass dish, steps inside.

"You should really keep that locked," he says.

"Huh?" I blink up at him. "Oh, yeah. I went out for the paper and forgot."

I take one of the cups of coffee, hold it up to my nose, and inhale, hoping the smell will help wake up my sluggish brain. The coffee is black and strong, the way I like it, and from my favorite neighborhood café, Hello Monday.

"Are you sick or something, Raquel?" Steve drums his fingers on the countertop, a nervous habit of his.

"I'm not sick. I'm having a very productive Sunday morning." I hold up the ruined pot so he can see just how I've been making use of my time. "Why do you ask?"

"You're still wearing pajamas?" he asks.

"These aren't pajamas." I'm wearing saggy charcoal-colored jersey pants, a pink built-in-shelf-bra tank top, and a pilly cardigan sweater. "It's called loungewear."

"Could you sleep in it?" he asks.

"I could comfortably take a nap in this outfit," I concede.

"Like pajamas," he says, pointing out just how flawed my flawed pajamas versus loungewear distinction is. "Cricket sent something for you guys to eat."

"That's so nice of her. How is she?" I ask.

"Fine." He shrugs but in a way that indicates there's more to the story and he wants to tell it to me. "She's thinking of buying a franchise. Cupcakes or something like that. Cricket loves cupcakes. Or maybe a Curves, you know, the workout place? Anyway, I'm going to look up some stuff at the library for her—demographics, financials. The UCLA library."

I merely nod at these pieces of volunteered information, unsure if my brother wants me to say anything.

"Yeah, so that's why I'm here, going over to UCLA, but thought I'd check in first. So are you sick?" he asks again.

"Lady problems," I lie.

"I didn't get a chance to ask how you and Mom are doing," Steve says, pretending that I haven't given him a menstrual-related answer to his previous question.

"We're doing great," I lie again. I know I just need to say the word and he'll take her off my hands. My brother would become catatonic if he had to live with two women both bent on each other's destruction. I admit to being selfish, but I don't think I'm a cruel person.

I lift the foil and poke at the casserole. It's bumpy, light beige, and punctuated by bits of green and red. Bell peppers, I hope. We'll eat it, taking forkfuls here and there, but there will be no setting of the table and serving it on plates, as I'm sure Cricket expects her food to be treated.

"It's not bad. Cricket made one for dinner last night," Steve says. He's nervous and jumpy.

"Tell her thanks," I say and leave it at that. I would never have taken my brother for a cheater, but he does seem to be sneaking around.

"Raquel? You don't have to eat it if you don't want to," Steve says, confused and guilty at the same time. "It's not that bad, really, if you put some salt on it."

I look up at my big brother, who has enough on his plate as it is. "Why are you here, Steve? Really?"

"Can I talk to you about Cricket?" he asks. It's as painful for him to say these words as it is for me to hear them.

"Uh, sure. Let's go outside so we don't wake Mom. She's been in such a mood lately, and I don't want you to set her off. Hurry—"

From the bedroom come noises of my mother rousing herself for her early afternoon of complaints and libations. Both Steve and I stare at the door, frozen for what feels like an eternity.

"You should go unless you want to stay for a while. And frankly, I can't stomach Mom fawning over you." I push my brother toward the door. "So go."

"Yeah, I'll call you later." Steve gives me a quick kiss on the top of my head and leaves.

I sigh at the closed door, leaning my forehead on it, and I sigh again as I hear my mother stumble out of my former bedroom.

"Was that your father?" she asks, looking rumpled and raw.

"No. It was my landlord. He says he'll have someone fix the garage door tomorrow." I hold up my cup of coffee toward her. "Want one?"

She wanders through the living room, stopping to peek out the window. "You should make him put in a new showerhead. The one you have now has no pressure."

"If I ask him for that, I'll have to put out. But if it'll make your showers more pleasurable, I'll let Mr. Kashini do dirty things to me, Mom."

"Very funny, Raquel." She settles down on the couch, kicking off her terry-cloth slippers. She picks through my magazines, setting them down after giving each a quick riffle of pages, impatient for me to pay attention to her.

"So, Mom, what's up with you?" I ask with no emotional inflection in my voice. I may as well be an automated phone recording, but it's enough of a springboard for my mother.

"Let's go out tonight!" She bounces up and down on the couch. "Let's go dancing! Let's go out and meet some men."

"Sorry?" Startled, I slosh coffee down my sweater. I'm so surprised, not only at what she's said but that she said it with some of her usual energy. "What did you say?"

"I can't stand your life, Raquel," she says as she watches me sop up the liquid with a wad of paper towels. "I'm bored to death. You used to be fun! Boys calling all the time, getting invited to two parties on the same night. Sneaking out. What happened to you?"

I keep myself from answering, "I grew up, Mom," knowing she's teetering between spending the day sober and not. Instead I just shrug and settle for the answer she expects and one that's even too true for me to pretend it is a joke.

"Old age, I guess," I say.

"Today is our anniversary." Her voice is thick with tears. She wipes at her eyes with each of her index fingers as if she were trying to clean up mascara smudges that aren't there. She reaches for a tissue and gives it a long, wet blow of her nose before she crumples it into a ball and tucks it into the sleeve of my former favorite sweatshirt. "I can't believe that asshole hasn't called me."

"It's still early, Mom," I say, coming over and sitting next to her on the couch. My pillow and blanket are still underneath us, but now doesn't seem the time to ask my mother to get up so I can tidy up. "I bet he's still sleeping."

"That man has never slept in past six in his life." She's stopped crying and has turned her attention to the TV, giving the remote vicious flicks with each press of the button as she flips through channels. "Not even on our honeymoon."

My phone rings. "It's Cricket," I say.

"Go ahead and answer it, or she'll keep calling back." My mother sighs.

"Hi, Cricket." I roll my eyes at my mother, who grimaces unattractively.

"Did I catch you on your way to church?" Cricket asks, even though she knows the Azorians are agnostics.

"Yeah, but I have a few seconds." If she's going to play dumb, I'm going to see her dumb with idiot. "What's up?"

"I was wondering if Steve was there?" she asks.

"Um . . ." I look over at my mother, who is listening intently but pretending not to. "No. I think he mentioned about going to the UCLA library."

My mother's brows go up as she deduces I'm talking about her perfect son.

"Oh, yeah, I forgot," Cricket says, even though it's obvious

that her steel-trap mind has never forgotten or forgiven anything or anyone in her entire life.

"Cricket? I'm sorry but I really have to go. Going to be
late for church." Another eye roll for my mother's benefit.

"Sorry to be such a bother," Cricket says just as brightly.
"Say hello to Marlene for me."

I hang up the phone and stare at the channels as they blip
past on the TV. "Mom?"

"Hmmm?" She's happy now that Cricket is no longer in
her space.

"We'll go out to dinner tonight. Somewhere nice. We'll get
dressed up and men will send us drinks, but I'm going to have
to pass on the dancing. I have to be in to work early tomorrow."

I know to expect an evening filled with more weepy, boozy
complaints about my father, Cricket, my nonexistent social
life, my diminishing prospects for marriage and pregnancy,
and how her brilliant Steve just needs to find a woman and a
job that match his capabilities.

"That sounds like fun, Raquel." My mother sniffles and
finally settles on a cooking show. "You can be my date."

"When you put it that way," I say as I fire up my laptop to
check for blog mentions of Rory, "I think we should set you
up with a Facebook account."

twelve | LOOSE ENDS

The Devil and Details . . .

I'm sitting in a pointless Cris Fuller meeting, and I'm wearing pants. Pants! When I got up this morning, the thought of shoving myself into one of my Soviet Bloc skirt suits made me want to gag. So instead I pulled out a pair of black (safe, yes) trousers that have been sitting in my closet for a couple of years, a long cardigan sweater, and a ruffled top in a happy pink. I'm also wearing the pointy suede heels because they're now officially my lucky shoes. My subversive act of fashion individualism hasn't gone unnoticed. Cris Fuller's eyebrows moved up a whole millimeter, and I'm sure I'll be hearing about it later.

Though no one talks to me and I'm relegated to a guest chair pushed up against the wall of the conference room, I can sense a growing dissent in the marketing department ranks. Even Bert, who's called more than his own share of pointless meetings, knew enough never to schedule one first thing Monday morning. People don't like starting their week this way.

No one is bothering to take any notes and, if I could hide my phone under the table, I'd be texting just as furiously as they are. Instead, I sit and stare at a point over Fuller's head and wait for him to run out of steam. He's been talking about nothing for the last twenty minutes.

"So we all on the same page?" he finally asks. People nod and stand up to leave, half expecting him to say something that will force them back into their seats. "Go work your magic, people. Raquel, I'd like to speak to you."

People hurry out, a few giving me a sympathetic glance as they leave, or maybe they're just noticing my outfit. I merely smile at them and cross my legs. Once the room is empty, I take a seat at the table and wait for Fuller to do his worst.

He sits forward, his hands in a pyramid, brow furrowed as much as he can manage. Overall, he's giving the impression of someone who's going to say something that he believes to be profound and that he's clearly rehearsed. The effort to appear vice presidential has caused a fine sheen of sweat to break out over his upper lip.

"Great meeting, Mr. Fuller," I say just to mess with his script.

He closes his eyes for a second to regroup, and I can't help but smirk. There's nothing for me to gain in baiting him. If anything, it's costing me time I don't have. My checklist of things to do is two pages deep.

"We should talk about what your plans are," he says.

"I have some memos to proof for Mr. Floss. And of course there's always filing."

"I think you know what I'm talking about, Raquel. Don't be stupid." He sits back but keeps his hands on the table.

Even if I could at least tolerate Cris Fuller, I'd still find his perfectly manicured hands off-putting. "Do you honestly think you can keep coming into work, sitting at your little desk, doing nothing and still getting paid?"

"I really don't see why not, Mr. Fuller. Plenty of people do that every day." Belmore, like any megacorporation, carries its own share of deadweight. "And I'd be more than happy to help out on any project. I'm sure Mr. Floss wouldn't mind since he's not in today."

"He's not in and he's not coming in." Fuller's face begins to redden. "He's done at Belmore.

"You are a negative influence on this department and, frankly, I just don't like you," he says, surprising me. I almost want to commend him for going for honesty, but I know he'd take it the wrong way. "I am willing to write you a letter of rec-ommendation, and you would get some severance, but I want you gone today. If you say no, then I'll make it my number one priority to see you leave Belmore with nothing."

"As tempting as your offer is, Mr. Fuller, I'm going to have to decline." I give him a nod and stand up. I'll never leave under his conditions. That he's even offering me a deal is laughable and just shows how desperate he is to get rid of me. Bert always says that desperate people do stupid things.

"Are you very sure about that, Raquel?" he asks. His color has gone back to normal, and for a second this worries me. It's almost as if he expected me to tell him no.

"I believe I am, Mr. Fuller," I say.

Instead of going back to my desk, I head to the commis-sary. I haven't eaten breakfast, and I can't face my day with only a Diet Coke to look forward to. I've given up the Pop-

Tarts, but it doesn't mean I've changed the way I eat. I want pancakes doused in syrup and covered in powdered sugar. And I want sausage, big, fat, greasy sausage, washed down with a massive cup of strong black coffee.

When I get there, it's fairly empty. A few people look up from where they're dawdling over fruit plates but go back to chatting once they see I'm no one special. My infamy, it seems, is so very last week. I've gone back to being another nameless girl. With the way I'm dressed, they probably think I'm some green intern. I grab a tray and push it down the line until I come to the pancakes. I load up my plate with three and add a few strawberries to cut the grease on the sausage. I hand the cashier my ID to scan and then sit down at an empty table on the fringes of the room, where no one can see me. I eat quickly, not really tasting anything, and by the time I put down my fork and knife, I feel not as happy as I thought a stack of pancakes would make me feel.

"Great," I say as my stomach rumbles ominously. "Now I'll never be able to look at pancakes the same way again."

Feeling sicker by the second, I press the button for the elevator, my hand over my mouth, trying to think only of the Tums in my desk drawer. The elevator is packed with women who are all talking at once. What gets to me, though, is the heavy perfume they all seem to be wearing. I grit my teeth, look down at my shoes, and hum quietly, not caring if I'm giving the impression that I'm some sort of nutcase. If my humming will keep me from projectile-vomiting all over them, they should be rubbing my back instead of giving me dirty looks.

I get off as soon as the doors open, not even bothering to check what floor I'm on, and rush into the bathroom. As soon as I close the door of the stall behind me, I throw up.

It's quick, no prolonged dry heaving, and I feel immediately better if a little woozy. I flush and, instead of hurrying out, rinsing out my mouth, and getting to work, I lean against the far wall, my forehead on the cool tiles.

"Get it together, Azorian. This isn't rocket science. You've done this before," I say to myself. Slightly bolstered by my attempt at a pep talk, I'm ready to face whatever Cris Fuller has in store for me when a clatter of high heels hits the marble floor. I peek under the door and see red-soled Christian Louboutins. Whoever they are, they don't work at Belmore. Crap.

"So she's really serious about him?" the woman in the black, strappy five-inchers says.

"Why do you sound so surprised?" her friend, dark purple, peep-toe platforms, answers in a voice that's tinged with a tad too much incredulousness to be genuine. "You know how she is when she sets her mind on something or someone."

"Oh, crap," I mouth. I've walked right into the monthly wives and significant others breakfast. They take over the tenth-floor conference room to talk about all the wonderful things they're doing for the community in the Belmore name. No wonder the commissary was practically empty; everyone is hiding out at their desks until these women leave.

"Don't get me wrong," Strappy protests, "he's gorgeous, smart, and I heard he has a magic cock, but don't you think she's being a little impulsive?"

"If you're trying to say she's using again, she's not," Peep Toe snaps. "There's too much at stake for her to fuck this up."

"So what's she going to do?" Strappy asks gently, not wanting to stem the flow of information by being too critical about whoever it is they are talking about.

"She has something planned but won't say. Christ, these

herbs my naturopath has me on . . ." Peep Toe's voice is muf-fled as she makes her way into the stall next to me. She con-tinues to speak as she pees. "I better lose those five pounds or I'm asking for my money back. Anyway, she's been very quiet, which is not at all like her."

"Half the time she's just, you know, faking that something is going on. She always likes to be mysterious."

"Not this time." Peep Toe pauses for the toilet to flush. "I wouldn't be surprised if the next time we see her she has a rock on her finger. A big one."

"Then I guess she'll be paying for it herself, because I heard he's got some monster alimony payments," Strappy says. "I can't believe I actually said that out loud!"

"You're such a fucking little bitch." Peep Toe laughs. "That's why I love you. But keep talking like that and you won't get an invite to the wedding. And, if she has it her way, it'll be shotgun."

Both women laugh, fuss in front of the mirror for a few more moments, and finally leave. I open the door, making sure no one is there, and walk to the sink, looking at my pale face in the mirror.

"You hear the most interesting crap in the bathroom," I say to myself and then bend my head to scoop some water into my mouth to rinse the bad taste of it all out.

Outsourcing . . .

Rory Tilley has done good. He's made appearances on major gossip blogs—Just Jared, PerezHilton, Dlisted, and Egotas-tic! where I notice a mention that Nicolette Meyers will be appearing in an upcoming issue of *Maxim*. Dlisted hasn't gotten his name right, and on PerezHilton there's a scrawled "Yum! Who is he?" in a balloon over his head, but I assume his budding manager, Kevin, is taking care of this. I won't bother to call and remind him that his new purpose in life is making sure Perez Hilton knows who Rory Tilley is. If Kevin can't do it, Frappa will find someone who can. Rory is now entering the celebrity chum machine, and this particular part of my plan now has other people to manage it.

What I need to do is get my hands on the master copy of *Fire House Hero* so I have something to hand over to the projectionist on Wednesday. I also need to hire at least a dozen people to scour malls, theaters, and college campuses to hand out passes. If this doesn't get done, not having something like the actual movie won't be a problem. I pull out the phone book I brought from home and flip through it until I get to the listings for temp agencies. I pick TempOne, merely on the basis of it having the nicest looking ad in the Yellow Pages. I rip out the page and shove it into my purse.

"You up for lunch?" Matthias asks from the doorway. He's leaning against it as if he's just entered a café in Capri. I half expect him to pull out a cigarette and light it.

"I can't. I have to go to the . . . bank," I say as I shove my arms into my cardigan. "Didn't your boss tell you to stay away from me?"

"He did, but he's not in. Some big meeting up on twenty-four." Matthias walks with me to the elevators, forcing me to slow down to his leisurely pace. "He ran out of here with his panties all in a bunch. Something about Walter Belmore and coffee. Who knows? Who cares?"

"Oh." Kyle still hasn't gotten in touch with me. If I had

any time to devote to this particular issue, I'd start to wonder if maybe I was nothing but a booty call. "He offered to send me on my way with a check and a letter of reference."

"I hope you told him to go fuck himself," Matthias says, but only after making sure the receptionist can't hear us. "I'm so going to quit, and so should you."

"Are you really going to quit?" I ask. Despite what I'm doing, I know I'm not brave enough to do that. If I quit, what will I do? With the way the job market is my best option would be to temp until I'm lucky enough to find a real job again.

"I can't quit, my parents would cut me off. Cris has to fire me so I can go back to New York," he says. "L.A. is just not for me. Too damn sunny, and I can't get a decent bagel. So you want me to come to the bank with you? Mein Fuller should be gone for a while."

"Not this time, Matthias," I say as the elevator doors open up into the lobby.

"Fine then. I'm going to go find Jessica. According to her, something juicy is going on with Kyle Martin, but Marisa, for once, is keeping her trap shut about it." He gives me a quick hug and then presses the button for the twenty-first floor. "Don't worry, I promise to share when you get back."

I walk through the lobby, taking a second to look around. If I didn't know what actually went on in the floors above this space, I'd be in awe of standing in the Belmore Corporation lobby. Now it's become just a place I have to stop while my employee ID is scanned so I can get up to work.

"Okay, enough of that," I say, shaking myself out of my stupor. Within minutes I'm in my car and heading toward an address that's in the shadow of the Belmore Tower. I park and dump all my loose change into the meter.

"Hi, I'm interested in—"

I'm stopped midsentence when a clipboard is shoved at me. A chewed-up ballpoint pen cap dangles from a frayed and grubby length of yarn.

"Write your name here," a dour-faced receptionist says without bothering to look up at me. "Then fill out those forms." She points her hand in the general direction of a once cheery wicker letter basket stacked with photocopied and stapled papers. "If you need to borrow a pen, you have to leave your ID with me. You get your ID back when I get the pen back."

"I have one," I say, instantly feeling stupid. I try to cover it up by printing my first name and the first initial of my last name and the time on the sign-in sheet with my own pen.

"Good. Someone will be with you in a . . ." She looks over her shoulder at the women seated at desks, sipping coffee or talking on the phone. "Someone will call your name."

I smile at her even though she's already bent her head back to whatever task she'd been doing when I came in. I reach for a packet of forms and, quick as a snake, she replaces it with another from behind the desk, not once looking up.

I take a seat in the far corner so I can see who comes in but they can't necessarily see me. I look down on the form and realize it's an application to work for the agency. I'm about to take my chances on approaching the receptionist again when someone calls my name.

"Raquel?" The woman sounds bored and annoyed at the time. She could give my mother lessons. "Is there a Raquel A. here?"

She stands near the reception desk, tapping her flip-flopped foot while trying to pretend she isn't scrutinizing what the woman behind the desk is doing. She's wearing a navy blue blazer with "TempOne" embroidered in red over the left breast pocket.

"Is there a Raquel A. here?"

"Right here." I raise my hand and hurriedly gather up my stuff. "I didn't fill out the paperwork because—"

She starts walking toward the back even before I've finished speaking. "Don't worry about it, it's just for you to use when you input your info into the computer. You do know how to use a computer, don't you?"

"Yes," I say, trying to keep out of my voice any hint of sarcasm that has been raised by her question and by the fact that she didn't bother to put on proper shoes this morning. "I've used one before."

"You'd be surprised." She turns around and starts walking again. "We get these people with Hollywood dreams thinking they can just waltz in here, earn a little extra cash, and flake on assignments when they have an audition. A little thing like not knowing how to do much more than update their Facebook page is no big deal because they're going to be rich and famous next week . . . Oh shit! You're not an actress, are you?"

"No." I reach into my purse and hand her my card. "I'm also not interested in signing up with your agency. What I want to do is hire at least a dozen people for a spot job I need done for Belmore."

"Oh!" Her hand flies to her mouth.

"As long as you make sure they're not total dipshits," I say as I pull out my list, "everything should be okay."

Futile Endeavors . . .

My humble Honda Civic joins the conga line of Mercedeses, BMWs, and a couple of Bentleys as they make their way to their Bel Air mansions and private-chef-cooked dinners. At Bert's gate, I punch the numbers into the pin pad, thanking my father for bestowing upon me his great memory. It takes me only a minute to get up the drive, but Bert is already waiting for me on the front porch. He's dressed in shorts and a Belmore T-shirt, and instead of sunglasses he's pulled his baseball cap low. This is a good sign, I think, and also kind of sad to see him dressed like a toddler.

"Hello, Raquel."

"Hi, Mr. Floss. I'm sorry I didn't call, but I wasn't sure you'd pick up the phone," I say as I get out of my car and walk toward him.

"I probably wouldn't have," he says. He takes a seat on one of the chairs on the porch, and I do the same. "What can I do for you?"

"Lots, but let's start with this." I hand him what I have of the *Fire House Hero* report and sit silently as he looks through it.

"Ah, yes. I remember this. Your memo was very positive," he says, handing it back to me. "Is this what Fuller is working on now?"

"No. It's what I'm working on. I've scheduled a screening, and I need your signature to release the master film." I hand him the memo I've drawn up. "To me."

"Raquel." He sighs. "You don't need me to sign this. You've been signing my name for years."

"You're right, but I want you to do it. I want you to see

what I see and know that, even though it's not much, it might be enough to get Cris Fuller to back down." I feel like crying but know I can't. Bert doesn't like people who cry; he thinks they're wimps. "I know the numbers will be good."

"Good enough to save my job?" He's humoring me, but I'll take it.

"Maybe good enough to not get you fired, but you'll have to save your own job," I say. "I've realized there's only so much I can do, Mr. Floss."

Bert looks over at me in the amused way he would after I proposed an idea that didn't entirely suck. Once he gave me that look, I knew everything would be okay. This time, I'm not so sure. This time I think he just finds me nothing more than amusing.

I hand him the report and a copy of the movie. "There's something there. I know there is. You taught me to trust my instincts, and I think you owe me at least the chance to see what happens."

I stand up to leave. I'll just forge his signature and do this on my own. I don't need Bert. I've gotten this far by myself, and I'm prepared to see it through, no matter what happens. But I do need Bert there to call the meeting; there's no way I can bullshit that, and he knows it.

"Hold on, kid." He reaches for his pocket for a pen and, realizing he has no pockets, looks up at me helplessly. I hand Bert his Montblanc pen and watch as he scrawls his name on the memo. "Good luck, Raquel."

"I'll need a lot more than luck." I pinch the sheet of paper between my fingers, careful not to crease it. I hold out my hand for the pen. I went through the trouble of filching it off his desk and will put it back in its place once I'm done with it. "What I need . . . What I need is a miracle, Bert."

thirteen | CLOSE ENCOUNTERS OF THE FAMILIAR KIND

Home on the Rage . . .

I finally come home, but only because I can't face another hooker shower in the ladies' room. Aside from sneaking into Bert's office for his pen, I've stayed away, well away, from anything I'm not supposed to touch, including the copy machine. I paid three hundred dollars to have survey sheets printed out and boxes of golf pencils sent over to where the screening of *Fire House Hero* will take place in a couple of hours.

What I need to do now is shower, change, hope traffic cooperates, and then, once I get there, wait in the lobby while my fate is decided by people who didn't have anything better to do on a Wednesday night. After I collect the surveys, I'm heading back to Belmore to compile the numbers, put the finishing touches on my marketing report, and then figure out what the hell to do with it.

I click the garage remote, not expecting much, and am pleasantly surprised when it rumbles open.

"That's a good sign," I say, pleased at the small gift the universe has bestowed upon me and momentarily distracted from my reality. When I click it again, it makes a loud metallic moaning noise, and the door doesn't close. It just gives a few jerks and stays there. "Thank you for reminding me who the boss is, Universe."

My phone rings, and I answer it, even though I just want a few minutes to myself. By this time tomorrow, I remind myself, I can relax.

"Hello?" When I lift my arm, I get a whiff of what I smell like. "Oh, yuck."

"Yuck what? Is it food or person? Whatever it is, don't tell me. I'm on a liquid detox and feeling very grouchy," Frappa says in her familiar rat-tat-tat cadence. "Listen, babe, I'm calling to let you know that I can't make it to the screening tonight, but I'll be there in spirit. I have Rory on lockdown until the weekend, so don't worry about him showing up on any blogs."

"No, not a problem," I say, even though I'm a bit disappointed. If Frappa doesn't come, I'll be forced to make conversation with the temps who I'm paying with my father's wedding money. "I figured you'd be busy anyway. And I'll call you as soon as, um, as soon as I get the verdict."

I climb out of my car and close the garage door the old-fashioned way, taking my time, and nod to a couple who I have a vague idea are neighbors of mine.

"I know it's going to be great, and even if it isn't, I already have a meeting set up for Rory. People are going to want to see more of him," she says after she takes a long gulp of something. "Ugh. That tastes like some old man's jizz, and it cost me twelve dollars. Anyway, he's definitely on people's radars, which can only work to your advantage. So call me and forgive me?"

"Yeah, I'll be at Belmore, probably all night." I keep myself from heaving a sigh, knowing the last thing I'll get from Frappa is pity. "If you need to reach me, try me at my desk."

"Hang in there, doll," Frappa says, ever supportive and brimming with confidence I can only hope to one day possess a cup's worth of. "You're almost at the finish line."

I drop my phone into my purse and stop to yank out the contents of my overstuffed mailbox. With the garage door opener almost fixed, I'll have to wait at least a month to approach Mr. Kashini about maybe installing a bigger mailbox. Not wanting to deal with digging my keys out of my purse, I ring the doorbell and go through my mail as I wait for my mother to let me in. After the fourth press of the buzzer, I accept the fact that I will have to let myself into my own home like an adult.

"Hello? Anyone home?" I call from the door, hoping to give my mother a minute to pull herself together if it turns out that she's "fallen asleep" on the couch. Nothing. No odor of microwave popcorn. Even the TV is off.

I walk around my empty home, familiarizing myself with it. My place is clean, dust free, and the kitchen smells of citrus cleaner. I wander into the bedroom, tiptoeing just in case, but find it just as empty and tidy as the rest of the place. The bed is made, books and magazines neatly stacked on the nightstand, and a fresh box of Kleenex on just about every surface.

All these clues can only lead to one conclusion—Cricket has been inside my home, and after cleaning it she absconded

with my mother back to her roomy South Pasadena Craftsman.

"Thank you, Cricket!" I do a little dance and strip off my
clothes, eager to get rid of the stale smell of being in the same
pants and sweater since Tuesday.

Enveloped in my plush mint green terry-cloth robe, I pull
on the matching slipper socks to complete the ensemble.
I'm about to flick off the light of my closet when I notice the
tracksuits my mother has been living in are neatly folded on
a shelf.

"Crap," I say and shut the door. "Cricket's just taken her
on a playdate."

I hear a car pull up and go peek out the window, creeping around as if I've broken into someone else's house. I wait
for a few moments, expecting them to walk through the door,
and when they don't, I let my robe fall open and kick off the
slipper socks. Naked, I walk to the bathroom and sing Céline
Dion songs at the top of my lungs for the duration of my ten-
minute shower.

When I come out, I'm still alone, but now slightly
annoyed. I open myself a can of Diet Coke and take a more
critical look at my clean apartment. I know my mother didn't
do this. She can barely manage to buy cleaning supplies,
much less use them. But someone was here who knows how
to use a mop, and it's my best guess that my mom is with
them. I still have her keys in my tote bag, and my tote bag is
locked in the trunk of my car, which is why my car smells like
stale coffee.

"What the hell?" I ask myself, not used to the sound of
only my voice in my apartment. I dial Steve's cell, and it kicks

immediately over to voice mail. I try my mom's, and the same thing happens. With no choice, I dial Cricket.

"Hello," she answers ever chipper. "This is Cricket Sherman Azorian."

"Hi, Cricket." I say a quick prayer that this will be a normal phone call, consisting of a greeting, inquiry, and then sign-off. "It's me, Raquel."

"Oh, I didn't recognize the number," she says. I can hear her turning the sound down on the classical music she plays for the twins.

"I'm calling from my home number; my cell phone is almost out of battery. But rest assured, Cricket, it's me. Not some pervert. Anyway, I'm wondering if you have any idea where my mom might be. Is she with you? Or with Steve?"

"No. I'm here alone with the babies," Cricket says in a tight voice. She's obviously been at home alone with them for a while. "Steve went to check in on Marlene, but he was supposed to be home hours ago."

"Oh, I guess they're out or something," I say, trying to keep any hint of a cringe out of my voice. "I know! They're picking up dry cleaning or . . . dinner."

Cricket is pissed at Steve and isn't bothering to hide it. Up until now, as much as she's tried to act like the sister I never wanted, there was a buffer of polite distance between us. Either Cricket feels that we're now close enough so she can vent to me or she's really, really pissed at Steve.

I wander over to the fridge to look for a note. Steve's usually very good about stuff like that. All I find is an expired pizza coupon and a to-do list in my mother's handwriting for me. Number two on the list after "Pick up more Diet Coke" is

"Find a husband." I peek into the fridge, my stomach giving a loud growl I'm sure Cricket can hear.

Not finding anything that suits my mood, I raid the pantry. Jars, cans, and packages are neatly arranged, more evidence that someone has been here and cleaned up.

"Raquel? I'm hoping we can talk sister to sister," Cricket asks, her tone dipping into the uncomfortably confidential. "I'd appreciate getting your take on a little something that's been bugging me."

"Oh . . . okay."

I look at the clock above the stove; it's ten minutes fast, but I'm sure Cricket won't need long to come around to what she wants to talk about. Cricket doesn't want to ask for my opinion or hear any advice. She wants me to be in league with her. Cricket believes there is strength in numbers and the more people she has on her team, the stronger her position is. In this way, she's very much like my mother: they both see conflict, slights, and insults everywhere.

I sit down with a jar of Nutella and begin to spread a thin layer of it on a half dozen saltine crackers and top them with another six—my version of a salty and sweet, crunchy and smooth sandwich. I arrange them on a plate so they form a circle, corners touching, and scoop a dollop of Nutella in the middle of the plate for dipping.

"I'm not sure if you know, but Steve and I have been trying for another baby." Cricket says this with absolute conviction that she's nothing but justified in exercising her right to procreate.

"Oh, really?" I play dumb, as is my right. I pour the rest of my Diet Coke into a tall glass and feel almost civilized. "And how is that working out?"

"It's not." I hear one of the twins coo in the background, and Cricket pauses from our adult conversation to address either Saylor or Rhys. "Is Mommy's angel making a poo-poo? Yes, I smell it. A little present for Mommy?"

"Cricket?" I nudge her back into our conversation. I don't necessarily want to have it, but it won't end anytime soon if she's distracted.

"I went to the doctor, my ob-gyn, and she says there's no reason why I can't get pregnant or shouldn't be by now." She pauses so I can absorb the enormity of her news. "Everything is in working condition, if you know what I mean."

"Uh-huh." I decide this is information that should just skim the surface of my consciousness and then disappear into the ether of my soul. Poor Steve. Poor me, but I'd forfeited my right to remain neutral by calling her up in the first place. "That's, uh . . . Yeah."

"I just don't understand why it's not happening. I've had a regular period now for months even with breast feeding twice a day," Cricket continues, sounding falsely concerned about her fertility and very proud of everything her body can do. "The doctor said to just relax and give it time."

"Yeah, sure," I say because I'm expected to say something.

"Obviously, the problem can't be with Steve . . ."

She trails off, planting the seed that Steve's seed is indeed the problem. I say nothing, dip a corner of one of my home-made cookies into the Nutella, and try to chew it as quietly as possible.

"Anyway"—Cricket moves the conversation briskly along without any prompting from me—"what I was thinking was that just me and Steve could take a little weekend trip to Palm Springs or Santa Barbara."

"I love Palm Springs. You have to make sure to stop at the outlets on the way." I push my dinner away, already planning what I'm going to wear to the screening and what I'll pack to wear tomorrow at work. "And if you have time, play a round of craps for me at the casino. Good times all around."

"I was talking with a girlfriend of mine, and she suggested that maybe a break from our routine will inspire us," Cricket says, ignoring me. She's having a monologue, and I keep interrupting her with my inane comments. "Except we have no one to watch the twins . . ."

"That sucks," I say, ignoring my cue to offer my as yet untried babysitting services.

"I've already asked Marlene, and she promised to pitch in. You two can stay here, and it'll be like a weekend getaway. Your own private B and B in South Pasadena." Cricket moves on to logistics. My agreement is a foregone conclusion. She just wants to hear me say yes I'll do it and yes, I think it's a great idea that she get pregnant again. "Doesn't that sound heavenly?"

"I couldn't imagine anything more heavenly," I say in the same false voice she employed.

"Not that I want to be parted from my babies, but I'm sure a little weekend away will hardly scar them for life. Plus, the air is so dry there it wouldn't be good for their little noses."

"And bringing them would defeat the purpose of a romantic weekend," I say.

"Exactly!"

For a moment I think of tipping what's left of the bottle of Baileys into my mouth and buying a ticket to ride my mother's crazy train. I'm about to remind Cricket I have to get back to work when my doorbell rings and then rings again, as if someone is leaning on it. I pull the phone away from my ear and hold it out so she'll be sure to hear it on her end.

"Cricket, my pizza is here. Give the twins a kiss from their aunt Raquel and I'll get back to you about . . . Okay! Bye!" I hang up the phone just as my tipsy mother stumbles through the doorway. "Where have you been?"

"Next door, talking to Vashti." At my quizzical look, my mother says, "Vashti Kashini. Your landlady?"

"You've been at the Kashinis'? How long?" I ask.

"For a few hours. She came by to ask me to unlock the garage door and helped me tidy up a bit. Anyway! Guess what, Raquel. Her husband is an even bigger asshole than your father!"

"I'm not surprised, Mom, not at all," I say. I take one last look at her and then go into my bedroom to get dressed.

Blank Spots . . .

My tires kick up a fair amount of gravel as I pull into Steve and Cricket's driveway—I don't have time to be sneaky and park half a block away. All the same, I don't bother with the front door and go directly around the back. If my brother is home and not out "jogging," he'll be in his office. I put my head down and take the distance at a fast walk. I don't need to go that far; I bump into Steve, who's carrying a trash bag full of yard clippings to the shed the garbage and recycling cans are stored in along with the other gardening supplies and gear.

"Hi, Raquel."

Steve doesn't look at all surprised to find me running headlong into his backyard. He sets the bag on the ground and then maneuvers a wheelbarrow out, being careful not to run over either of our feet.

"Is Cricket around?" I automatically glance up, half expecting to see her face pressed against one of the windows. She must have heard me drive up, and I'm surprised she hasn't rushed out yet to micromanage my visit and slip me some pro-procreation talking points she wants me to bring up to my brother.

"She's inside with a migraine," he says. "She's feeling pretty lousy."

I watch as Steve easily shoulders a bag full of grass seed and then reaches in for another of fertilizer. He sets them carefully on the wheelbarrow, taking his time. If his wife is feeling lousy with a migraine, he seems to have decided the best way to deal with it is not to.

"Kind of late to be doing yard work unless you like to work by flashlight," I say. It's dark outside except for the bare overhead bulb in the shed.

"I'm just getting stuff ready for tomorrow. I promised Cricket," he says. "She's sort of upset with me. You want to go inside?"

"I think it's best if we talk here," I say. "I want to ask you something."

"Yeah, sure." Steve frowns as he turns his attention to emptying the clippings bag into the bin without dumping any leaves on the ground.

"Are you cheating on Cricket?" This is a very basic question, and it pains me to ask it, but I ceded all neutrality when I called Cricket looking for my mother.

"Not anymore." Steve grunts as he lifts the handles of the wheelbarrow, setting it beside the shed. "I was seeing someone, but she broke it off with me. It wasn't anything serious. We never even, you know, slept together. It was just . . . It was nothing, and it's over now. Please don't tell Cricket."

"I won't, and thanks for being honest. I've almost forgotten what it sounds like." I rub my temples, feeling the onset of a horrendous headache. "Why are you hiding out by the trash cans?"

"I'm not hiding. I'm prepping for tomorrow." Steve shuts the door to the shed and then leans his forehead against it. "Cricket wants to have another baby."

"Yeah, I know." I glance toward the windows, nervous that we've been left alone for this long. "She mentioned something about it."

"It's all she talks about, all she wants to . . . do." My brother's shoulders sag under the weight of his wife's expectations and needs.

"So, knock her up and shut her up." I have no idea if my brother wants any more children or if he ever even wanted the ones he already has. He always seemed happily resigned that they, like Cricket, were around. This almost-affair that he's confessed to is just that. My brother would never go through with trying to have another relationship when he's so obviously failing at the one he has now. "What's one or two more?"

"I can't," he says in a defeated voice. "I can't do it."

"You mean you can't get it up or you can't because you don't want to contribute to the overpopulation of the planet." I'm trying to find some humor in his situation for both our sakes. If I don't, I'll start crying like he is.

"Can't as in can't." Steve slumps into me, and I hold him up as best as I can, patting his back. He takes a few deep breaths before he can manage to talk again. "I had a vasectomy a week before the twins were born."

I don't have to ask if he's shared this news with his wife or if he ever will. Steve made a decision, maybe a little late for everyone involved, but he's done with fathering children he isn't capable of providing anything more than financial security to. My brother has done the right thing for him, not his marriage, and it makes him a coward because he'll never admit to Cricket the true reason why he won't give her any more babies.

I feel his tears wet the shoulder of my dress as he cries. When Cricket calls his name, her voice sharp as our mother's has grown over the years, Steve straightens up and walks toward her without a word.

I stand there, by the garbage cans, feeling my bottom lip begin to quiver.

"What is it with you people?" I ask, my exasperated voice muffled by the aluminum walls of the shed. When I feel nominally better, I get into my car and glance in the rearview mirror just to make sure I'm as alone as I feel.

General Consensus . . .

By my fifth paper cut I have to stop to find more Band-Aids. It's after one in the morning, and I have just enough numbers from the evaluation cards that trend to *Fire House Hero* ending up with a high favorability rating, and it's solid when broken down among target audience groups (women, teens, men, et cetera). The majority of the comments single Rory out as the highlight of the movie and say that they want to see more of him.

"This is good, very good," I say to myself, whispering even though I'm the only one here. I do a tired little happy dance in my chair and reach for a stack from the nine o'clock showing to reconfirm my numbers and look for the comment card that asks for a Rory Tilley butt shot or at least a little haunch.

"What's good?" a male voice I haven't heard in a while asks.

"Holy crap, Kyle! You scared me." I stand up, fumbling to turn off my computer monitor. It's a reflex and lets him know there's something I don't want him to see. "What are you doing here?"

"I looked out the window of my hotel room and saw your light was still on," he says as he approaches my desk. Wherever he came from, it wasn't his suite at the Century. He's still wearing his suit and is carrying his briefcase. "What are you doing here?"

"Working on my résumé," I say, which is basically true. Despite the subterfuge and some very minor forging of documents with Bert's signature, my marketing report for *Fire House Hero* is my ticket out of assistantdom. "What are you doing here? Raiding the supply closet for rubber bands and Bic pens?"

"I've missed you." He puts his briefcase on my desk and topples a small tower of evaluation cards. "And I'd kiss you if I wasn't afraid you'd punch me in the face."

"Why would I punch you?" I say, feigning indifference I don't feel. Even as tired as I am, freaked out about what tomorrow will bring, and slightly high from the rush of being this close to pulling everything off, I can't ignore that my feelings have been hurt. "You're a busy man, I'm a busy woman, and one of us obviously forgot how to dial a phone."

"You could have called me," he says. "I was hoping you would."

"And if I had?" I don't pull away as Kyle puts his arms around me. "Would you have dropped everything and rushed over?"

"Maybe, but we'll never know." He buries his head in my neck and inhales. "I've missed your smell, your skin, the way you feel."

"Kyle. Wait." I push him away enough so I can see his face. "So why haven't you called? Not to sound like a clingy girlfriend or whatever, but you just basically disappeared."

"Life just got a bit more complicated, but I don't want to think about that right now." He sits down in my chair and pulls me into his lap. I have to admit it feels pretty nice. "Right now I'm just really happy to see you."

I don't say anything and let myself relax into his embrace. When he starts kissing me, not only do I let him but I kiss him back. I'm due for a break, and Kyle can have the concierge send up a box of Band-Aids.

"Have you ever seen the view from twenty-four at night?" he asks, nibbling on my ear.

"No," I admit as a wave of contentment flows through me. I think this might qualify as having my cake and eating it, too. "No, I haven't."

"Let me show it to you." Kyle stands, holding on to me tightly. "Yeah?"

"Sure," I say. "Why not?"

fourteen | MAGICAL REALISM

Games of Chance . . .

Other than having gotten laid more than once in the last few hours, nothing is currently going my way. A Belmore security guard who takes his job very seriously won't let me back into the building no matter how nicely I ask.

"I was just here, not even a few hours ago. I stepped out to get some fresh air, and no one told me the building was going to be locked down." I don't care if he's wearing a company-issued uniform with patches on each shoulder and a shiny badge on his chest—I'm not calling him Officer. "I was right in the middle of printing something."

"Sorry, miss, but I got my orders. No one goes in or comes out until the doors officially open, and that will be in"—he checks the cheap watch on his hairy wrist—"one hour and fifty-four minutes. You're welcome to wait in the lobby."

"No thanks," I say, trying to keep my temper in check. He has my name, and I don't need him writing me up for being rude. It's just the kind of thing Fuller would find in my file and use to justify putting me back on the reception desk.

I walk out, my shoes making audible squeaks on the polished marble floor. Outside I rub my arms to keep warm and debate my choices. I could go home and tiptoe around my apartment so I don't wake up my mom. Or I could catch some sleep in my stale-coffee-smelling car. My last option is to go back to Kyle's suite and climb into bed with him, take another shower, order room service, and still be at my desk by eight.

"Really, dummy, is there any debate about what I should do?" I ask myself. I'm about to head left toward the Century when my cell phone gives a powerful buzz in my purse, and it turns out both of them are going off. I answer the one closest to my hand, suddenly very nervous when I see that Frappa is trying to reach me.

"Frappa? Is everything all right?" I ask as my other phone goes silent.

"Yes and no," she says, her voice tense. "Our little diamond in the rough Rory Tilley has gotten himself in a pickle. Actually, it's his pickle that's gotten him into a pickle."

"What he'd do? Bar fight?" I ask, my heart kicking up about a dozen beats in under a second. "Did his face get hurt?"

"Last night, after I told him to stay home, he went out and sometime between two and three got himself a blow job while driving down PCH courtesy of either Cat or Cara. If not both. I'm still trying to get the details out of one of them, but she's locked herself in my bathroom."

I laugh out loud, startling a couple of landscapers who are fiddling with sprinklers a few feet away. "I'm sorry. This is not funny. What can I do?"

"I need you, really need you, to go down to the Malibu police station and bail Rory out with as little fuss and muss as possible while I deal with either Cat or Cara."

"This might actually work to everyone's advantage," I say as I run to my car. "It'll give him some street cred, instant notoriety, not to mention boasting rights for the next five years, but it'll trash the wholesome Ward twin brand. On the other hand, they've wanted to sex up their image, right?"

"I know that, but not this way," Frappa snaps, clearly short on her usual charm. "I can't manage the story with him out there. I need his cute ass in your car before some bottom-feeder gossip blogger picks up on this. I'm at my office, bring him here. Please, Raquel. You're the only one I trust on this."

"Don't worry. I'll have him at your door as soon as possible. Bye." I hop into my car and peel out of the garage, going well above the fifteen-mile-an-hour speed limit.

Even though it's early, it takes me almost an hour to get to the Malibu police station, and by the time I do, I can see a couple of paparazzi milling about in the parking lot.

"Frappa isn't going to like this," I mutter as I make my way past.

"Hey, you here about the Ward twin arrest?" one of them calls out, pointing a camera at my face.

"No. I'm not," I say, even though I know I should keep my mouth shut. "My grandmother got picked up for speeding."

"If you see anything in there, come out and tell us. We'll pay you," he says. "Cash. No one has to know but us."

He shoves his card into my hand, and I take it. I'd never sell him information, but it might be worth my time and energy to find out where this guy is getting his from.

Inside the station, I approach the counter, unsure if I should play it nonchalant or admit that I've never been in a police station before, much less bailed someone out of jail. Looking at the officer, a walrus of a man, I think helpless and polite is my best bet.

"Hello, Officer," I say. This guy has the patches, badge, and a gun, but more important, he has Rory somewhere in the building. "I'm here to . . . I guess *pick up* isn't the right term for it. I'm here for Rory Tilley."

The police officer clacks on his keyboard as he looks me over from the top of his glasses. "You a friend of his?"

"I'm just doing this as a favor to a friend of mine who, um, works with Rory. Do I have to give my name?" I say, looking over my shoulder at where the paparazzi are milling around like piranhas on asphalt.

"We're going to let him off with a warning. This time. Seems Mr. Tilley has friends in high places." He looks around to make sure no one is listening before he adds, "You tell him we don't want to see him back in Malibu until he learns some manners."

"Of course, Officer, I'll tell him." I take a seat on a hard plastic chair and call Frappa while I wait for Rory to make his appearance. "Hey, it's me. They're letting him off with a warning and he should be out in a few minutes."

"Good. That's good. I got Cat out of the bathroom, and Cara is coming over to drive her home. But . . ."

"What?" I ask while I watch Rory's tousled head of hair as he makes his way toward me. "What's wrong?"

"Nothing I guess, but I got a call not two minutes ago from an Officer Elliot Shipper apologizing for the mistake and asking me very nicely to come get my client."

"That's weird," I say. I take another look outside and see that a few more paparazzi have joined the scrum. "What do you want me to do about the photographers outside? They're asking about the Ward twins, not Rory."

"Say nothing. Just let Rory do his walk of shame and you stay out of the picture," Frappa says, sounding more like her in-control self. "And thank you, Raquel. I know today is your big day. I owe you one, and I always pay up on my debts."

"No, really, don't worry—" I start, but Frappa hangs up, saving both of us the embarrassment of me not letting her acknowledge my favor.

Rory sits down heavily next to me, head bent, hands dangling between his knees. "I'm sorry, Raquel. I guess I really screwed up."

"Other than for making me drive all the way over here to pick you up, I'm not the one you should be apologizing to, Rory." I look at him and can't help picturing the expensively bleached blond head of Cat Ward in his lap. "You were supposed to lay low for the rest of this week."

"Yeah, I know, I know. But she's so hot, man. She called me up, and next thing I knew she was handing me the keys to her Porsche," he says, giving me a quick look to gauge how pissed off I am. "I've only washed cars like that, never driven one."

"Much less gotten a blow job in one, I bet." I give him a nudge on the shoulder. "You'll have to be smart about this, Rory. People are going to start throwing things and themselves at you, but you can't drop your pants each time some hot piece of ass winks at you or a producer tells you he sees great things for you."

"Do you think Frappa is going to drop me?" he asks as another car roars into the parking lot.

"She might if you don't do exactly as I say. Walk out there, smile, but don't say anything but good morning. Don't give your name or even hint who you were hanging out with last night. And for God's sake, don't try to hold my hand. Got it?"

"I got it," he says, standing up. He takes a couple of deep breaths. "Ready?"

"Me?" I say, touched that he's thought to ask.

For a moment I wonder if we, Frappa and I, are doing the right thing. Sure Rory isn't turning his back on a promising career in cancer research, but maybe he could make something true and honest of his life. Then I watch as he checks the state of his hair in the fish-eye mirror mounted above the door and realize he's already made his choice.

"Right now this is all about you, Rory." I adjust his T-shirt so it hangs just right. "So go. I'll be right behind you."

Return of the King . . .

I walk through the Belmore lobby feeling inconspicuous in my jeans, red flats, and cardigan sweater. I half expect one of the security guards to make me stand off to the side while they triple-check that I really do work here, but no one stops me and I almost sprint to the bank of elevators. I can't help but feel a little paranoid, though, when the phone on the security guard's desk rings not even thirty seconds after I swipe my badge.

During the sixty seconds or so it takes for me to get to 17, all I think about is my change of clothes hanging on the back of my office door and whether I turned on the fax machine before I left with Kyle. As soon as I step onto the marketing department floor, I know things are not the way they should be. People are scurrying around, darting in and out of offices and cubicles. I stop by the reception desk, where the new temp is finishing up a call.

"Hi. I'm wondering if you know what's going on," I say, swallowing my pride—she definitely knows more than I do.

"Are you Raquel Azorian?" She checks me out and ignores my question.

"Yes. I am. Is there something—"

"Raquel!" Matthias hurries over, wearing what looks to be a regular suit—no ankles or wrists to be seen. What's more, he's carrying my shoes and garment bag.

"What is going on?" I ask as he yanks me down the hall toward the ladies' room. "Did someone die? Oh, my God, Mr. Belmore!"

"Just the opposite." As soon as we're inside, he starts to undo my sweater until I bat his hands away. "Bert is coming in, and he's going to save us from the tyranny of self-tanner and overaccessorizing."

"Bert? My Bert?" I ask, now jerking my own clothes off. "Who told you this?"

"Cris called me a half hour ago. He's still not here, so he doesn't know that you're late or that you're dressed like you are. Why were you late anyway?"

"I had to run an errand for a friend." Not caring that he's watching, I slip out of my jeans and into my skirt. "Bert hasn't called me. Should I be worried?"

"I don't know, but Cris Fuller is pooping in his pants. Whatever is going to happen, it's going to be big." Matthias throws his hands in the air and gives a little hop. "And I know you have something to do with it."

"Me?" My mind immediately goes to my *Fire House Hero* report. My computer is password protected, but I know this isn't much of a barrier for anyone seriously motivated to access it. "Why would I have anything to do with anything?"

"Cris asked what you were doing. I told him you were getting something to eat in the commissary, but I think he knows I was lying." Matthias turns his attention to straightening his tie in the mirror.

"Thanks, Matthias." I button my blouse, having to do it twice to get everything lined up correctly. I twist my hair up, only to have it uncoil down my back. There's nothing I can do about it until I can get to my desk, where I keep an old Altoids tin full of bobby pins and clear rubber bands. "How do I look?"

"You look very Belmore. By the way, nice rack," he says, patting me appreciatively on the shoulder. At my shocked look, he gives me a wry one. "Just because I don't fart sports and swing my dick around like it's some sort of cave man club, know how to dress, and have manners, I'm not necessarily gay, Raquel. People just assume, and I let them. You think Cris would let me get away with half the crap I do if he didn't think he had a chance of getting into my pants?"

"Smart man, Matthias. If you weren't leaving, you'd do very well at Belmore. And thanks for noticing, but I doubt my rack will help me with whatever is going to happen." I take the lead and hold open the door. "Anything else I should know?"

"Yeah, there's a department meeting at ten. Bert called it."

"You're serious," I say, feeling paranoid at being so far out of the loop. For the first time since Bert hired me as his assistant, I get here a smidge after nine and this is what happens?

"Tell me about it," Matthias calls over his shoulder. "Maybe I'll put off getting fired until next week."

I rush toward my desk and wiggle the mouse to wake up my computer. My report is ready to go; all I need to do is print it out, put it in a binder, and pray. I'm about to open the document when Bert strides in.

"Oh my," I say, before snapping my mouth closed.

Bert's dressed in his usual suit and custom-made Italian loafers, but instead of his head of sandy brown hair, he's sporting a monk fringe. There's nothing on top but a smooth, shiny scalp, and the rest of his hair, what there is of it, is bleached almost white.

"Good morning, Raquel," he says as he passes my desk. "Print out your report, make sure *Fire House Hero* is ready to play in the conference room, and have my usual breakfast sent up."

"Of course, Mr. Floss."

I open the sole document on my desktop, *FHH*, and send a request for eight copies to the high-speed printer in the supply closet, which will collate and bind them in under three minutes. I hurriedly pin back my hair and swipe on some lip balm as I make my way to the hulking printer. I grab the copies, not even giving them time to cool.

At Bert's door, I close my eyes for a few seconds before I knock and enter without waiting for an answer. I set a copy of my report on his desk and walk out, leaving the door ajar so Catering knows it's okay to come in with his glass of carrot juice and bowl of dry bran cereal.

In the conference room, I flip on the lights, bring down the screen, and carefully put *Fire House Hero* into the DVD player. I set a copy of my marketing report in front of each place and then, out of sheer nerves, straighten chair backs so they all line up. I force myself to go through the motions even though I'm jacked up on adrenaline. All I can think about is what I should have done better and if I kept all the receipts so I can get reimbursed for what I spent on the test screening. I look up when I hear the sound of slow, sarcastic clapping coming from the doorway.

"Hello, Mr. Fuller. The meeting isn't for another forty minutes. Would you like me to save your seat?" I ask with extreme politeness (Helen Mirren would be proud), knowing that he's just there to put me in my place.

He circles the table, plops down on Bert's empty seat, puts his feet on the table, hands behind his head, and leans back. It's what I imagine he'd like the picture in *Los Angeles* magazine to look like when they finally get around to doing a feature on him. I concentrate on the patch of white skin on the inside of his wrist where his spray tan didn't take.

"It looks like I underestimated you, Raquel," he says after a few moments.

Cris sits there with his patch of pale skin and in his $2,500 suit with his feet on my marketing report, still secure in his delusion that he'll one day run the marketing department, if not Belmore itself. Whatever this is, he's going to pretend he's not worried about it, but he is. Even a face full of Botox can't keep his left eye from twitching.

"Looks like you did, Cris," I say, using his first name.

"Kudos to you for having a fat friend in the right place." Fuller waits to see if he'll get any reaction from me by insulting Frappa. "A fat friend who has the right friends. Friends who can get a certain no-name pretty boy out of jail."

"Thank you," I answer. I won't dignify his comment about Frappa, but I hope he'll keep talking about friends of friends. He knows something I don't, but he doesn't know the whole story. For once, if we work together, we can figure out what's going on around here.

Fuller, a jerk but no dummy, tries another tactic. "Maybe if you start caring about how you look, I might consider keeping you around when I take over this department, Raquel," he says, with his usual ratlike smile. "Unless you're going for a Soviet Bloc beauty queen look? If that's the case, congratulations. You've really nailed it."

"Really, Cris, is this all you have?" I ask, frustrated that he can't see beyond his own pettiness. "Bert's back now, and if you don't want me to tell him that you've been harassing me and offering me deals behind his back, you'd better get out of here, and don't come back until it's time for the meeting."

I turn my back on him and fiddle with the DVD player for lack of anything better to do. I can't leave the room before he does since he'd basically be chasing me out.

"Everything ready, Raquel?" Bert asks.

"Yes, everything is fine, Mr. Floss. Is there anything you need?" I ask, already going through my mental checklist of what I have to do before the meeting gets started.

"I'd like to have a few words with Fuller," he says, coming into the room, my report in his hand.

"Of course," I say, snatching the copy at his place out from under Fuller's shoes.

"No, I want you to stay," Bert says, closing the door. I pull out the chair I'm digging my fingernails into and sit down. Instead of kicking Fuller out of his, Bert takes the one opposite me.

"I want to commend you, Fuller, for taking charge of the department in my absence," he says. I feel my eyes widen in disbelief at his words, but I force myself to stay silent as he continues.

"Thank you, Bert." Fuller's not even bothering to keep the gloating out of his voice. "I'm glad you're finally acknowledging my contribution to this department."

"*Fire House Hero* will be the next project we focus on," Bert says, moving on. "Raquel, I need you to schedule meetings with Development, Creative, Finance, Public Relations, and Art. Cris, get your team on the report. We need more demographics and another round of screenings. The usual."

With those words, Bert has let me know that there will be no promotion without actually saying it. I am once again just Bert's assistant, exactly where Cris Fuller wants me to stay until he takes over the department and fires me.

"Of course, Bert," Fuller says. He picks up my report and thumbs through it. "*Fire House Hero* is the right project for this department to focus on. I'll have my team start working on it now."

The rational part of my brain understands why Bert has taken my project and handed it over to Fuller. He's the one who needs to be appeased. I held down the fort, scrambled, and didn't panic when my boss was away having a mental breakdown. It's all he can offer me and it's not much of a bone, but it's all I can expect for being a good assistant.

"Raquel?" Bert asks, finally meeting my eyes.

He's begging me to go along with what he's proposing. Really, it doesn't matter if I don't. He can fire me, and that will make Fuller just as happy, but Bert thinks he's doing me a favor. He has his reasons for not acknowledging what I've done for him. There's nothing I can do but step aside and let the train leave the station without me.

"Yes, of course," I say.

And with those three words, I go back to being "Bert Floss's assistant, Raquel." Back to writing uncredited memos, facilitating meeting coordination with the other executive assistants and departments, answering his phone, and waiting for my chance to make a small contribution to the bigger picture that might someday lead to a promotion.

I get up and gather up my reports. They, just like me, won't be needed for the meeting.

And So It Goes . . .

I stand in front of the frozen pizza case at my local supermarket. I wonder if it would be some sort of sign of depravity if I bought three different flavors, baked them, stacked one on top of the other, and then ate them while watching reruns on SOAPnet.

"Maybe, but it sounds like a fun night to me," I say.

"Rachel?" A young woman calls from in front of the frozen vegetables. Mentally I try to imagine what different flavor combos will taste like and decide that Hawaiian will not be making it into my shopping basket. "Rebecca?"

The vaguely familiar voice is now a few feet away, and I realize she's trying to talk to me. I shove my head farther into the freezer, acutely aware of how I must look in my corporate lady clothes topped with my Belmore fleece zip-up vest and Belmore cap pulled low to obscure my face. My eyes are puffy from crying and my nose red from having to wipe it with fast-food napkins I found in my car.

"I'm sorry but . . ." She trails off, not taking me wanting to climb into the freezer case as a sign that I don't want to talk to her. With no choice but to acknowledge that my camouflaging trick has failed miserably, I turn to face the person who recognized me. "Are you . . ."

"Raquel?" I offer up, as if I'm not sure what my own name is.

"Raquel? Oh, my God, it *is* you! Raquel! Do you remember me? Nicolette Meyers? *Risk Management III*. We met at the premiere?"

"Yeah, hi, Nicolette. I got your card," I say, unsure of where she expects this to go. "Congrats on the movie doing so well."

"Thank you," she says in a breathy voice that only very fresh young starlets can get away with. She stands tall, shoulders back and serene despite her hyperkinetic state. She looks like what I feel like after a couple of strong cups of coffee but with better posture.

"Well, I guess I better get going. My, um, cat is—"

"Really, you saved my life," she says. "Those red carpet pictures have opened so many doors for me. I even scored a meeting with Frappa Ivanhoe? She's a really powerful agent."

"I think I've heard of her," I say. "Good luck with your meeting."

"Things are happening, and it's all because of these," she says as she cups a breast in each hand.

"Oh," I say, feeling myself blush, "I'm sure talent has something to do—"

"I love them. Totally love them." To give me a better look, she unzips her designer tracksuit hoodie to reveal a tissue-thin T-shirt she might as well not be wearing. "My ex-agent pressured me into doing it, but it was the best thing he ever did for my career. If he wasn't such a prick, I'd send him a card or something."

"Oh, my," I say, staring at her chest.

I shut the door to the pizza fridge—the cold air is doing wonders to Nicolette's nipples. She has the kind of breasts songs and poems are written about. Too perfect to be real so that they look like unbelievably great tits.

"I don't even have to bother with a bra." She proudly gives each of them an affectionate squeeze.

"Congrats. Again." I touch her arm so maybe she'll consider putting them away.

"Here," she says, maneuvering them into my personal space, "have a feel. I mean after all, the entire whole world is going to see most of them in *Maxim*."

"Okay." I reach out a finger and gently press the left one near the top. "Thanks, and I really should be—"

"Not like that, Raquel. Really grab them." She takes my hands and clamps one around each breast. "I never found out what you do at Belmore. I had to ask around forever to even find out your address."

"Me?" I continue to feel up Nicolette, unsure what the time limit is from being dismissively rude to being a pervert. I give them a final squeeze and then clasp my hands behind me. "I work in the marketing department and . . . Well, that's about it. I just work a normal job."

"You don't know how good you have it," Nicolette says, finally zipping up. "It's just awful out there. Backstabbing, gossiping, and the competition is beyond cutthroat. Sometimes I wish I just had a normal job."

"Funny," I say, "sounds almost like working at Belmore."

I smile at Nicolette, feeling something close to pity for her even though her career is taking off and mine has effectively come to an end. Except in her case, when reality comes knocking at her door, not even another boob job with bigger implants will be able to help her. Nicolette's career, with her pretty but bland California girl look, will peak by the time she's twenty-five. All she has going for are her pretty face; her boobs, which aren't real; and her good manners. Soon she'll start messing around with her face and forget to thank the little people. As for me, I think I'll be fine. Belmore is a big company, and if my future isn't in Marketing, there are twenty other departments I can try.

"It was nice to run into you," Nicolette says.

"Yeah, good luck again." I turn away from the frozen pizzas and push my cart toward the checkout stand.

When I get home, the first thing I notice is that Mrs. Kashini hasn't been around. My mother's presence is noticeable everywhere. From the magazines left open on the floor to the discarded clothes draped on the backs of the dining chairs. There's also an almost empty bottle of Baileys next to a completely empty bottle of wine on the counter. Next to the bottles is an arrangement of pink and white tulips. No card, just the flowers in the vase I keep on top of the fridge.

"Raquel?" my mother calls from the bedroom, sounding hopeful that I won't answer.

"I'm here, Mom. In the kitchen."

I stash a case of Diet Coke into the fridge along with a half dozen Granny Smith apples and arrange a dozen Lean Cuisines into the freezer. Promotion or no promotion, I'm going to lose those fourteen pounds and start hitting the Belmore gym every morning. At least this is a goal I know I can meet.

"You're home early from work." Her hair is wrapped in a towel, and she almost looks like her old self. "Good. We can go out. I don't want to be around when your father calls. It'll give him something to worry about."

"Uh-huh," I say, not wanting to stir that particular pot.

My mother views me as nothing more than her sounding board. We don't have actual conversations. It's more me just waiting for her to stop talking, but she never runs out of things to say. I wonder if she's even noticed that I haven't been home much longer than an hour or two the last few days.

"Someone came around looking for you. A man." She looks smug, as if she thinks she's finally caught me.

"A man? For me? Was he tall, obviously rich, and without a predisposition toward male pattern baldness?" I keep my back to her as I fuss with cans and packages. "If so, I hope you tied him up and threw him in my closet."

"He was a very good-looking man," she says with grudging approval. "Tall, but not too tall. It always bothered me that your father was freakishly tall."

"Handsome and tall, but not freakish. Sounds promising," I say, my anxiety level rising with every word she says. "Let's go wedding dress shopping."

"If you're going to be a smart-ass, I'll just mind my own business." As my mother has no business to mind but my own, we both know this is a promise she won't keep.

"Okay, sorry, Mom. What did this guy want? Was he selling magazines? Bottled water service?"

The only way I can get through this conversation is by resorting to juvenile tactics. I can feel her eyes burning into the back of my head. She has me caught. I'm not doing anything but confirming her suspicions by acting like I have something to hide.

"He said he was a friend of yours and asked if you were home," she says.

"Sounds kind of creepy. Are you sure he was looking for me?" I turn around, hand her a Diet Coke, and set one on the counter for myself. "There's some actress, and by actress I mean call girl, a few doors down. Maybe it was one of her johns? If you're telling me you don't mind me marrying a man who frequents prostitutes, I could have gotten engaged a while ago."

"At your age, Raquel, you really can't afford to be picky." My mother pops the tab on her soda and takes a deep swallow even though it's at room temperature. "I had a very interesting chat with Cricket."

"You guys compare broomsticks?" I snap, but not very loud, so my mother can pretend she didn't hear me.

"She thinks you're seeing someone and that it's serious. I told her if you were, I would know. A mother can sense these kinds of things. Anyway, he was sorry that you weren't home."

"Poor him." I walk into the living room and kick off my shoes, adding them to the small pile of my mother's under the coffee table.

"What kind of guy comes to your door with flowers?" she asks, amazed at this small act of romance.

"A flower delivery guy," I say and roll my eyes.

"He was wearing a suit and driving a Ferrari." She sits down next to me and picks up the remote. "He didn't look like any flower delivery guy I've ever seen."

"Things are different on the west side of Los Angeles, Marlene," I say, leaning my head on her shoulder. "They're extra fancy."

fifteen | HAPPILY NEVER AFTER

End of an Error . . .

The only way I can tell that Bert is back from padding around his mansion is by the half dozen Post-it notes stuck all over my monitor. I left early yesterday, came in at nine today, after nixing any idea of going to the gym, and so far haven't seen him at all.

"Who cares," I say as I move on to the next Post-it task.

I have no more illusions of what Bert can and can't do for me, but the excitement around *Fire House Hero* proves, at least to me, that given the chance I do have a future in marketing. Maybe not at Belmore, but there are other companies out there . . . who aren't hiring right now. I'm going to follow Matthias's lead, hang out at Belmore until I can leave for something better.

There's a short, hard knock on my door, followed almost immediately by a throat being pointedly cleared.

"Excuse me?" The new receptionist stands there smack in

the middle of the room, looking like she has no plans to leave anytime soon.

"Oh, hey . . ." I keep my eyes on the yellow square of paper. Seems Bert wants a memo on the status of the *Extracurricular Activities* logo color change done by the end of the day.

"There's a meeting," she says, taking a long, curious look around her.

"Thanks, yeah, I know. Thanks," I say. I'm a bit on the busy side and well aware there's a meeting since I'm in charge of scheduling them.

"They're all waiting for you," she says, unwilling to veer from her own agenda, "in the Big Conference Room."

"The Big Conference Room?" I ask, looking up from the monitor. At the same time, a reminder for the daily marketing debrief pops up on my screen with a loud ping.

"They're waiting for you," she says again. She clearly has her orders, and I'm not making her job any easier by asking stupid questions.

"Who's waiting for me?" I ask, unable to help myself. My hand reaches for my phone, itching to dial Matthias to ask what he might know.

"I really don't know, Ms. Azorian. I got a call at my desk telling me to tell you to go to the Big Conference Room."

I instantly regret not wearing something more appropriate. Instead of my usual skirt suit, I woke up feeling defiant and rediscovered parts of my wardrobe that I'd long ignored for the sake of crafting my image as an up-and-coming Belmore employee. Wanting to give the whole of the marketing department, and Bert especially, a big fuck you, I'd stepped into a black pencil skirt, dark purple wrap sweater, and black suede boots.

"Has the morning debrief been changed to the afternoon?" I ask as we make our way down the hall toward the reception desk and elevators.

"The morning debrief has been canceled," the new receptionist says with all the subtlety of a guillotine blade.

A meeting is never canceled at Belmore without first holding a meeting to decide whether to cancel the meeting or not. Bert has never called one off. If anything, he's more likely to call for another meeting before starting the one we were all sitting down to.

"Mr. Floss canceled the morning debrief meeting?" I ask her, even though it's my job to know everything Bert is going to do before he does.

"Yes," she says, sparing me a glance while she presses the up button.

We step out of the elevator, she speeding up her gait to stay ahead of me, and make our way down the hall in uneasy silence. I have no idea why she's escorting me, and I don't want to ask. She opens the door to the Big Conference Room and holds it open.

"You can go in now, Raquel," she says when I don't move.

"I know that," I snap and force my feet to move forward.

Unfriendly Persuasion . . .

I walk into the Big Conference Room and take in what's before me with what I'm sure are very wide eyes. Around the custom-made conference table are the VPs from Human Resources, Legal, Accounting, and Bert. They're seated in order of corporate importance and in mirror image of how their cars are parked in the structure outside.

At the end of the table there's one of those flimsy folding chairs I've only seen in the basement security office, and it's obviously meant for me.

The receptionist gives a little dip of the head, backs out quickly, and closes the door behind her with what to me seems like a thundering click.

"Raquel. Please sit down," Dr. Winterbourne says.

She's the vice president of Human Resources, has a doctorate in psychology, and likes to be addressed as Doctor rather than Ms. She also sports one of the most severe sets of eyebrows since Joan Crawford walked the face of the earth.

I sit and stare straight ahead at the empty Big Chair. In the middle of the table are evenly spaced muffin and pastry platters, ringed with sliced fresh fruit and pitchers of ice water, with lemon or cucumber floating in them. A small plastic bottle of water, one of those mini eight-ounce ones, is set in front of my seat. Just the bottle, no cup or even a straw.

"You may be wondering, Raquel, why we're here," says Dr. Winterbourne. I look at her, trying to judge just how dire my situation is by the arch of her caterpillar brows.

"I am," I answer after finding my voice, "wondering. Yes."

"We'd like you to tender your resignation and immediately vacate your office." Mr. Tately, the vice president of Legal, jumps in, which doesn't surprise me. Dr. Winterbourne frowns in Tately's direction but makes no move to contradict him. As well as being a fool, he's a third-rate lawyer who keeps in his office a framed cover of *The American Lawyer* where he appeared a decade ago in a group shot. "And we'd like you to tender it immediately."

"You are, all of you, you're all here to fire me?" I ask, my mouth somehow forming the words. I look over to where Bert is slouched in his seat, assiduously avoiding eye contact with me by concentrating on his dissection of a blueberry muffin.

"We're not firing you," Tately says. "Unless you came here with the intention to quit? If that's the case, we'd happily accept your resignation."

"Are you serious?" I sputter, unable to contain my incredulity at the sheer stupidity of his words.

"Raquel, what Mr. Tately is trying to say is that we find ourselves in a very serious situation," Dr. Winterbourne says carefully. "With repercussions that affect your continued employment with Belmore."

"What is it, exactly, that you're saying?" I blurt out.

"What we want," Tately says, grimacing with the effort to choose his words a little more wisely, "is for you to voluntarily submit your resignation."

"You want me to fire myself?" I can't help but sit up a little straighter when Bert chuckles, finding amusement in my reply. "Is that even possible? On what basis would I resign?"

"We have grounds, believe me," Tately says, looking like the smug lawyer he is, "to make sure you never work in this town again."

"So why not just fire me?" I ask him.

Dr. Winterbourne, sensing that this meeting is going in an unavoidably tawdry direction, tries to diffuse the situation with more human resources tactics. "Raquel, we're a fair company—"

"Oh, so you're afraid I'll sue?" I say.

"Sue?" Tately's voice goes up a full octave. "Good luck on finding a lawyer that'll—"

"Gloria Allred," I say, invoking the most unholy of the unholy.

There's a collective sucking in of breath that's only slightly louder than the sound of my heart thudding in my chest.

"We're prepared to offer you a month's salary and accrued vacation time," Dr. Winterbourne says quickly and slides over a sheet of paper that details the company's offer.

I pick up the sheet, pretend to study it for a few moments, then push it away. "I don't think so."

"Raquel," Dr. Winterbourne starts but is cut off with one look from Tately.

"This is not negotiable," he says with immense confidence that I hope will one day rupture his aorta cleanly in two.

"Everything is negotiable." I stand up and go, as my high school jock boyfriend used to say before a big game, all balls out. "I want a year's salary with medical coverage, a fair and accurate letter of recommendation."

Tately leaps to his feet just as if he were in a TV courtroom. "I really don't think you are in any position to—"

I raise my hand to shut him up and continue once he settles back down into his cushy leather seat.

"Or I let slip that a certain teenage movie princess's recent hospitalization for emergency appendicitis was actually a coerced abortion even her parasitic parents don't know about and, oh, I don't know, the truth that the star of our, sorry, your very macho movie franchise has that little habit of engaging in risky gay sex when he's on location overseas. Maybe I'll start a blog. I have lots of material for a blog. I might even get a book deal out of it. I was an English major, so I don't have to hire someone to write it for me like who was it? Oh yes, that feel good man of the people politician who was nominated for a Pulitzer for penning his autobiography, which should be shelved in the fiction section and is a project now in development that just screams 'Oscars for everyone.' So yeah, do me a favor and don't negotiate with me, because I could already sue this company three ways from Wednesday for this clusterfuck firing you're trying to pull."

By the time I finish, I'm close to peeing myself, but I wiped the smug look off of Tately's face. I wouldn't swear to it in a court of law, but I think that Dr. Winterbourne actually gave me a smile before schooling her eyebrows back into their usual angry position. Bert looks up at me with something akin to pride in his eyes.

"It would be in your best interest, Raquel"—Tately enunciates his words very carefully, as if doing so will make what he's saying all the more authoritative—"if you thought very hard about opening up this particular Pandora's box."

"Consider it open," I say just as slowly, causing a ripple of suppressed laughter at his expense.

"If that's your choice, Raquel," Tately says, ignoring a sound of protest from Dr. Winterbourne.

He nods, and behind me I can hear the screen lower from the ceiling. The lights dim, and the company logo appears on the screen as it does before any Belmore PowerPoint presentation.

Everyone shifts in their seats and stares over my head. With all the dignity I can muster, I pick up my chair and turn it to face the screen. After a few blinks, the Belmore Corp. logo disappears and then fades into the image from the slightly grainy security camera, complete with the date and time in the corner. It's of the empty Big Conference Room, and the camera is positioned at an odd angle, about waist high. I gulp. And since there was no sound to go along with the security tape, it's the loudest gulp I've ever heard in my life.

A man, obvious from his suit pants and stylish square-toed leather lace-up shoes, walks into the frame. He takes a seat, and almost everyone in the room gasps when they realize he sat in the leather chair reserved for Mr. Belmore's and only Mr. Belmore's ass. A woman, wearing exactly the outfit I wore on the night of the *Fire House Hero* screening, steps in between his legs and hands him an open bottle of wine. The woman lowers herself to her knees, her shoulders and head still out of the frame, but her hands are clearly visible as she unfastens the man's belt and then pulls down the zipper of his pants. She then bends her head toward his, her long, dark hair obscuring her face until he gently moves it aside.

"We can stop this now, Raquel," Dr. Winterbourne says. Her offer is a little late, but I suppose some iota of sisterly concern has finally compelled her to say something.

"That would be nice," I say, looking at her. She's the only one not watching the footage with rapt interest.

Dr. Winterbourne nods, and I turn back around to see the image of me, mouth open with a more than average-size cock heading straight for it, frozen on the screen.

"As you can see, Raquel, we have evidence of multiple

infractions of your employee contract," Tately says after clearing his throat a couple of times. "First one is being in an unauthorized part of the building after hours, as you can see from the time stamp. And then there is the matter of the alcohol on company property."

"Let's not forget that," I mutter. I reach for my puny bottle of water before I stop short. The last thing I need is to draw attention to my mouth and swallowing abilities. I set it back down on the table and fold my hands right behind it. "I could sue for—"

"You really don't want to do that, Raquel." Tately points to the screen behind me. "Remember Monica Lewinsky? Remember what a hard time she had?"

"Let's leave her out of it," I snap.

"If you sue," Dr. Winterbourne says carefully, trying to tread the fine line between loyalty to the company and loyalty to her duty as a doctor who practices in the field of human resources, "this will become very public."

"What about him?" I ask, jabbing a thumb behind me. I know enough to not come out and give a name to the penis. There are still feelings of loyalty, even though he's spoken volumes by not being here. He's putting distance between himself and me and my ignoble departure. "Is he also being encouraged to resign?"

"We have no way of knowing who the other party may be, Raquel." Tately dusts imaginary crumbs off the table in front of him. We all know that the penis on the screen is attached to Kyle Martin, and none of them, even me, have the balls to say it. "Security was unable to capture the scene from any other angle."

"I'm sure," I say, standing up and trying to position myself in front of the picture of me mid-fellatio, "if we really, really thought about it, we could figure out some way to identify him."

Everyone knows whose face belongs to that penis, but if I say his name, they'll call me not only a slut but a lying slut. It'll become a messy game of he said/she said, and what I have to say doesn't matter.

"If we all put our heads together and thought about it long and hard, we could come up with some way to figure it out," I say.

"The other party will be dealt with." Dr. Winterbourne says this with a twist to her mouth, as if the words are causing her physical discomfort. Belmore is an old boys' company, and by even hinting at any sympathy for me and my predicament, she's putting her future at stake. After a moment she continues with a more neutral expression on her face. "We'd like to keep this incident as discreet as possible."

"For your sake, Raquel," Bert adds. No one is going to hold him responsible for what I did. If anything, it just proves their case. My boss is out on a vague medical leave and I start boozing it up and sucking dick while he's gone.

"So I'm supposed to accept my big fat scarlet letter A and just disappear? Really," I say, pulling the threads together, "if anything, this is something I can build a whole career off of. Talk shows, books, a reality show. It's a good old-fashioned Hollywood sex scandal. Who doesn't like that?"

The phone, set between the empty chairs of Walter Belmore and Kyle, rings. Everyone stares at it for a second like it's the burning bush. Before the second ring, Tately reaches forward to answer it.

"Hello?" He listens for a moment and then hangs up the

phone, his face pale. He leans over and whispers into the ear of Dr. Winterbourne, who nods. Tately clears his throat and says in his best lawyer voice, "We can offer you three months' salary, no medical, and we keep one copy of the tape in the company vault. More than generous, considering the circumstances."

"My lawyer will be in touch with you by tomorrow." I reach for the bottle of water, causing Tately to rear back as if he expects me to lob it at him. I set it down again, push my chair away from the table, and make to leave the room. "And I'm sure Gloria Allred will be able to come up with a way to compare and contrast company dicks until we figure out who the other party is in that video. Now that's a subpoena I'm certain *Variety* will reprint in its entirety."

The phone rings again, and Dr. Winterbourne snatches it up before Tately can get his sweaty paws on it.

"Yes, sir?" She makes some notes on the pad in front of her and then passes it off to Tately, who merely nods, face pale once again. "Yes. Yes. Of course, sir . . . Raquel? Mr. Belmore would like to speak to you."

I stand up, walk over to the phone, and put it to my ear. I take a deep breath and look at the faces staring at me and not at the image on the screen. Tately has visible beads of sweat on his forehead and upper lip.

"This is Raquel Azorian."

Hard to Swallow . . .

I say yes and no where I have to and, when asked politely and authoritatively, hand the phone to Dr. Winterbourne. After a couple of minutes of listening, she finally says, "Of course,

Mr. Belmore," and sets the receiver down with a delicate click.

"We're authorized to offer you a year's salary along with two weeks' salary for every year worked, paid in full today, medical coverage for the rest of the year, and the sole copy of the tape to reside in a safety deposit box with one key remaining in your possession, another with the company, and the third with the bank."

"What about my shares?" I ask, not willing to give everything up for a one-time, monumentally stupid mistake. "I'm vested in six months, and my last work performance review was excellent. Wasn't it, Bert?"

We all look over at him, slumped once again in his seat. He grunts and nods but doesn't look up.

"You may purchase them at the current price, of course, and sell them as you wish," Dr. Winterbourne says. "But you must do so today. The purchase price will be deducted from your . . . package."

"You either buy them today or they revert to the company," Tately adds unnecessarily.

"I'll buy them," I say, not bothering to explain myself. They are my shares, something I can take away with me. If I want to donate, burn, or sell them, they are mine to do with as I wish.

"And you sign a retroactive confidentiality agreement," Tately says.

I'm about to give my answer when Dr. Winterbourne stops me with a look of concern that I'm sure will cost her all hope of moving up a seat anytime in the near future.

"Do you understand what you're agreeing to, Raquel?" she

asks. "If you violate the confidentiality agreement, the company will hold you liable for any payments made out to you and it is very likely that the tape will be made public. Do you understand that?"

"Yes, I understand," I say. My voice sounds thick and labored, even to my own ears. I have a lump in my throat the size of a tennis ball, but I can't seem to work up enough saliva to swallow it.

We sit in relative silence as numbers are compared and confirmed, language checked and approved and, finally, a two-page separation agreement is put in front of me. There's a space for me to sign, as well as one each for Bert, Dr. Winterbourne, and Tately. The VP of Accounting cuts my check in front of me. When I put pen to paper, everyone around the Big Conference Table lets out a collective breath of relief. I swallow a hiccup.

I stand up, back straight, eyes forward, gait purposeful, but covered in goose bumps and seconds away from breaking into a cold sweat. All I want to do is get the hell out of there before that stupid phone rings again with Kyle on the other end suffering from an attack of sentimentality and louses up my deal.

Right outside the door the receptionist is hovering, waiting for me.

We ride the elevator down to Marketing in silence, the receptionist keeping her gloating to herself lest she let loose with some nugget the people in the elevator car with us can make use of. Information like this, almost firsthand for her, is valuable, and she's smart enough to know to parse it out in selective chunks to those who can make a move from the reception desk to one of her own happen.

"I'm going to need your ID badge, key cards, and commissary debit card, Raquel," she says as she trots behind me in her Steve Madden peep-toe heels and pressed Gap skirt while we make our way onto the marketing department floor. "And the key to Mr. Floss's office."

Though I am in no position to give her any attitude, I do. "You can wait until I get back to my—"

I stop in front of what had been my desk. A maintenance guy waits with a dolly and boxes, ready to help me pack up, but there isn't much. I grab a box and begin to jam in personal photos and other assorted career-related debris. People make unnecessary trips to the copy room and bathroom to try to gather early intelligence.

In less than five minutes my desk is stripped of any evidence that I ever spent most of my waking hours there for the last three years making sure the important marketing work of Belmore Corporation got done.

"Raquel? I need your phone," the receptionist says, already sizing up my ex-office as her own.

"Yeah, sure." I dig through my purse and hand it over, watching as she checks it off her list.

"By the way, Raquel?" She waits to continue until I look up from fussing unnecessarily with my purse. "Happy birthday."

"Thanks, really, whatever your name is." I turn on my heel and walk toward the elevator bank as quickly as what remains of my dignity and pencil skirt will allow.

I'm spared a security escort—technically I'm not fired, I've resigned—but word is spreading fast. I wait for the elevator, gripping my box of stuff and trying to keep myself from doing something stupid like crying.

cry and
pologize
f going
ga DVD
with my

one in a

ce," she

le wrap
air is up
or a day

"Raquel?" Matthias steps out of the elevator I'm about to get into. "Where are you going?"

"I'm not really sure." I put the box down and give him a quick hug. "It's over for me at Belmore."

"I'll walk you out." He blinks back tears and picks up my box. In the lobby, Matthias stops just before the security desk so he doesn't have to swipe in again. "Are you going to be okay?"

"I think I am. Either way, I don't think things can get any worse." I give him a quick peck on the cheek and walk out to my car.

I drive away from Belmore, not looking back, and take deep breaths that sound more and more ragged to my ears. To distract myself, I flip on the radio, hoping some background noise will drown out my racing thoughts.

"Breaking news today from Hollyweird," the DJ intones, obviously enjoying the sound of his own voice. "Belmore Corp. has named Kyle Martin the new president of the company." He pauses to allow for a few seconds of canned cheers and clapping. "Martin says he's looking forward to taking Belmore into new ventures and continuing the Belmore legacy. Walter Belmore, the current president, will step aside but remain on as chairman of the board." A snippet of "Hail to the Chief" plays and then fades out.

"But that's not all, folks. Industry tongue waggers are in hyper mode spreading the *other* news that Kyle Martin, new prez of Belmore, is a bachelor no more." There's the sound of a woman's theatrical weeping. It's not mine, even though I'm pulling my car over and feel very close to crying. "Yep, representatives for Phoebe Belmore, niece of Walter Belmore, confirm that she and new head cheese Kyle Martin were married over the weekend." The opening notes of the "Wedding March" fill my ears. "And the lovely lady, giver of mucho glamorous parties and a budding humanitarian, will now be known as Mrs. Phoebe J. Belmore-Martin. Hey, if anyone knows what the *J* stands for, call in and you'll win a couple of concert tickets. So, ladies who lunch Hollywood style, update your databases. Here's to the new Hollywood power couple." More canned cheering and clapping. "Also in the news—"

I switch off the radio, preferring the sound of my own crying to the awful truth of it all.

sixte

sixteen | THE TRUTH IN CONSEQUENCES

Awkward Overtures . . .

In the four months since my departure from Belmore, my mother has had good days, when she seems excited and hopeful about her future. She'll enjoy one or two glasses of wine with the dinner she cooks for me after a day wandering between malls and she'll go out of her way to fix herself up. What I like most is that she'll hardly mention how miserable she is, and if she does it's wrapped in a wry joke we can both laugh at. Then there are the bad days, which can be very bad for both of us.

She won't say a word to me until she has her mug of Baileys-spiked self-esteem in her hands and will stay indoors in a haze of artificial sweetener and just enough alcohol to numb her to the reality of her situation. On those days, I check in with her every couple of hours and rush home from wherever I find myself to make sure she's okay. Occasionally, I'll stay home just to sit with her, even though I know she'll cry and complain about anything, everything, and then apologize before "falling asleep" around dinnertime. Instead of going out for what's now my regular nightly run, I'll do a yoga DVD with the sound off to unwind and not risk waking her with my need to find peace and serenity.

Today, though, looks to be a good day. The first one in a while.

"You look cute, Raquel. Dressing your age for once," she says as she watches me fix myself a brown bag lunch.

Under a plain white apron I'm wearing a simple wrap dress; I'm also wearing peep-toe wedges. and my hair is up in a messy bun. I look as if I were about to set out for a day of shopping, not work. My mother must know, on some level, that I no longer work at Belmore. Not with the relatively normal hours I've been keeping, the days off I've taken, and what I wear on my way out the door on the mornings I do go to work. But she only sees what she wants to and is blind to everything else.

"It's new," I say of my dress. "I had some time yesterday after lunch and there was a little shop not too far from where I was."

Where I ate was in a small park across from an office complex where I was known as Tracy because the last receptionist was named Tracy and everyone loved her. As it was only a one-day assignment, I really couldn't rustle up the energy to care.

"Hmm," she says as I carefully spread some avocado on a slice of multigrain bread before I top it with sliced turkey and tomatoes. "That looks good."

"I'll make you one and leave it in the fridge."

After I deposited my check from Belmore, I took a long, hard look at my finances and decided that, along with Diet Coke and Kyle, there were many other things I could live comfortably without. Buying lunch was one of them, and making my own food has made me aware of what I actually put in my mouth. Suffice to say, hot dogs or sausage of any kind has not been on the menu around the Azorian apartment.

"Oh, that's nice of you, honey." Mom settles herself on one of the rarely used barstools that sit under the raised counter looking into my galley kitchen. "I think I'll walk to the mall later."

"Sounds like fun, Mom. It's a nice day out. If I didn't have to go into work to take care of some things, I'd go with you." I'm practically begging her to ask me what is going on, but I know she won't, and if I were her, I wouldn't either.

My father is going to start divorce proceedings. He told me so a couple of weekends ago, when I helped Steve move his stuff back into his old room and turn mine into his work space. Out went the princess bed and up went the shelves of humming computers. He kept the Hello Kitty curtains, though. Steve isn't getting a divorce, Cricket won't hear of it, but their marriage is over. Cricket has put her efforts into opening up her own cupcake shop. She's okay with having her husband live a few miles from her as long as she gets to keep the house, the kids, and the façade of status my brother's money can bring her. She can deal with being married to my brother, even if it means he won't live with her, but the thought of being a divorced woman is inconceivable to her.

When my dad told me he was going to divorce Mom, he didn't try to explain himself and I didn't ask him to. He has his reasons, and I respect them even if I don't want them spelled out for me.

My parents speak on the phone every couple of days, and usually Dad is the one who calls, which my mother always takes as a sign that she has the upper hand. She'll start girlish and flirty before ending up weepy and bitter. After half an hour, the longest my father can tolerate talking to her, she'll slam down the phone and declare that she'll never set foot in his love nest again. (My father made the mistake of letting it slip that Jerri had been paying him visits, even though he made it clear he wasn't interested.) After these phone calls, my mother commandeers my laptop to look up divorce attorneys and tactics, has a drink or three, and naps in front of the TV but grunts awake the second I even think about reaching for the remote.

I dig through the fridge and knock over the very last can of Diet Coke. It rolls off the shelf and lands squarely on my toe.

"God damn it!" I yelp, embarrassed at how quickly the tears come to my eyes. I've been on the verge of crying, bawling really, for weeks, and to have it happen because of a can of Diet Coke is just pathetic.

"Raquel, turn around and look at me," my mother says, sounding, for once, like a mom. When I don't move, she comes up behind me, puts her hands on my shoulders, and physically turns my body so I face her. She puts a finger under my chin and lifts. "You can tell me the truth, Raquel. You know that, right?"

I look at her, my lip and chin quivering like Jell-O, and shake my head. What can I tell her? The truth? What is the truth anymore? Oh, God, I'm getting existential over a can of Diet Coke. I pinch the bridge of my nose, and once I feel a bit more in control, I answer her with a question of my own.

"Can I really tell you the truth, Mom?"

"Oh, Raquel." She folds me into her arms, setting my head on her shoulder. "I'm so sorry. For everything."

"I am, too, Mommy." I hug her back, tight. "And don't take this the wrong way, but I really need you to move out."

Temporarily Insane . . .

I luck out and snag a parking spot with a busted meter a half block away from TempOne. I drop my signed time sheet off with Allison, who's manning the reception desk as usual, and head straight for one of the terminals. I log into the system, update my status as available, and then pull out a copy of *The Secret*. Assignments are tight with layoffs happening right and left, but if I camp out at a terminal, I up my chances of landing one. I read and watch as people shuffle in nervous and annoyed to sign up with the agency. I can't feel bad for them, and I know the smart ones will learn to work the system or else not work.

My money situation is worrisome but not dire. Though I won't be getting a new car anytime soon, I make enough through TempOne to cover my monthly expenses without having to touch what's in my savings account. I've adapted to doing things on the cheap. Instead of buying books, which

I'm consuming with a voracious appetite, I check them out from my local library. Magazines I read at Kool Nails #3, where I can get a mani-pedi on Tuesdays and Thursdays between 9:30 and 11:30 for 30 percent off the regular price. I haven't downgraded my satellite TV package, knowing my mother would notice, but I discovered that McDonald's makes a decent cup of coffee.

The feeding and care of my mother is by far my most pressing expense, both financially and emotionally. Still, no matter how many assignments I take, I come nowhere near making what I'd been making at Belmore or clocking in the hours I need to stay away from home long enough to make it bearable to be around her.

After fifteen minutes of reading, I check in with Allison, who lets me peruse the latest assignments while I cover the desk so she can have a pee, a smoke, and a cup of coffee. I scan the listings and find mostly a string of one- or two-day desk jobs that will be nothing but headaches. They won't last long enough for me to figure out what needs to get done, and I'll spend most of the time trying not to confuse Dan from Shipping with Dan Accounts Receivable. Still, an honest day's wage is just that, and I'll ask Allison to schedule me for a two-day assignment starting tomorrow.

"Thanks for covering." Allison hurries in clutching a Venti latte from Starbucks to fuel her until lunchtime. Of all the assignments TempOne hands out, covering the reception desk is the crown jewel for those who want a blue blazer. Allison's one of these people. She fits the headset over her ears and asks, "Did you see anything?"

"Looks pretty dead, but the one I highlighted seems decent enough. At least it'll take me into the weekend."

"Guess what I heard . . . Good morning, TempOne. Please hold; a liaison will be with you in a moment . . . One of the gals back there is going on maternity leave, so I have my fingers crossed that they'll ask me to cover her desk . . . Good morning, TempOne. Please hold; a liaison will be with you in a moment . . . I should know by Friday."

"Congrats, Allison. That's really great," I say, happy for her even though it means I've lost my in with the one person who can make my life as a temp tolerable.

Allison's pinned all her hopes, built up over her short, nineteen-year life span, on landing a job at TempOne. And really, is it so bad to have such modest goals in life? I could learn a lot from her.

"I swear . . . Thank you for holding. A liaison will be with you in a moment . . . I can't take another time-sheet Tuesday," she says. "You want to get some lunch?"

"Can't. I have this thing I'm doing," I say. I momentarily consider canceling my other thing to hang out with her, but I know I can't. I've put it off long enough, and it's time to deal with it.

"Call in later. Maybe something will come in for next week . . . Good morning, TempOne. Please hold; a liaison will be with you in a moment."

I sprint to my car and jump in just as a parking enforcement officer pulls up next to it. I zoom out into traffic, cackling maniacally, my heart racing at the near miss. I weave through traffic and reach the parking lot of Hello Monday only a few minutes after I was supposed to be there.

"Hey, baby," Kyle says. He's standing by the entrance of the café, waiting for me.

"Hello, Kyle."

He gives me an overlong hug, ignoring the looks from the people around us. His face has been all over the news, but he's still anonymous enough not to have industry bloggers following his every move. He's a big piece of cheese in Hollywood now, the president of Belmore Corporation, but inside Hello Monday he only stands out because he's wearing a ten-thousand-dollar suit and it's his Ferrari in the parking lot. Kyle walks with a swagger as he follows me to my favorite table, his hand on the small of my back. He knows he doesn't have to hide anything anymore. No one from Belmore will dare call him out on being seen with me. Kyle exists in an entirely different universe than the rest of us.

"You're a hard woman to reach, Raquel," he purrs into my ear.

"There might be a reason for that." I smile at the cashier as I pay for my glass of iced green tea and wheat-germ cookie. "So why have you been trying?"

"Do I really need to say why?" He chuckles, aiming for debonair but hitting pathetic square on the nose.

"Maybe you shouldn't say it, Kyle," I say. "Didn't I just read in *People* magazine that you and your bride, Phoebe Belmore-Martin, are in the process of overpopulating the planet? I'd think you'd be too busy with that little project to do much else."

Kyle sighs and runs his hand through his hair. It's a gesture that used to make me sigh, too, but I now know it means he's trying to buy himself some time. "You shouldn't believe everything you read, Raquel."

"The pictures of your wife standing in her professionally decorated nursery are pretty easy to believe," I say. "And I believe they reported that you and your wifey-poo are expecting triplets with an Indian surrogate."

"Twins, and our surrogate is in Indiana," Kyle corrects me. "That's a fucking fiasco in the making."

"Tell me about it," I say.

There's no reason for me to talk to Kyle. I owe him nothing, but I can't help it. He's called me at least once a day since the day I left Belmore, and I feel entitled to be as bitchy as I want to be. He needs to see me as much as I need closure.

"I've missed you," he says and seems to genuinely mean it. "I think about you all the time, and not just in that way."

I smile at him but keep my reply, which would only be trite, to myself. Instead I ask him the one question I know he'll never be able to answer. "Are you happy, Kyle?"

He frowns. I put my book on the table to indicate that I don't expect an answer and I'm ready to move on even if he isn't. He comes around to my side of the table and kisses me full on the mouth. It's a friendly kiss, there's nothing sexual. Except for a little sadness behind it, I can't say it has any impact on me and I'm not sure if it's coming from me or him. Really, it doesn't matter.

"You're special, Raquel." He kisses the top of my head, and for a moment, breathes in the scent of my shampoo, and I let him. "Believe it or not, you made me happy, Raquel."

"That's sweet of you to say, Kyle." I pull away, ready to turn my attention to my book. He places a manila envelope on the table. "What's this?" I ask.

"It's for you," he says and watches while I open it. Inside is an internal Belmore memo signed by Kyle detailing the causes for the firing of Cris Fuller. The memo makes a perfunctory mention of an out-of-court settlement for sexual harassment of Matthias, but he's officially being let go for unauthorized construction in his office.

"I've missed you," he says again. "Run away with me? I'm fucking serious. Let's go away somewhere, anywhere you want. Just pack a fresh pair of panties and I'll take care of the rest."

"As tempting as you think that sounds, I believe you've taken care of enough things for me. I'll pass. Shouldn't you be, I don't know, looking down some starlet's dress at a party celebrating how you have Hollywood by the short and curlies?"

"So mean, Raquel," Kyle says. "You know I like it rough."

"You must," I say. I look around, wondering what the usual crowd at Hello Monday makes of us. I suppose we just look like a normal couple who are catching a late morning coffee break before heading back to work.

"Can I see you again? Please?" He blinks his eyes as if trying to hold back a rush of tears. "Don't you miss me?"

"No and no." I say it without hesitation, and it feels good because I know it's the truth.

"Why not?" His desperate eagerness sends a jolt of electricity mixed with pity through me. "I know I ruined what we had, but there's still something between us. Tell me you don't feel it."

"You're married, Kyle. You're going to be a father. Doesn't that mean anything to you?" I ask.

"Yes, it does, but you of all people must know why I did it." He's hurt that I'm not giving him a free pass. If he has the gall to say he did it for me, I'm hurling my iced tea into his face. "It is what it is."

"Maybe if I was totally heartless, insanely ambitious, and pathologically opportunistic, I could understand why you've married a woman you don't love and are having children with her, but I know I could never do what you've done," I say. "Whether you like it or not, Kyle, you're married."

"Phoebe has been acting crazy lately," he complains, ignoring my righteous tirade. "Constantly calling me, asking me where I am, who I'm with, when I'll be home."

"Maybe it's the hormones?" I suggest, playing along. If he doesn't want to have a serious conversation, that's fine with me. "Though I'm not sure it's possible since she's having a long-distance pregnancy."

"The babies are due in the summer," he says, as if the reality of his bargain is finally hitting him. "A boy and a girl. If I divorce her, I lose custody of the kids and Belmore."

"Congratulations, Kyle." I reach over and punch him on the shoulder. "You're beyond sold out."

Kyle hangs his head. I take a sip of my tea and then set the glass down delicately on the table next to my uneaten cookie.

"Don't look like a wounded puppy. I'm done," I say with a laugh.

"I just needed to see you . . . to tell you . . ." He looks me straight in the eye. For the first time since I laid eyes on him, I can tell I'm finally seeing the real Kyle. He's nothing more than a very good-looking and charming man who is in way over his head. "I need—"

"Okay. I'm here," I say. "I'm listening, and for the next five minutes I will keep my mouth shut. Talk."

"I don't know where to go, Raquel. You can't imagine the

kind of pressure I'm under. I'm walking on knifepoint at Belmore. They're out for my head, waiting for me to screw up. I can't sleep on weekends, dreading the box office numbers on Mondays. Christ, they even announce them on *Good Morning America*. Why would some chain-restaurant-eating Midwestern corn farmer care how much money a Belmore flick pulled in? Last week some woman goes and gets herself raped at Belmore Gardens Park in Florida. Raped on a half-price Thursday and files a multimillion-dollar suit against us on Monday. And she names me as a defendant. Like I'd ever put one finger on a peroxide blond truck stop waitress."

He takes a breath and continues. "I have the old man yelling in one ear that he just saw one of the young lady interns wearing dungarees in the mail room and the veep of Digital whining in the other about how his budget needs to be increased so he can hire Pixar-level talent." Kyle slumps back in his chair, spent. "How is any of this my problem? And what the hell are dungarees?"

I wait until his face is a couple less shades of red and then say in my most soothing voice, "You're the de facto head of the Belmore Corporation, Kyle. Everything is your entire and complete fault. And as a stockholder, I want to know what you're going to do about it!"

Despite his desire to wallow in self-pity, Kyle smiles at me. "I've missed you."

"You hardly knew me, Kyle," I scoff, feeling myself blush at my corny comeback.

"I know you taste like honey, you groan like a wild cat when I put my mouth on that spot on your shoulder, and you're the only person I ever trusted at Belmore. Maybe ever."

"It wasn't trust, it was sex, Kyle. I enjoyed it, and so did you. I made a mistake, and it cost me my job. You slept with someone's assistant, did nothing while I took the fall for it, and got promoted." It's a lame summary of everything, but it has to be said. I'll leave out the adultery part—he already has a lot on his plate.

"I need you, Raquel," he says, sounding as if he's considering dropping to his knees in front me. "Every day, every second that passes brings me closer to assuming full control of Belmore, and all I can think of is how your hair feels in my hands. But if I can't have that, please tell me you'll be my friend. I need a friend now more than ever."

I reach into my bag, pull out an old Belmore business card, and scribble the e-mail address I use for online shopping. "If you really need to talk, e-mail me and we'll take it from there."

Kyle takes the card and stares down at it. I realize he's memorizing the address and will toss the card before he leaves the café. I laugh softly at first, and then, when I can't hold it back, I laugh until tears roll down my cheeks.

"What's so funny?" he asks, confused.

"Oh, Kyle," I giggle, "what about this whole thing isn't funny?"

Hollywood Ending . . .

I sit behind the reception desk of an imploding mortgage company. When the phone rings, people poke their heads above their cubicle walls and give me a pleading look so I won't transfer the call to them.

I keep my head down and my eyes on the phone system,

taking my time to transfer the caller to the right extension even though most of the desks are empty. Desperation is thick in the air, and it's as if everyone expects the feds to rush in and close down the place any second.

"If I ever needed a Diet Coke, it's now," I say under my breath. Besides answering the phone, there's nothing for me to do, but I suppose the company needed to maintain the appearance of still being in business, so they called TempOne to send someone, anyone, out for the day. All they (and I) have to do is make it to six o'clock, and then the phones can be shut off, the lights dimmed, and we'll all get a weekend reprieve from the bullshit that has become our respective existence.

I doodle in my journal, and when I fill one page, I turn to the next. I have two hours to go. Another two hours of playing hot potato with phone call transfers and doodling. All in all, my misery will earn me around seventy-eight dollars to deposit into my bank account.

"So not worth it," I say to myself, and I write those words down on a fresh sheet of unlined paper. When my cell phone vibrates in my bag, I answer it without even trying to hide that I'm taking a personal call.

"Raquel speaking. Is this salvation on the line?"

"Yes and no," says Frappa.

I can lie to my mom and even to myself, but I know that's impossible with Frappa, so I've been avoiding her calls. As I get deeper into temp mode, I want to exist in my bubble, where I won't be reminded of what I'm doing with my life. And as Frappa is the only person who knows something close to the truth about what happened those last two weeks at Belmore, she's a prime candidate for avoidance.

"Are you going to pretend you're getting bad reception or are you going to finally show some backbone and talk to me?" she asks.

"No. I can hear you just fine," I say, ignoring a glare from the office manager. "I'm sorry I've been such a wimp, but I have my lame reasons."

"Of course you do, but get over it, Raquel. I just wanted to let you know that *Fire House Hero* is going to be huge," she says, respecting me enough not to cushion the blow of the news. "They tested the new cut last night, and the numbers are off the charts. Rory is the name on everyone's lips."

"I knew it." My gossip blogs are filled with pictures of Rory's toothy grin as he escorts Cat and Cara down the red carpet and ducks into one club after another holding the hand of Nicolette Meyers. "Much good it did me, though."

"Shut up and let me talk," she says. "My dipshit assistant has mono or crabs, something STD related, but is most likely hungover. I'm firing her today if she ever makes it in. If not, first thing Monday morning. So what do you say? I'm no Belmore, but the pay is decent, plus you'll get to hang out with me twenty hours a day."

"That's really nice of you, Frappa. Really. But I don't want to turn into one of those people who live off their successful friends."

"Will you give up on being humble and self-righteous, for fuck's sake? I talked to Bert, and he basically filled me in on the parts you left out of your why I left Belmore story. Aside from all that, he also told me you were the best assistant he ever had and would have made a damn fine executive."

"You're making me blush, Frappa, for more than one reason," I say. "About what happened . . . You can understand why I was a little reluctant to 'fess up to everything."

"No shit," she scoffs. "Listen, as much as I love you and would love to function as your life coach, I sort of have my hands full right now with the ménage à twats going on between my newest, two biggest clients and that slut Nicolette Meyers. So are you going to come work with me or what?"

"Really, Frappa. Like I said, I appreciate—"

"Shut up, Raquel, and listen very hard to what I'm going to say. I have a job you can do and you can grow into something bigger. I don't expect you to answer my phone forever, and I know what you can bring to my company. Considering how everything else is going in your professional life right now, what do you have to lose? Trust me, Raquel."

"I've always trusted you; it's your judgment that I'm questioning. How long do I have to think about it?"

"About three seconds," she says, and she means it, too.

"Consider me hired," I say, knowing it's the first right thing I've done in a long time.

"Good. Be here Monday at nine. And if you show up in one of your Belmore skirt suits, you're fired," she says and hangs up.

I stash my phone and journal in my bag, smooth back my hair, and stand up. "I'm leaving now," I announce, to what's left of Sterling Mortgage and Loan. "You can call and complain to the agency if you want, but I won't be submitting my time sheet, so consider this a freebie. Good luck, you guys, with whatever it is you do here."

I walk out into a sudden rainstorm. Instead of running for my car, I take my time and enjoy it for what it is.

acknowledgments

Many thanks are due to the friends and family who suffer as much as I sometimes do. Writing is a process and it's made all the easier when shared with people who understand.

My sister Monica, sometimes you ask questions that annoy me, but that's only because you really listen. From nixing or approving character names to correcting my grammar, thank you for not making me feel crazy when I talk about my characters like they're real people. You lived through this book with me chapter by chapter, and I owe you big-time for all the help you gave me. I'm hoping an acknowledgment *and* dedication settles our account. Heather, Paula, and Anne, we might not sit around someone's table and talk for hours anymore, but you're never more than an e-mail away. A writer needs a support system, and, ladies, you're mine. My dear friend Maria, you remind me I can always come home again and there'll be a banana shake or cup of tea waiting for me. And finally to Sulay, you give me a push in the right direction when I think I've hit a wall. Working with an editor who actually edits is every writer's dream and I don't ever want to wake up from mine.

"Raquel?" Matthias steps out of the elevator I'm about to get into. "Where are you going?"

"I'm not really sure." I put the box down and give him a quick hug. "It's over for me at Belmore."

"I'll walk you out." He blinks back tears and picks up my box. In the lobby, Matthias stops just before the security desk so he doesn't have to swipe in again. "Are you going to be okay?"

"I think I am. Either way, I don't think things can get any worse." I give him a quick peck on the cheek and walk out to my car.

I drive away from Belmore, not looking back, and take deep breaths that sound more and more ragged to my ears. To distract myself, I flip on the radio, hoping some background noise will drown out my racing thoughts.

"Breaking news today from Hollyweird," the DJ intones, obviously enjoying the sound of his own voice. "Belmore Corp. has named Kyle Martin the new president of the company." He pauses to allow for a few seconds of canned cheers and clapping. "Martin says he's looking forward to taking Belmore into new ventures and continuing the Belmore legacy. Walter Belmore, the current president, will step aside but remain on as chairman of the board." A snippet of "Hail to the Chief" plays and then fades out.

"But that's not all, folks. Industry tongues are in hyper mode spreading the *other* news that Walter, prez of Belmore, is a bachelor no longer, courtesy of a woman's theatrical weeping. Before I'm pulling my car over and feeling faint, representatives for Phoebe Belmore confirm that she and new head cheese Kyle Martin were married over the weekend." The opening notes of the "Wedding March" fill my ears. "And the lovely lady, giver of mucho glamorous parties and a budding humanitarian, will now be known as Mrs. Phoebe J. Belmore-Martin. Hey, if anyone knows what the *J* stands for, call in and you'll win a couple of concert tickets. So, ladies who lunch Hollywood style, update your databases. Here's to the new Hollywood power couple." More canned cheering and clapping. "Also in the news—"

I switch off the radio, preferring the sound of my own crying to the awful truth of it all.

Good-bye to All That

Raquel Azorian has finally found her niche: the habitual temp worker is just days away from a promotion to junior executive at the prestigious Belmore Corporation. However, right before her big break, her boss suffers a terrible meltdown that precipitates a chain reaction of rotten luck for Raquel. Her sister-in-law, Cricket, won't stop calling; her brother is showing hints of unfaithfulness in his marriage; and her mother and father separate, leading Mrs. Azorian to spend her days boozing on Raquel's couch and eating Raquel's food.

Two men seem poised to change all this. Raquel begins sleeping with Belmore vice president Kyle Martin and discovers marketable hunk Rory from the little-known film *Fire House Hero*. Raquel hopes that her relationship with Kyle and the unearthing of Rory will put her back on the fast track to corporate stardom. Will this finally be her big break, or will Belmore prove to be just another paragraph on her professional and personal résumé?

FOR DISCUSSION

1. We are introduced to Raquel as her client Belmore starlet Nicolette Meyers is taking her first turn down the red
carpet. In contrast, Raquel explains that she has long
since "stopped swimming in a sea of pretty and settled
firmly in the land of frumpy" (page 5) because she feels
she will be taken more seriously this way. Do you think
Raquel's attitude toward her own looks and style evolves
throughout the novel, or will she always continue to put
work first?

2. Raquel's sister-in-law, Cricket, seems to have everything
that Raquel doesn't: a nice husband, money, two babies,
and a beautiful new house. As the story goes on, the
glossy exterior of her life is slowly chipped away. Do
you see Cricket as a cautionary tale, a victim of her own
idealism, or is she as dysfunctional as the rest of the
Azorians?

3. Raquel subsists largely on Diet Cokes and strawberry
Pop-Tarts. What do her unhealthy eating habits reveal
about her character? Are her eating habits indicative of
other problems in her life?

A Conversation with Margo Candela

What inspired you to tell this story of a temp worker's foray into the corporate world? Were you interested in exploring the consequences of a tryst in that particular environment, or did the two themes blend together once you started writing?

I've worked from home for the past few years, and as a consequence I've developed a fascination with office life. For someone like Raquel, whose office life and personal life have become intertwined, having her get involved with someone she worked with seemed only natural. She loves Belmore and could never be with anyone who wasn't also, in a sense, married to the company, too. Plus, it makes for a lot of interesting complications to play with.

How has your background in journalism helped you as a novelist? Do you see yourself ever venturing into the world of nonfiction?

Journalism has absolutely structured the way I write, from giving myself deadlines to meeting word count goals—it all goes back to what I learned in Journalism 101. I do give myself a bit more leeway with structure, but I think my style will always lend itself to shorter chapters.

If the right nonfiction project presented itself, I'd love to take a crack at it. It would mean a different approach to writing—more research and actually talking to real people—but it might be a nice change as well as a challenge.

Your first three novels all took place in San Francisco. *Good-bye to All That,* **of course, is set in your hometown of Los Angeles. Why the change of scene? Did you find your native city creatively inspiring, or was it a struggle to bring it to life?**

I lived in San Francisco for a decade and the city was a good fit for the characters in my first three books. *More Than This* is my sort of love note to the city. I had a wonderful time there and visit as often as I can. When it came time to move back to Los Angeles, I knew my own life would change and so would the characters and stories I would write. I realized how very different L.A. is not only from San Francisco but also from how I experienced it when I was growing up here. In some ways, Raquel is also experiencing that same culture shock. Like her, I grew up in northeast Los Angeles, which is not at all like Westside L.A. The part of Los Angeles I live in now is nothing like where my parents still live, even though it's only about twelve miles away.

Have you ever worked as a temp or in the corporate world? If not, how did you go about conducting your research for the novel?

I was a horrible temp, which is why I only managed to do it for a few months, maybe weeks, right out of college. Some people thrive on hopping from job to job, but it made me feel unmoored. I relied on friends who have been much more successful at temping and made the transition to full-time jobs at the companies where they'd temped. Everyone likes to talk and complain about their jobs, so I was able to form a very distinct impression of what life in a company like Belmore would be like.

Your third and most recent novel, *More Than This*, has brought you a considerable amount of accolades and critical attention. Is it difficult to write with these new expectations, or do you feel a certain amount of freedom now that you have established yourself as a strong literary voice?
I took a break between writing *More Than This* and *Good-bye to All That*, and it's one of the smartest things I've ever done, writingwise. I knew I needed to step back and give myself time to think and get used to living in Los Angeles again. When it came time to start something new, I had to figure out what kind of story I wanted to tell. It took more than a few false starts, but it was worth all the hard work. *Good-bye to All That* is its own book and I hope readers can find value in that I've tried something new but familiar and entertaining.

How do you come up with the great names for your characters like Frappa Ivanhoe, Cricket, and the twins Cat and Cara? Are the names of your characters important to you and to the telling of the story?
I spend a lot of time on naming characters. More than once all work has come to halt when I realized someone didn't have the right name. In real life people get stuck with the names their parents give them at birth, even if it doesn't match up to the

person who they turn out to be. As a writer, I get to think of a character, realize what kind of person she is, and give her the perfect name that goes with her personality. It's a lot of fun and I always try to pick names that are unique but believable.

Did being a mother yourself influence the way you wrote the truly hilarious character of Raquel's mother?
Raquel's mother was more of a result of observing other people's behavior and realizing that a person doesn't stop being herself, for better or worse, the second they become someone's mom. Raquel realizes this about her mother and it helps her accept Marlene as a person.

What sort of books do you read for pleasure? Do you feel any of your literary influences seeping into your own writing?
I read just about anything and everything. One of life's greatest pleasures is finding a good book when you least expect it, so I try to keep myself open to all genres. Personally, I admire tidy writers like Delia Ephron and Anne Tyler, who write about messy life situations. As a reader and writer, their styles really appeal to me.

Your blog is a lot of fun, and seems to feature a number of nascent ideas that may eventually turn into subjects for future novels. Has the popularity of blogs and the opportunities they create changed your trajectory as a writer at all? Do you ever prefer writing blog posts to writing fiction?
Blog writing and book writing are two separate things. Some days, writing a blog can fire me up for a day of working on a

Enhance Your Book Club

1. Check out the latest news from Margo Candela herself on her blog, www.margocandela.com. You can e-mail her questions, read interviews she has done, and keep up-to-date on all of her current projects.

2. One of the most entertaining characters of the novel is Raquel's mother. Consider a tribute to Marlene at your book club by spiking your coffee with some Baileys, uncorking a bottle of cheap red wine, or ordering a pizza and keeping it all for yourself.

3. If you liked *Good-bye to All That,* delve into Margo's other books. Check out the much-lauded *More Than This, Underneath It All,* and *Life over Easy.*

4. Raquel goes to great lengths to get her marketing report for *Fire House Hero* ready to be presented upon Bert's return. Using what you've learned from the descriptions of Raquel's preparation, create your own minimarketing report for one of your favorite movies. Try to make a hard sell to the other members of your book club. Why will this movie be appealing? Is there a budding young star/starlet? Who's the target audience?

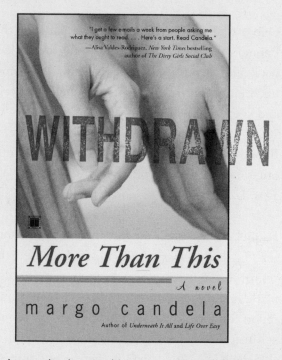